OUTLAWS
AND
LAWMEN

La Frontera Publishing Presents
The American West
Great Short Stories from
America's Newest Western Writers

Edited by

Michael T. Harris

LFP

La Frontera Publishing

Cheyenne, Wyoming

Outlaws and Lawmen
La Frontera Publishing Presents The American West
Great Short Stories from America's Newest Western Writers

An Anthology

Copyright © 2012 La Frontera Publishing

Stories presented in the *Outlaws and Lawmen* anthology are works under copyright by their respective authors. Authors retain all rights, and are used by La Frontera Publishing with permission. The authors and their works include "Introduction" by Johnny D. Boggs, "A Blood Red Moon" by D.B. Jackson, "A Cool Hand" by Jerry Guin, "Dead Women Tell No Tales" by W. Michael Farmer, "Don't Judge A Book" by Dave P. Fisher, "Escape From The Hell Hole" by John Duncklee, "Marshal Of Arizona" by Douglas W. Hocking, "Riding Lonesome" by Jason H. Campbell, "The Day Delgado Rode In" by Lori Van Pelt, "Ground Truth" by Rob Kresge, "The Road" by Wesley Tallant, and "Wild Bill, A Comedy In Three Acts" by James Hitt.

Cover illustration from the original painting by
L.D. Edgar "Stolen Horses - Borrowed Time"
Butch Cassidy and the Sundance Kid © L.D. Edgar.
All rights reserved, used with permission.

Cover design, book design and typesetting by
Yvonne Vermillion and Magic Graphix

Printed and bound in the United States of America

First Edition

First Printing October 2012

Library of Congress Cataloging-in-Publication Data

Outlaws and lawmen : great short stories from America's newest Western writers / edited by Michael T. Harris.
    p. cm.
  Includes bibliographical references and index.
  ISBN 978-0-9785634-9-3 (alk. paper)
  1. Short stories, American--West (U.S.) 2. Western stories. 3. American fiction--21st century. 4. West (U.S.)--Social life and customs--Fiction. I. Harris, Michael T., 1947-
  PS648.W4O98 2012
  813'.087408--dc23
                    2012028807

Published by La Frontera Publishing
Cheyenne, Wyoming
(307) 778-4752 • www.lafronterapublishing.com

Dedicated to all those who love the
American West and its many tales, lores and legends

PREFACE

If I were to ask you to name a Western fiction author, most likely the first name you'd say would be Louis L'Amour. Pressed to name another, you might add Max Brand or Zane Grey. Asked to go beyond these three, however, and you might need some hints.

L'Amour, Brand (pen name for Frederick Schiller Faust) and Grey are no longer with us (L'Amour died in 1988, Faust died in 1944 and Grey died in 1939), but their novels and short stories continue to sell, partly because they are well written and good tales, but also because the public recognizes the author's name. L'Amour, Brand and Grey have become synonymous with trusted, dependable storytelling about the American West and the frontier.

But beyond these three literary giants, there is a wonderful world of Western fiction available to fans of the West. A lot of really good writing from living Western authors is waiting for each and every one of us to discover.

That's one of the reasons I started La Frontera Publishing in 2005. I wanted our company to bring to the public great Western stories from today's talented writers. I'm proud to say we're off to a good start.

In 2010 I had the privilege of working with the Western Writers of America to publish an anthology showcasing some of the talented members of that excellent organization. *Roundup!* was well received, and encouraged me to look at publishing additional collections of short fictional stories from today's new Western writers.

Our hope is that our new series, "La Frontera Publishing Presents The American West," will serve as a stepping stone for some of today's storytellers who may become tomorrow's Western literature giants.

This anthology—*Outlaws and Lawmen*—includes samples of short stories done in the traditional style, as well as three that we think of as more contemporary. The theme of good versus evil, right versus wrong, is a classic of Western storytelling, so we selected it to be the theme of our first anthology in La Frontera Publishing's "The American West" series.

By the way, I'm also proud to say that my company is a member of the Western Writers of America, and I'm even more proud to tell you that six of the authors represented in this anthology also are members. It's a great group, with high standards for Western writing.

I also want to thank all the authors who are represented in *Outlaws and Lawmen*. The selection process we faced was a tough one; we received many more well-written submissions than we could present in this collection.

Lastly, I want to thank you for purchasing this anthology, and supporting La Frontera Publishing.

Here at La Frontera Publishing, we believe there are more histories to discover, there are more tales to tell, and there are more stories to write. *La Frontera* is Spanish for "the frontier." We hope you will continue to join us here — on la frontera.

Michael T. Harris, publisher

TABLE OF CONTENTS

INTRODUCTION

By Johnny D. Boggs

My favorite Western novel is A.B. Guthrie Jr.'s *The Big Sky*, and I've written more than 40 books and novels, but the literary form that drew me first to the American West was the short story.

Specifically, two collections: *The Hanging Tree* by Dorothy M. Johnson and *The Collected Stories of Jack Schaefer*. When I read their short prose, I knew: That's the kind of literature I want to write. Elegant, rich prose that moves the reader, that lifts the Western above the formulaic genre.

Not that I've succeeded, but I'll keep trying.

Chances are, as you're reading this my nose might be buried in a story by Jack London, Ernest Hemingway or, my favorite writer of any form, Mark Twain.

When I was beginning to blaze my own literary trail, I wrote short stories. People often asked when I planned on tackling a novel, and I always replied, "I can't keep a train of thought long enough to write a book."

I thought I could hone my craft on short fiction, and, maybe, at some point, move into tackling a novel. So I wrote, and wrote, and revised, and revised, and rewrote, and spent a fortune on ribbons for my manual Smith Corona typewriter, and, later, ink cartridges for an Apple computer. I sent stories out, and accumulated rejection letters before someone took a chance on publishing this no-name

1

writer. Other editors encouraged me; some even published me. A few even dared to pay me.

Eventually, I moved to long form fiction, and when editors or publishers came back to me requesting a new, original short story, I started sweating. Profusely. Because after writing novels, I realized that those warnings I'd heard earlier from masters of prose like Elmer Kelton and Loren D. Estleman were absolutely right.

It's harder to write a short story than a book.

In fact, I'll go on record as saying the short story is the hardest form of literature there is.

Think about it. You have to cram everything into a few thousand words – science-fiction genius Isaac Asimov even boiled down some of his stories into mere sentences. Everything. Character, plot, drama, dialogue. You can lose the reader with one bad or boring phrase, one misplaced, ill-thought-out word. Every single word has to work. There is no room for error.

That's not always the case in book-length prose. I remember people telling me when I had just started reading Larry McMurtry's *Lonesome Dove*: "Oh, the first 100, 200 pages drag, but keep with it." (Confession: I, however, became hooked on that novel from the opening, "When Augustus came out on the porch the blue pigs were eating a rattlesnake—not a very big one.")

Short stories stick with me longer than novels. Louis L'Amour's "The Gift of Cochise" over his novelization of the screenplay for *Hondo*. Elmore Leonard's "The Boy Who Smiled" over *Hombre*, which is a fantastic novel. Owen Wister's "Timberline" over *The Virginian*. John Jake's homage to German writer Karl May, "Manitow and Ironhand," over *The Bastard*. And those masters of the short fiction form, Schaefer ("Sergeant Houck," "Hugo Kertchak, Builder"), Johnson ("I Woke Up Wicked," "Lost Sister"), London ("To Build a Fire," "All Gold Canyon"), Twain ("Buck Fanshaw's Funeral," "The Celebrated Jumping Frog of Calaveras County"), Fred Grove ("When the Caballos Came," "Comanche Woman"), Bret Harte ("How Santa Claus Came to Simpson's Bar," "Three Vagabonds of Trinidad") and O. Henry ("The Reformation of Calliope," "The Ransom of Red Chief").

Stephen Crane, Eugene Manlove Rhodes, Zane Grey, Luke Short, Max Brand, B.M. Bower, Will Henry/Clay Fisher,

2

Wayne D. Overholser and even Brian Garfield all wrote short fiction set in the American West. Annie Proulx and Sherman Alexie still do. A lot of great novelists, on the other hand, never could master short fiction. For one simple reason: It's a brutal, unforgiving form.

As a child of the 1960s, and novice writer in the 1980s, I missed those golden years of short Western fiction, when writers had high-end markets such as *Collier's, Argosy* and *The Saturday Evening Post*—the later still out there, by the way—not to mention a plethora of pulps, including *Ranch Romances, All Western, Western Story* and Max Brand's *Western Magazine*. By the same token, I'm a sucker for hard-boiled pulps like *Black Mask* and mystery writers such as Dashiell Hammett, Raymond Chandler, William P. McGivern and Raoul Whitfield (nobody remembers Whitfield) who did their best to prove that genre writing can be great literature. As did Guthrie, Schaefer and Johnson in the Western field.

These days, it's hard for fans of short Western fiction to find new stories. Likewise, it's hard for writers to find those markets, too. Fewer and fewer magazines are publishing fiction, especially fiction set in the American West. Anthologies of original works are even rarer. That's why I'm pleased to introduce you to *Outlaws and Lawmen*.

This anthology from La Frontera Publishing is divided into two categories: traditional and contemporary. That makes me happy. For years, I've argued with editors and publishers that the American West didn't begin in Texas after the Civil War, that it's alive and vibrant and relevant today. On the other hand, solid-researched traditional settings never fail to transport me back in time.

In these stories, you'll find familiar and unfamiliar names. The writers and the characters they're writing about.

John Duncklee—one of the modern West's great poets and curmudgeons—has won a Spur Award from Western Writers of America. So has Lori Van Pelt, who always amazes me with her short fiction. D.B. Jackson is a rising star in the field. Douglas Hocking knows his stuff. Jerry Guin, James Hitt, Jason H. Campbell, Rob Kresge, Wesley Tallant, W. Michael Farmer and Dave P. Fisher have their own unique voices and original or traditional approaches to storytelling.

The only thing these writers have in common is their love of the American West, then and now. And their love for the hardest form of fiction there is to write.

Enjoy the journey.

Editor's Note: Johnny D. Boggs (www.johnnydboggs.com) is a past president of Western Writers of America and winner of six Spur Awards. His first came in 2002 for the short story "A Piano at Dead Man's Crossing." Another story, "The Cody War," was a Spur Award finalist in 2008. He lives in Santa Fe, New Mexico.

TRADITIONAL WEST

A BLOOD RED MOON

By D.B. Jackson

Chapter 1

John Paul Riggins rode with his back to a wind that blew down from the north country careening through thinly treed granite passes like some errant freight train racing the long shadows of a dying day. He turned in the saddle and checked the carcass of the deer, gutted and field-dressed, and slung across the back of his packhorse with nothing to cover it but its own hide, haired-out and ready for winter.

A sky, the color of a bottomless lake, backlit the saw-toothed horizon where the sun began its descent and burned a line that made the clouds appear to be on fire from north to south, as far as the eye could see.

He nudged his saddle horse down across shale scree and through the dark, forested woodlands of the upper elevations to emerge in the last light of day onto a clearing from which he surveyed the land below. A modest cabin and a barn, as out of place as the man himself, stood as stark reminders of the solitary life he preferred over the company of people.

Behind the barn in a split rail corral stood a mare and her wobbly-legged foal. In the meadow beyond, cattle grazed and some took shelter in the brush for the night.

Riggins descended the trail to the barn, put up the horses, tended to the venison, and called to the dog. The man and the dog entered the cabin through a door with no lock, and the man built a fire in the river-rock fireplace that made up one wall.

He skewered the heart and tongue of the buck for the dog and a cut of the hindquarter for himself. The fire sizzled and crackled with the drippings, and the dog watched without moving.

After they ate, the man sat with his boots crossed before the fire and stared into the flame as though the act itself was the product of some primeval calling of his ancestors from a thousand years before. He set the coffee cup on the hearth near his feet and his head nodded as he dozed and the dog slept near the heat of the fireplace.

Neither the dog nor the man heard the guarded shuffling of boot heels upon the plank-board porch outside the door. When the door exploded from the hinges, both man and dog awoke to the thunderous blast of fire and smoke from the muzzles of shotguns that fired indiscriminately in upon them.

The first blast lifted the dog and sent it across the room in a trail of its own blood. The blast from the second shotgun twisted Riggins where he stood and dropped him with his shirt bleeding from half a dozen holes. The gunmen turned and continued firing until the air was no longer breathable and the shooting obliterated the fixtures of the cabin.

When they left the violators took with them food and whiskey and two fresh saddle horses. They rode through the night beneath a moon that came up blood red and, when they stopped just before dawn, they did so looking down upon a poor homestead occupied by a preacher, his wife, and their fifteen-year old son.

They sat on their horses in the moonlight and neither spoke. Tom Gorman and Randall Shaw wore ill-fitting coats procured along the way, and beneath the coats, prison shirts. They passed the whiskey bottle, reloaded, and carried their shotguns cross-saddle as they descended the narrow trail in silence.

At the cabin a dog barked, the horses whinnied, and a sleepy-eyed preacher, unarmed and dressed in nightclothes, stood with the door ajar as he gazed out upon the two riders who stood their horses and looked down without comment. The preacher waited, and then he spoke.

"You're welcome to make your beds in the barn yonder, and share breakfast in the morning."

Fire from the muzzle of Gorman's shotgun lit up the porch, ripped away a portion of the door, and soaked the preacher's nightshirt in red. The preacher slumped as his wife emerged from the darkness behind him, screaming and wailing at the sight of her husband.

Another explosion from the 10-gauge held by Shaw sent her reeling back into the darkness from which she came, and both men dismounted.

They entered the cabin where the young boy knelt over his mother. Her eyes, blank and empty, stared up at the dark ceiling.

Shaw nodded toward the boy.

"Bring him with us."

Gorman pushed the boy away from his mother with his boot. "Get some clothes on."

When they rode out the boy sat astraddle the family's buggy horse, his hands tied behind him and a rawhide lace looped about his neck and bound to the saddle horn.

At midday they stopped to rest and water their spent mounts. They lay down beside a still stream in a meadow of tall grass and slept a whiskey-induced sleep with the boy bound to the wrist of Gorman, and the horses hobbled to graze.

John Paul Riggins awoke with the sun in his face and sat with his back to the fireplace, his breathing shallow and the burn of infection beginning to settle into the weeping holes that pockmarked his midsection.

He rose to his feet, checked the dog, then collected his hat, his frayed coat, and his rifle and wobbled to the splintered door and out to the corral. His movements came slow and pained, but he managed to saddle one of the worn out horses left behind by the shooters. He turned the horse's head toward town, slumped in the saddle, and prayed he could stay mounted.

Sheriff Clinton Grant stopped midway as he crossed the street and watched the solitary figure riding slowly in his direction, the rider tilted forward in the saddle with a rifle tied on across the saddle in front of him. The sheriff walked toward the approaching horse and caught it up by the headstall when it stopped in front of him.

Riggins lifted his head.

"I've been shot up some."

He pitched sideways and the sheriff lowered him to the ground as several others gathered around them.

Riggins awoke in the evening darkness of a room he recognized as the parlor of the doctor's house. His wounds had been treated and dressed and, but for the soreness that attended the wounds, he felt his strength returning. He sat up in the makeshift bed when he heard the familiar voice of the doctor.

"How you feeling?"

"Better than I expected."

"I don't know what happened, but you're a lucky man, John. I removed six shot, two of which penetrated deeply, but caused no significant damage. If you'd have gotten here much later, we'd be fighting a serious infection—as it is, that's not the case."

"When can I ride?"

"The only thing that will slow you down is the pain. Your injuries are minor. If that shot had gone a few inches to the right, we'd be considering what to put on your gravestone."

Riggins spent the night. In the morning he made his report to the sheriff. Grant deputized him and they made plans to find the shooters. By noon, he and the sheriff were back at the cabin setting out on the trail of the two men who did not attempt to conceal the direction in which they rode. Their reckless manner left the sheriff with grave concerns about their intentions.

The sun rode high in the sky when Sheriff Grant and John Riggins pulled up on the trail above the homestead of Preacher Jennings. Grant cursed when he looked down through the trees at the sprawled body of the clergyman lying on his back with his arms and legs twisted in disarray and his nightshirt soaked red with blood.

"There's no damn call for that."

Riggins shook his head and they nudged their horses forward.

They searched the cabin and found the body of Mrs. Jennings, but no sign of the boy.

The sheriff was the first to speak.

"They took Levi with them."

Riggins nodded in the direction of the corrals.

"The boy's riding their old buggy horse."

They wrapped the bodies of the preacher and his wife, laid them side by side upon their rickety bed, soaked the place in kerosene and burned it to the ground. When they rode out on the trail of Gorman and Shaw, they did so knowing the life of the boy hung in the balance.

Chapter 2

The boy's nose bled and his eyes peered out through a puffy face, bruised and beaten by the rough-knuckled fist of Gorman, who jerked the boy to his feet by the rawhide lace about his neck. The boy stood and coughed, and caught his breath.

Gorman shouted at the boy.

"Get them horses saddled."

Shaw looked up at the boy over his coffee.

"You'd like to shoot him, wouldn't you?"

Levi shook his head.

"You wouldn't kill him for what he did to your daddy?"

"No."

"That's mighty big of you, son."

Shaw stood and put a boot to the boy's backside and sent him sprawling.

The boy stood and Shaw dealt him a heavy blow to the jaw and spun him backwards off his feet. The boy lay dazed and, when his head cleared, he stood again and glared at Shaw.

"You going to turn the other cheek, are you?"

The boy turned his cheek and Shaw dealt him another crushing blow, and this time the boy did not get up.

Gorman stood over the boy.

"I told you to saddle them horses."

The boy rose on unsteady legs and wobbled to the saddles piled with the blankets and bridles near where the horses grazed. He caught and saddled first one, then another of the horses and, when he was finished, he turned back to Gorman, who sat near the fire.

"Is that it?"

Gorman rose, strode quickly to the boy and backhanded him causing a welt to rise over the cheekbone beneath the bruises and wobbling him back off his feet.

"Don't back talk me, boy."

Gorman bent over, caught up the rawhide lace and dragged the boy to his horse.

"Get on."

The boy mounted and Gorman knotted the lace through the gullet of the saddle. He looked up at the boy.

"You don't have any more sand than your daddy did."

The boy glared down at him and, this time, the passive look in the boy's eyes took on the dark defiance of hatred. He kicked violently, caught Gorman on the jaw, and dug his heels into the sides of the horse. The horse bolted and, as it did so, Shaw raised his rifle in a slow and deliberate manner, centered the sights on the heaving ribs of the horse and shot it out from under the boy.

The horse dropped lifeless to the ground and scarred up a trench where it skidded to a stop, throwing the boy forward and snapping him back at the end of the rawhide lace that bound him to the saddle. Gorman rushed forward, checked the boy, then began laying his boots on him as Shaw pulled him off and wrestled him away from the boy.

"Leave him be."

The boy coughed and gasped. His shirt hung on him in shreds and blood ran from his arms and chest.

When they mounted up, the boy rode behind Shaw. He chanced a furtive look in the direction of Gorman, who did not speak, but glared at him with an expression vindictive and hateful.

The loud report from Shaw's rifle had echoed through the granite canyons and traveled on the quiet mountain air a long time after the bullet that killed the boy's horse left the barrel. When the sound reached Riggins and Grant, they both pulled their mounts to a halt and attempted to determine the direction from which it came.

Grant pointed up country.

"It's them."

Riggins nodded.

"How far away do you reckon they are?"

"Not far, as the crow flies—maybe half a day on the trail."

Riggins confirmed Grant's estimate and added, "If we press it, we should close the gap sometime after they make camp for the night."

Grant looked at Riggins.

"They don't seem too concerned about anyone catching up with them, do they?"

Riggins shook his head.

"They got nothing to lose, and they're holding all the cards."

The moon came up full, outlined in a crystal halo that appeared to have been put there as a tribute to the moon's place in the order of celestial bodies that presided over the heavens from the time the moon and stars came to be.

The two lawmen who rode the lunar trail did so grateful for the light it cast upon the ground before them. They followed the moonlit shadows and the light of the campfire down to the small clearing where Gorman and Shaw slept with the boy tied out to Gorman's wrist.

The boy lay on his back, his face swollen from the beating he took, and his eyes red from the tears he shed for the parents he lost and the soul he was about to lose. He lifted his head and looked over at Shaw, and then at Gorman. Both men reeked of alcohol and wood smoke. Their breathing was heavy and deep.

He rolled on his side, lifted the pistol from Gorman's holster, and held his breath. Neither of the men responded when the boy sat upright and drew back the hammer with no pretense of concealing its sound. He did not weigh his next move but, when he squeezed the trigger, the explosion of thunder and fire sent the bullet spiraling into the chest of Gorman, and Shaw jumped to his feet, clawing for the pistol at his side. When the boy fired the second shot and sent the bullet whining past him, Shaw turned and ran for the cover of the trees.

The smoke cleared and the boy stared wide-eyed and fearful into the surrounding darkness, waiting for Shaw to return in a fury of gunfire. He sat there tethered to the body of the man he killed, and his hands shook and the pistol waved wildly about as though he had lost all ability to control it.

His heart pounded and he listened for that which he could not see, and he imagined devilish creatures of the night lurking in the bushes watching him through eyes red and on fire.

Sheriff Grant stepped into the clearing, his shadowy figure outlined in the silver light of the moon and his face shrouded in darkness. The boy swung the pistol around and squeezed the trigger. The sheriff turned to face the sound of the gunshot and the boy recognized him in that instant of an eternity in which it was too late to undo that which had been done. He wished it otherwise but, in his mind, he could see the bullet spiraling and buffeting the night air as it flew with frightening accuracy toward its intended victim.

The boy waited. He heard no sound when the sheriff doubled over, gut-shot and spewing blood from his shirt. He did not hear the sheriff when he screamed a warning to Riggins and, when the impact of the bullet sent the sheriff sprawling into the brush, the boy had shut out the reality of it all in a silence so complete he was certain it was a dream.

Levi Jennings dropped the pistol and tore at the rawhide lace knotted about his neck. His hands shook and he struggled with the unmanageable knot. He leaned across Gorman's body and reached for the belt knife pinned beneath the dead man.

The boy watched the brush as he tried to roll Gorman over and, just as he grasped the knife, Shaw burst forth from the darkness and caught the boy up by the tether. The boy attempted to draw the knife free, but Shaw jerked him backward before he was able to do so.

Shaw raised his pistol to strike the boy when Riggins, carrying a rifle and hunkered low, stepped forth from the shadows near where the sheriff lay. To protect the boy, he fired a warning shot high over Shaw's head, and then dropped to one knee and pressed his fingers to the side of the sheriff's neck.

Shaw rolled back to the cover of the saddles and left the boy tethered to the dead man.

Riggins shouted to the shadows that concealed Shaw.

"The sheriff is still alive. We can end this here."

The boy rocked back and forth on his knees, and tears rolled down his cheeks. Shaw's sobering voice behind him came cold and unexpected.

"Give it up or I'll kill this kid."

14

The boy reached for Gorman's knife, took it up and began sawing at the rawhide lace.

Riggins looked up and called out to Shaw.

"All that'll buy you is more trouble, and they'll dig your grave when they dig his."

Shaw's voice was calm and frighteningly final.

"Mine's already dug."

The rawhide lace dropped free and the boy threw down the knife and stood to run. Two shots lit up the darkness behind him and the bullets that whined past his head in the night did so in such close proximity to him he dropped to his knees. Both rounds shattered the tree limbs near where Riggins knelt, and Riggins lay flat on the ground in response.

Shaw stepped up, snatched the rawhide lace, and dragged the boy back into the darkness.

The picketed horses of Shaw and Gorman pulled back, tossed their heads and stomped their feet. Riggins looked in the direction of the horses, and then back to the black void in the brush where he imagined Shaw and the boy to be. There was no sound, and nothing to suggest their whereabouts or their intentions.

Riggins shook his head in disgust. He rose up slightly and fired two shots in rapid succession, dropping both horses, with their heads held up by the lead ropes that bound them to the picket line.

"Dammit," he cursed.

Then he moved back into the brush where he and Grant tied off their horses earlier. He led the horses closer to where the sheriff lay and shouted back into the blackness across the fire.

"You just ran out of options."

The silence that followed hung in the cold night air a long time. Finally, Shaw responded.

"You want the boy—I'll trade him for a horse."

"No deal."

The boy screamed in pain.

"It's all the same to me, but you're going to end up with a dead kid and a fifty-fifty chance of dying yourself."

Riggins bent down close to the sheriff, whose breathing was shallow but steady. The bleeding of the gunshot wound seemed to have stopped. His eyes fluttered at Riggins' touch, and they opened when he lifted the sheriff's shirt to examine the wound. He bent low over the sheriff and spoke in a hushed voice.

"Clinton, can you hear me?"

The sheriff nodded, and his eyes appeared to be clear.

"I hear you—I heard him too. Trade the boy for the horse."

Riggins nodded, then sat up and called out to the night.

"All right, you got a deal. Send the boy out."

"No, you walk that horse out and tie him up close."

Riggins looked down at the sheriff.

The sheriff shook his head, but did not speak.

Riggins waited a long time before he responded, then he did so in a manner that did not invite a counter.

"You'll not get a horse until I get the boy."

"Have it your way. Come daylight you'll have a dead boy and a dying partner to deal with."

Chapter 3

The fire in camp burned down to ash and coals, the moon receded into the cover of the pre-dawn sky, and the black of the granite peaks that stood above them to the east were now visible by the thin gray line that outlined them.

The boy shivered and hunkered down into his coat. Shaw sat with his rifle across his legs. The new position they had taken up in the night looked down upon the camp and concealed them in a cluster of granite boulders that kept them from the wind.

Below them, Riggins and Grant held a vigil over the camp and over the brush-covered location in which they supposed Shaw and the boy to be.

When the sun came up full, the grotesqueness of the two horses lying dead with their heads held aloft by the lead ropes tied to the picket line and Gorman's blood-soaked shirt clinging to his cold body caused Riggins to look away. He glanced over at the sheriff, his expression one of disgust and frustration.

"I had to shoot my own damn horses last night, and we still don't know for sure what's become of the boy."

The sheriff nodded.

"Sometimes, there ain't nothing about this job I like."

16

A band of sunlight crossed the granite fortress where Shaw and the boy sat out the night. The boy, his hands bound behind him and the tether now off his neck and about his ankles, pushed against the dirt with his boots and adjusted his position to move himself into the warmth of the sunlit patch of ground.

Shaw shifted his gaze to the boy without moving his head.

"Your daddy was a preacher?"

The boy nodded.

"What's your name?"

"Levi Jennings."

"Levi is a Bible name—your daddy tell you that?"

"Yessir."

"Did he tell you Levi was a good man?"

"Yes."

"Did he also tell you Levi and his brother Simeon murdered people?"

"He didn't murder no one."

"He damn sure did—says so right in the Bible."

"How do you know that?"

"My daddy was a preacher, same as yours."

Shaw stopped speaking and let his words sink in with the boy. Finally, Levi shook his head.

"I don't believe you. If he was, why do you kill people?"

Shaw looked at the boy, his expression grim and with no sign of concession about it at all. He tilted his head in the direction of Gorman stretched out dead before the ashes where he died.

"Same as you—we all got it in us."

The boy glared at him, but did not respond.

"How old are you, boy?"

"Fifteen."

"Fifteen, a preacher's kid, and look at you, a full-born killer yourself. You suppose the angels rejoiced when you, with no more forgiveness left in you, shot and killed a man while he slept?"

Levi hung his head and the knot in his throat prevented him from responding, so he just shook his head. Shaw held his gaze and Levi turned his eyes up and stared directly into those of Shaw, and he saw no malice there, only the reflection of himself bound for the same hell.

"You and me—we get no free pass for studying the scriptures and putting in the years of trying to live a righteous life," Shaw

17

said. Then he shook his head as though the action itself confirmed the final condemnation of a young man's soul to eternity.

Levi's eyes, rimmed in red, bore the hopelessness of his circumstance. He spoke in a low voice.

"How many people you killed?"

"Two, before yesterday...one that got me sent to prison and another in prison—neither one my doing."

"You reckon you're going to hell?" The boy asked.

"You reckon I'm not?"

"I reckon you are."

The boy looked at him a long time. He appeared younger than he did in the dark of night. There was nothing soft in his eyes, and no sign of a future in them the boy could see.

"Can you untie my hands?"

"What for?"

"My wrists hurt and I gotta pee."

Shaw cut the rawhide from the boy's wrists and freed his hands.

"You try to run off or untie your ankles, I will shoot you."

Levi stood and turned his back to Shaw. When he turned back and buttoned his trousers, he sat down in the sunlight again.

"You planning to kill me?"

"What would you do about it if I was?"

"There ain't much I can do."

"Your daddy make you sing much in church?"

"Yessir he did, some."

"Mine too. You got a favorite song?"

"I'm partial to *A Shelter In The Time Of Storm*. We sang that one a lot."

"Yeah, we sang that one too...it was a good one."

Levi turned his head from Shaw and stared off into the blue haze of the distant mountain peaks. Tears dropped in ones and twos from his eyes and ran down his cheeks, but he did not cry and he did not let Shaw see the tears. He wiped his cheeks on the back of his hands and looked out onto the camp a long ways below.

"They're gonna kill you," he said.

"They'll try, but they'll be killing you too."

Levi looked back at Shaw, his eyes cold and empty and nothing hollow about his words when he spoke.

"I'm like you now...I'm dead anyway."

They sat a long time in silence. Below them the sheriff and Riggins ate from their saddlebags and drank from canteens. Shaw and the boy had neither. Levi sat with his knees up to his chest and his head resting on his arms.

"You think they're gonna give in?" He asked.

"I don't suppose they will."

"How long we gonna wait?"

"When I'm done waiting, me and you are going to walk out there, and I'll get a horse or they'll be packing you back down the mountain."

"You'd for sure kill me?"

Shaw unholstered his pistol, opened the loading gate, and spun the cylinder. He looked up at the boy and nodded he would, then he ejected the empties and replaced them with live rounds.

The boy bowed his head and folded his hands. When he finished, he said *amen* and raised his head.

"Reserving you a spot in the afterlife?"

"No."

"What are you praying about then?"

The boy shook his head as though to dismiss the question.

"I asked you a question."

The boy spoke in a voice not much more than a whisper.

"I asked forgiveness for what I done."

"That's it?"

"No."

Shaw waited and his silence asked the question as though it came directly from his lips.

"I forgave you and him for what you done."

"We just killed your ma and pa—we made you an orphan."

"I know you did. Last night I wanted to shoot you when I shot him," the boy said, tilting his head in the direction of the body lying near the ashes of the burned-out campfire.

"Why didn't you?"

"I tried. You run off."

"No, I mean, why didn't you shoot me first?"

"Of the two of you, he was the worst."

Shaw sat back and chewed the inside of his cheek as he contemplated the boy's words. The boy stared down at the camp and shifted his head for a better look.

"They killed your horses."

"I know, I seen them last night—funny thing, they wasn't even ours."

The boy raised his head and, when he sat back down, he looked directly at Shaw's downturned head until Shaw looked up at him from under his hat.

"What?" Shaw asked.

"Those are Mr. Riggins' horses."

"Who's Mr. Riggins?"

"He's the man down there you been talking to."

Shaw raised his eyebrows.

"We killed the man owned them horses."

"You didn't kill him very good, 'cause that's him."

Shaw laughed.

"It's a small damn world, ain't it?"

They sat in silence a long time before the boy spoke. When he did speak, his voice was quiet and sincere.

"It's not too late."

Shaw stared down at his boots without looking up at the boy.

"Not too late for what?"

"For you to redeem yourself."

Shaw shifted his gaze to the boy, but did not turn his head.

"You mean give up?"

"Yes."

"You never been to prison, have you?"

"No."

Shaw's voice softened when he responded.

"I'm not going back to that."

The boy took a deep breath and let it out slow, as though he understood.

"He ain't going to forgive you. You could just go off now and he can't come after you. There'd be three of us and just two horses, and the sheriff is shot up."

"All your concern for me, or are you just trying to save yourself?"

The boy spoke up in a direct manner that caught Shaw off guard.

"Both. I don't want to die, and I don't want you to die. We'll both have to answer to God over all this anyway."

Shaw was quiet a long time. He looked off into the endless treetops and the forbidding rise of mountains in every direction.

"It's a long damn ways out of here—I ain't going it on foot."

Shaw looked down at his boots, then across that great expanse of trees to the ridgeline that made up the horizon in every direction. He sat in deep contemplation and the boy watched without speaking. Shaw stared a blank stare at the ground around his boots, and stayed that way a long time.

Finally, he turned and rose, then positioned his rifle over the top curve of the great boulder that sheltered them, and took aim in the general direction of where Riggins and Grant made their stand during the night.

He fired a random shot and the bullet screamed overhead dangerously close to the two lawmen. Riggins looked about attempting to locate the point from which the shot had been fired.

With disregard for concealing his position any longer, Shaw called out.

"I'm coming down with the boy. Walk a horse out and we'll trade. And I will kill this boy if it comes to that."

Riggins looked over at the sheriff and the sheriff nodded his approval. Riggins shouted back in the direction of the granite fortress.

"Bring him down—I'll get the horse."

Riggins slid his rifle over to the sheriff, who now sat upright, held there by the slender sapling against which he leaned. Riggins knelt beside the sheriff.

"Clinton, we can't let him ride out of here, boy or no. I'll stop the horse so as to give you a shot. You decide when to take it."

The sheriff nodded, levered in a round, and put the rifle to his shoulder to measure his shot if he was to take one.

Riggins led the horse into the clearing of the camp and positioned the animal to put Shaw in the sheriff's line of fire. He lifted his own pistol from the holster, let it drop lightly back in place, and waited.

Shaw leaned his rifle against the rocks and threw his knife to the boy.

"Cut yourself loose."

"Aren't you afraid I'll run off?"

"You think you can outrun a bullet?"

"I reckon not."

While the boy took up the knife and sawed on the rawhide lace about his ankles, Shaw unholstered his pistol, unloaded and reloaded it. With the boy in front and Shaw following and brandishing the pistol, the two emerged from the high ground and thick brush into the edge of the clearing from a direction Riggins did not anticipate. They stopped when they saw Riggins standing beside the horse with his pistol drawn.

Shaw spoke first.

"Put up the gun, we're coming in."

Riggins holstered his weapon.

"Now you do the same," Riggins called back to Shaw.

Shaw held the boy by the back of his shirt, holstered his weapon, and then pushed the boy before him as they began to close the distance to Riggins and the horse. Riggins' hand shook as he measured the distance to Shaw and the boy. The sheriff held his breath and kept Shaw in the sights of his rifle, adjusting his position with each step Shaw took.

Shaw slowed the pace and Riggins felt his chest pounding. Shaw's demeanor, as cold and unwavering as a deadly serpent, challenged every instinct of self-preservation within Riggins. Riggins' hand dropped and he let his fingers rest against the worn grips of the pistol, and Shaw stepped forward slowly.

Shaw stopped and time seemed to have stopped with him. The sheriff bore down upon the trigger of the rifle and waited. Riggins felt his fingers tremble, and he resisted the almost uncontrollable urge to draw and fire. He waited. Shaw did not move, and the boy stood where Shaw stopped him. Shaw turned his head slowly to survey all that lay before him: the dead horses suspended from the picket line, Riggins, deputized and waiting, the unattended body of Gorman, and the prize—a waiting horse, saddled and ready. He turned his gaze towards Riggins, and Riggins saw the vacant look in Shaw's eyes.

Then, with no warning, Shaw pushed the boy and sent him sprawling violently to the ground as Shaw cleared his holster and an explosion of fire from the barrel sent a bullet screaming in Riggins' direction, but off-target by a dozen feet.

As quickly as it started, it was over. The sheriff's shot exploded in Shaw's chest and the round fired by Riggins entered near the jawbone and exited near the base of the skull. Moments later, Randall Shaw, child of the clergy, lost soul of those dispossessed of virtue, lay dead, with a young boy weeping at his side, and the two lawmen standing over him.

They removed the coats of Gorman and Shaw and covered the bodies with them. When the two men and the boy stood back, Riggins shook his head.

"He never meant for that shot to hit me."

Sheriff Grant stood favoring his wounded side and looked to the place Shaw had been standing.

"He could have let his nerves get the best of him," he offered.

Riggins stepped forward and retrieved Shaw's pistol from the ground where it fell. He opened the loading gate and spun the cylinder. His expression was void of victory when he snapped the loading gate shut. He looked from the sheriff to the boy.

"He never meant it to go any other way. He had one spent cartridge and five empty chambers."

A COOL HAND

By Jerry Guin

Bat Masterson looked up from his desk when the board door to the sheriff's office was opened. A slight of build woman clad in a plain cotton dress stepped through the door way. She had an ill-fitting small ladies' hat atop her head that did little to conceal her hurriedly combed hair-do. Sunlight glittered off loose strands of gray-blonde hair that stuck out near her ears where she had attempted to arrange a bun. She hesitantly stepped forward; her face drawn, carrying a worried expression. Bat stood as the woman approached. He recognized Evelyn Tiggs from a previous encounter with her son Russell, a few weeks ago.

"Mrs. Tiggs, how are you doing today?"

She gave a futilely-attempted smile by drawing her facial muscles a little which only served to show her distress.

"I'm fine Sheriff, fine."

Bat held a hand out to a ladder-back chair in front of the desk.

"Would you like some coffee, Ma'am?"

"Oh, no, no thank you," she muttered then sat down in the chair. Bat sat down as well. When the woman remained silent, Bat asked, "What can I do for you Mrs. Tiggs?"

Evelyn Tiggs sat back in the chair and placed her small handbag onto her lap. She casted her eyes away, not looking at the sheriff directly.

"It's about Russell my son," she began, "I'm afraid for him. There's a man that came out to the house looking for Russell; said

25

he was a bounty hunter. He said he would shoot Russell if he didn't give himself up!" Then Evelyn Tiggs burst into crying pitifully.

Bat stood and pulled a handkerchief from his jacket pocket and offered it to the distraught woman. She took it and wiped at her eyes and nose.

"I just don't know what to do. I haven't even seen Russell since last week; before this whole thing began. I heard about you bringing in Emmett and Mica."

Bat sat back down.

"Those three were bound to get into a lot of trouble the way they were acting around town. I don't know why they were thinking that they could travel off to a different town, different county and try to rob a bank without being caught. I'd say it was real fortunate that no one, including any one of them got shot or killed. Bank robbery is a serious business. I know of the reward being offered by The Kansas State Bank. Five hundred dollars, I believe. They would like to retrieve the balance of the money that Russell got away with. And you say someone is already looking to claim the reward?"

Evelyn Tiggs nodded. "He came and beat on the door, demanding that I tell him where Russell is at."

Bat leaned forward in his chair. "I can't stop a bounty hunter from trying to lawfully collect a bounty but I can stop him from harassing you again, if you'll give me his name and description."

"I didn't get a name. He was a tall man needing a shave; dirty and mean looking. He rode a brown horse. That's all I know."

Bat almost smiled from the information the woman gave. Hell, half the men in town matched that description. Figuring further talk of the man's looks would be a waste of time, Bat turned to a different approach.

"I can only offer the protection of the law if Russell is in my custody. Do you have any idea as to where Russell may have taken off too? If I knew where he went, then I would go and get him. You folks have lived near Dodge for only a couple of years. Could Russell have gone on back to where you came from or some other place that he is familiar with?"

Evelyn Tiggs shook her head from side to side. "We came from Arkansas but there is nothing for Russell or me back there. It was hard living there; then one day we had a fire in the stove pipe; the whole place burned to the ground. That's when Ernest, that's my late husband's name, loaded everything we had left in a wagon and came out here to be close to his bother Willie. We had no other place to go."

* * * *

Six months prior to Evelyn Tiggs coming to the sheriff's office, Dodge City Mayor Jim Kelly had become very irritated by the actions of town Marshal Larry Deger. In addition to being the mayor, Kelly owned several saloons along the streets of Dodge. Larry Deger also owned at least one saloon so the two men were in direct competition. Deger was not above using his position as marshal to enhance the interest of his own business at the expense of Kelly's. He had arrested the bartender of the Red Hen, one of Kelly's saloons, on a simple charge of assault when the bartender threw a drunken friend of Deger's out of the saloon.

Kelly figured the charge was dubious, seeing how the saloon would have to close for lack of a bartender, who was sitting in jail while Deger's saloon next door was over active. Deger was a heavy man, often using his size to overpower and beat any drunken opposition to submission. His heavy handed tactics of arrest, however, were not sitting well with Mayor Kelly and the influential business interests he was trying to promote.

It was June of 1877 when a young Bat Masterson was in town having a few drinks to celebrate his return to Dodge. He was in the Red Hen Saloon along with several others. A local man named Bobby Gill embellished with a few too many drinks saw the rotund marshal walking nearby and made a few diminutive remarks about the marshal's size. Deger wasted no time in approaching the mouth piece, snatching him by the hair then delivering a thundering blow to the side of Gill's head.

When Gill hit the floor Deger commenced to kick him. One kick could have been sufficient but Deger kept up a merciless tirade of kicking. Bat Masterson did not like what he saw. He yelled out, "Enough!" Deger paid him no mind while delivering another kick to Gill. Bat jumped on Deger and locked an arm around his neck. Bat was not a large man himself weighing around 150 pounds. It didn't take long for the 250-pound Deger to fling him to the floor and direct his onslaught to Bat instead of Gill. Somehow Gill got to his feet and escaped through the back of the saloon. A dazed Bat was hauled off to jail.

Bobby Gill was caught and arrested by none other than Ed Masterson, Bat's brother working as Deger's newly hired deputy marshal. After a night in jail both Bat and Bobby were fined and let go.

The fiasco caught the attention of Mayor Kelly. He really wanted to find a way to rid Dodge City of the disliked Deger. Kelly held a meeting with Vice Mayor Chet Jackson and three other Dodge business men.

"The town is having growing pains gentlemen," Kelly said. "The cattle business has been good, thanks to the railroad coming here. We have other factions, besides cattle, to consider as well. Dodge has been a center for hunters to buy supplies and then bring in their hides for trade and transport. The Army has cleared the area of hostiles and opened up the land for settlers. There's an element of interest here and we get inquiries all the time about new businesses having considerations of locating here. We have to make some changes in order to entice new business."

"What kind of change are you talking about?" Jack Jones, owner of the Emporium hotel and restaurant, asked.

"Why, we need to soften our image, somewhat." Kelly said, "Dodge has a reputation as a rough frontier town, full of rowdiness. There's more to it than supplying gambling, whiskey and women to trail end cowboys looking to blow off a little steam before they go home."

"We're already supplying the Army with the stuff they need," Leonard Blake, owner of Blake's' Goods, said.

"That's true," Kelly acknowledged, "but don't you want your business to expand Leonard? What if all of sudden you had a number of farmers wanting implements and ladies wanting furniture and sewing goods. Why you'd be ecstatic and looking for a way to get the stuff here. What I'm talking about is presenting an image of a town that those farmers and ladies would be proud to call home!"

"What do we have to do to get them here?" Leonard asked.

Jim Kelly looked at him as if a bit amused. "Clean the town up," He quipped.

"What we need is a man to quell the violence and make the streets a safe place to walk."

"Marshal Deger's been busting a few heads," Leonard said.

Jim Kelly looked about to each man then spoke, "That's the problem, and Deger's too damned rough! He's a bully and I believe that he's more interested in the amount of whiskey he sells than keeping peace here about. The election for Sheriff of Ford County is coming up in November and I believe Deger is thinking of running for the office. If he wins the election then I believe that things will stay the same as now, a lot of rough housing. The next thing you know we'll be running things at his direction instead of the business leaders directing the affairs of the day. I don't believe that he's the man for the job."

"You got someone in mine Jim?" Chet asked.

"As a matter-of-fact I do. That young Masterson is gutsy enough to handle the job."

"Isn't he already working for Deger?" Leonard asked.

"I mean Ed's younger brother, Bat." Kelly answered then looked around for any rebuttal.

"I heard he was a gunfighter," Chet said.

"Well, he certainly has a reputation as such," Kelly said, "he's the one that was cheated out of wages by that railroad grading sub-contractor a few years ago. Broke as he was Bat got a job driving a freight wagon, for a month, until someone told him the man that ran off without paying up was coming in on the train next day. Bat met the train and spotted the man seated in a coach; he stuck a gun in the man's face and got his pay. He could of killed the guy, and been justified, but he didn't go to such extreme. And Bat is the same man that held out with thirty plus other buffalo hunters at Adobe Wells to send hundreds of war-hooping Indians away without losing a single man. Oh he did shoot a fellow, in self-defense I might add, a couple years ago down in Sweetwater, Texas. That fellow was a soldier from nearby Fort Elliot. Seems the soldier was as much a bully as Larry Deger is, especially so after a drinking episode. It is said that he disposed of several men by means of shooting them. One night after much drinking, he found his so called girl-friend, a saloon girl, curled up next to Bat. He drew a pistol and shot her. The bullet went through her and lodged in Bat's hip. Bat drew his own weapon as he fell and shot the man in the stomach. The man died and so did the saloon girl. Bat got the bullet removed from his hip, spending several weeks in recuperation. Then he came to Dodge and was an assistant marshal under Wyatt Earp just last summer. Bat and Wyatt both left when things got slow last winter."

"Why he sounds as bad as some of the riff raff we'd like to see gone." Leonard said.

"What you say has some truth to it," Kelly said, "but that's the point, we need someone that is a bad ass. Bat is a desperado, but a law abiding one. He can handle himself in a pinch without giving the town a reputation of being wild. Bat has lived with these guys. I don't guess that he's a cowboy, but he knows how to talk their language. He's lived on the range. Been a buffalo hunter, an Indian fighter, scout for the Army and has experience as a peace officer. He talks the talk and walks the walk. I believe he can drink right alongside the visitors to Dodge and hold down violence to a minimum."

Kelly watched as each man sat and listened to his speech, nodding after he had finished.

"I'd like your support in appointing Bat to the office of undersheriff of Ford County until the election is held. And if he does a good job, then we throw our support in his direction and get him elected." When there was no dissention to the mayor's proposal the meeting was adjourned.

The next day Kelly had a meeting with Bat. "I'd like you to consider running for Sheriff of Ford County," Kelly informed right away.

Bat was surprised by the consideration, "I don't see eye to eye the way Larry Deger carries out his duties but wouldn't that be quite a jump, I mean I've a little law enforcement experience, but I have no long-term experience to that effect. How would I begin to get enough votes to roust Deger from getting the office?"

"Your experience speaks for itself and you've nerve enough to do a respectful job," Kelly said, "First off I'll appoint you as Ford County's undersheriff; that alone will give you exposure until the election is held. I've already got the support of other business leaders of Dodge City in this favor. You'll have a good chance to win the election, but you also need to clean up your own reputation a bit and look the part of a man that is friendly to the affairs of Dodge instead of looking the part of a rough frontiersman."

Bat took the Mayor's advice and bought a business man's suit, a bowler hat and a cane. He already owned two .45 Colts, silver plated with bone white handles. Bat spent most of his time as undersheriff in and around Dodge, but managed to steer clear of Larry Deger. The two men eyed each other from a distance, but neither would approach the other, the only exception being legal duties.

It wasn't long before Deger went ahead and declared that he was running for Sheriff of Ford County. At Mayor Kelley's urging the *Dodge City Times* threw their support to Bat Masterson by publishing a campaign article paid for by Mayor Kelly. "Bat is well known as a man of coolness and unflinching nerve under fire or pressure. He is well qualified to fill the office of Sheriff of Ford County and will not turn away from danger."

On November 6, 1877, Bat Masterson became Ford County's sheriff after defeating Larry Deger by a small margin of votes. His first official duty was to fire Deger then appoint his brother, Ed Masterson, to fill the position of Dodge City marshal.

Dodge City was divided into two towns. North of the Santa Fe railroad tracks lay the business commerce of Dodge, lined with stores, eateries and hotels along Front Street. South of the tracks were gambling halls, honky-tonk saloons and shanties where ladies of the saloons kept busy after dark.

The two Masterson brothers worked to reaffirm the town ordinance of no guns on the North side of the tracks. Fired up with quick drinks of whiskey, trail end cowboys were allowed to whoop it on the South side, but anyone caught wearing a gun on the North side was stopped and reminded of the law. If for some reason they did not comply immediately then action was taken.

The brother lawmen agreed to give fair warning to any intrusion of the law, using force only when necessary, but not so much as to bully or beat an opponent senseless. Ed favored talking the offender into reason whereas, depending on the circumstance, Bat would simply club the offender over the head with cane or pistol, throw the drunk into a horse trough to wake him up then give the man a chance to sleep it off. If, however, he resisted then Bat would haul him off to jail, a tactic that he had learned from Wyatt Earp. "Never argue with a drunk. Tell him the way it is going to be and follow through," his words echoed more than once.

Within a few days, the word got out and no more guns were being packed around north of the tracks. Consequently there were no shooting-up the saloons or street gun fights as seen in the past. A drop in saloon brawls was apparent also as no one wanted to have either of the Mastersons standing in front of them.

Inside the Red Hen Saloon, Russell Tiggs, a youth of 18, embellished by a few drinks of rye, approached the suited man leaning his back against the bar. The suited man was Bat Masterson. Bat watched as the young man, with drink in hand, wobbled his way toward him. Tiggs, whose family homesteaded a farm just north of Dodge, had taken to drink and carousing with two hell-raising cousins near to the youth's age. Bat had visited the Tiggs' household just last week after complaints by a number of outraged town folk. Apparently the alcohol-fueled three youths had roamed the streets of Dodge, loosening the cinch on several horses, so that the riders hit the ground when attempting to mount. They also loosened or took off wheel nuts of wagons, causing much mayhem and anguish. Mrs. Tiggs was apologetic.

"It has been hard ever since Russell's father passed on last year. Russell has been difficult to handle, particularly when he takes to running with his cousins," she said. When confronted, the slightly built Russell merely said, "It will not happen again."

It seemed to Bat that Russell might be up to mischief despite the visit last week. Russell was sandy haired with a sprinkling of freckles on a discernible fair-skinned, oval face. He weighted maybe 130 pounds and stood five-foot four, having to look up to the five-foot nine sheriff, when he spoke. Russell was at a difficult age, old enough to think he knew it all and had nothing more to learn. He grinned before he spoke to Masterson.

"I heard that you are a gunfighter and that you are good with your guns, Sheriff. Word is that you spend a lot of time practicing, shooting at cans and bottles. Is that what makes you good, shooting at cans and bottles?" Russell smirked.

Bat eyed the young man, "Does your Ma know that you are in town, Russell?" He asked.

"I can take care of myself, Sheriff," Russell said flatly.

Bat figured the big eyed youth was full of exuberance and loaded with a few-too-many drinks so he decided to go along for the time being. He replied, "Just about anyone can learn to draw and shoot at a can or a bottle, but it takes a cool hand to shoot quickly and straight at a man that can shoot back."

"How's that?" Russell asked.

"Three things are important to a gun hand: speed is third; accuracy is second. The most important thing is your state of mind; the ability to stay cool under fire, making quick decisions, such as when to hesitate and when to draw and fire. Hesitating at the wrong time can get you shot in a heartbeat."

Russell was quick to answer, "But if you never hesitate, then you will always win!" He smirked.

Before Bat could say another word, Russell's two cousins, Everett and Mica, appeared. Everett stated, "We gotta go," then ushered Russell out the bat wing doors. Bat watched them go, hoping they would go home before some sort of misdeed, by one of the three, would force him to intervene.

* * * *

Ten days later at Kinsley, about 35 miles northeast of Dodge, in neighboring Edwards County, three bandits had held up the Kansas State Bank. In their haste to get away they dropped the bag with most of the loot, but still managed to make off with $5,000. The Sheriff of Edwards County, Jack August, sent a wire to Bat telling of the misdeed. Bat summoned a posse and took off, but not toward Kinsley, figuring the sheriff was covering that end. Instead, knowing the countryside from his scouting days, Bat headed the posse in a direction that he figured the bandits would go, which was south and west of Dodge.

It was early December and a driving snow storm was upon the posse at the end of the first day out. A darkened nightfall came early. They found shelter in an old drover's line shack. The horses, by now with backs bowed and tails tucked between their legs from the cold wind, were put into a lean-to shelter nearby the shack. The posse men had a fire going in the shack's stove and were getting ready to brew coffee when two riders rode into the yard, presumably, seeking shelter.

One of the riders yelled out, "Hello the cabin!" Bat yelled back to them without opening the door, "come on in, we got coffee in here!"

Bat settled in a chair next to a table with one of his .45s in hand under his coat. The two half-frozen riders opened the door to enter the shanty. It was semi-dark in the cabin; a single coal oil lamp flame struggled at its wick when the door was opened, while a puff of black smoke erupted from the top. The two hunched figures instinctively headed to the warmth of the little stove.

By the time they looked up and had recognized the new sheriff, Bat Masterson had moved his coat aside a little to show

33

the .45 pointed in their direction. Each man's hand began to lower over his pistol. Bat cocked the .45.

"I wouldn't do that, if I were you!" Bat said.

The two raised their hands when they heard four other pistols being cocked around them.

"Where's Russell?" Bat asked.

Emmett Tiggs looked at brother Mica then gulped and said, "He sent us in ahead, I expect that when we don't come back, he'll most likely go away."

"I'm sure he will!" Bat said, "I'm also sure that he's the one carrying the money."

Emmett silently nodded his head.

At first light, the posse hustled the prisoners to the Dodge City jail.

* * * *

It was exactly one week later that Evelyn Tiggs visited Sheriff Bat Masterson.

Bat felt sorry for the poor woman having first lost her home to a fire then losing her husband to a malady and now her only son and his cousins had robbed a bank. The cousins were in jail, but Russell was still at large and now had a bounty on his head and a bounty hunter hot on his trail. Bat figured the bounty hunter would narrow the search to Russell's home territory; perhaps even trailing him here.

Bat did the best he could to console the woman. "Mrs. Tiggs if the bounty hunter shows up again, tell him I said for him to come see me. If he comes around here, I'll order him to not pester you again. Now if, by chance, Russell sees fit to come home, I want you to talk him into giving himself up." Bat stood, "is that fair enough?"

Evelyn Tiggs stood, "Yes, Sheriff, that's fair."

"It would be the best thing for Russell to come in on his own rather than risk being shot at," Bat assured as he walked the woman to the door.

It was well past dark of the same day when Bat walked into the Red Hen Saloon. Al Green, the bartender, was busy worrying a cloth to a drinking glass when he saw Bat walk in. He put the glass down and hurried to the end of the bar where Bat stood. "Glad to see you, Sheriff."

Bat looked to Al, "are you having a problem Al?"

"No, no nothing like that, I just thought you'd be interested to know that we got a bounty hunter in town. He's sitting over there at table three, jawing with two cowhands."

Bat turned to look in the direction of table three near the back wall.

"Fella in the tan shirt and vest," Al said, "he's had a few and keeps telling everyone that he's going to shoot that Russell kid as soon as he sees him. Says he was run off from their place and someone took a shot at him as he was leaving. Now he hasn't caused any trouble in the saloon, but I just thought you'd like to know, Sheriff."

Bat nodded his understanding, "thanks Al, I do appreciate the information."

"Can I get you beer, Bat?"

"Yes," Bat said, "then would you go by table three and tell that fella that I would like a word with him?"

"Right away, Sheriff," Al said. He presented the beer to Bat then walked over to table three. Bat stood at the bar and watched as the man got up and walked toward him. A tall man, broad of shoulder wearing dirty and rumpled range clothes, scuffed boots meaning lots of time in a saddle, perhaps riding through brushy country. He had a flat face that needed a shave and with a nose pushed to one side having been broken some time ago. He stuck out a hand when he approached Bat.

"The name's Avery Welky, been aiming to come see you, Sheriff." His eyes were bleary and red rimmed, possibly from drink.

Bat gave him a quick shake, "heard you were talking about shooting someone," Bat said, "We frown on that kind of behavior around here."

Avery Welky took a step backwards and held his hands out, "I'm a law abiding man, Sheriff; my six-gun is hung on a peg over there on the wall."

"You said you were aiming to come and see me," Bat stated.

Welky stood still, "I was out to the Tiggs place earlier today and someone took a shot at me!"

"That so," Bat said, "what were you doing out to the Tiggs place?"

"I went out to serve a lawful warrant," Welky said.

"You mean a bounty?" Bat corrected, "If it was a warrant then an officer of the law would have done the serving."

35

"Same thing!" Welky shrugged.

"No it isn't!" Bat insisted. "Mrs. Tiggs did come to see me and said you were threatening to shoot her son unless he gave himself up to you. Is that right?"

"I might have said something to that effect. He's there, I know he is. I've been trailing him for most of week now. He spent a lot of time circling around in back country figuring someone was on his trail, I reckon. Anyway the trail leads right back here. I've got a dodger on him and mean to serve it. The lady wasn't very cooperative and when I took to leave, someone took a shot at me from a distance. I heard the bullet whiz past, real close like."

Bat listened attentively and when the man was finished he asked, "Have you ever done this kind of work before, bounty hunting?"

Avery looked at the floor, "No, no I haven't. I finished up a drive to town last week. When I heard about the robbery and the two others being caught and a reward being offered, well then I figured that I'm a good tracker and I could catch that other one, them all being just kids. It's a lot of money for a few days tracking."

Bat nodded his understanding. "That dodger you have doesn't give you a ticket to gun anyone down. It reads that the reward would be paid upon the arrest and confinement of Russell Tiggs. It doesn't say anything about dead or live! I'll give you a little bit of advice, Avery. It would be best if you left this up to the law to handle this matter."

Avery got a startled look on his face, "Are you ordering me to give up on collecting this bounty?"

Bat wasn't to be intimidated, "I said it would be best if you let the law handle the matter, that's all! You already have a complaint against you, now if you go out there again then there might be some blood shed for no good reason."

"What if I catch him off the homestead?" Avery asked.

"He's fair game to catch; not to kill! That's all!" Bat reminded.

Avery nodded then turned and walked back to his table.

Bat left the Red Hen to find his brother. He couldn't watch the man night and day, so if Ed and his deputies could keep track of the man until he left town then let Bat know, he would be able to follow up.

It was just past 8 a.m. the next morning that Ed sauntered into Maggie's Café to find Bat at his customary window table. Bat had just finished his breakfast and was supping coffee.

Ed took a chair across from his brother, "your man just checked out of the hotel and is headed to the livery. I'd say he's leaving town. Do you think you might be in need of some help here Bat?"

Bat shook his head no, "thanks Ed, but I can handle this one on my own."

"Do you want me to get your horse saddled and ready?" Ed asked. Bat pointed a finger out the window to a waiting sorrel, "he's ready to go. I was up early and figured the man would leave early on. If he's headed to the Tiggs' place, he'll ride right past this window."

Ten minutes passed until as Bat had said, Avery Welky rode his horse at a walk right past the window he and Ed were sitting behind. They watched until he was out of sight, then Bat got up and patted his brother on the shoulder as he walked out.

Bat mounted and urged the sorrel into a lope. He was careful to stay a distance behind Avery so that he was not detected. When the Tiggs' home came into view, Bat pulled rein on his horse to see if he could spot Welky's horse. It was there all right. The man had brazenly ridden right up to the hitching post in front of the house. Bat was still observing when the front door opened and Welky took off running from the porch. Something had put a scare into the man. Bat gouged his heels to the sorrel and got the animal moving quickly.

A shotgun blast suddenly ended whatever quietness that was about the place. Bat could see that Welky had fallen down in the yard. Evelyn Tiggs stood on the porch with the double-barreled shotgun still pointing at Welky. Bat pulled the sorrel to a halt just as the woman was walking down the steps. He could see that she had fire in her eyes and would undoubtedly pull the trigger on the second barrel if he didn't stop her.

"Stop it!" Bat yelled, "Evelyn, stop right there!" Evelyn took another step and it looked as if she was going to raise the gun for another shot. Bat grabbed his .45 from his right holster and fired a shot into the air to get the woman's attention. It worked. She stopped in mid-step then looked over to Bat and then let the shotgun down. "I told him not to come back!" she muttered.

Bat slid from the saddle and slapped the sorrel's rump to get it to move on.

Russell came out the front door. He had a six-gun belted on. He walked across the porch, down the steps then stopped next to his mother at a distance of about fifteen feet, facing Masterson.

"Are you looking for me, Sheriff?" Russell smirked.

Bat was aware of the youth's six-gun, the position of his hands, and his demeanor. Wary of any quick movements, his own right hand was close to the ivory handle of his .45. "There's been enough bloodshed, Russell. That man is hurt over there!" He pointed to Welky lying on his face a short distance away. "It would be best for you to surrender yourself and the money to me," Bat said.

"Do you think you are faster than me, Sheriff?" Russell asked, his hand hovering over his pistol butt.

Bat starred expressionless at the youthful face not yet hardened by toil. "I know things have been tough on you, with your Pa dying and all. Life doesn't seem fair when whatever money you got has been spent. At such a time a fella can get to thinking of another way of life, a way where money comes easier. Robbing a bank is not an easier way of doing things. That money belongs to others that worked and saved it. I know that you care for your mother and she has certainly demonstrated that she cares for you. I want you to surrender your pistol and allow the law to settle this matter."

"I'm not sure I'm all that trusting with you, Sheriff! The money would give me and my mother a new start, otherwise I wouldn't have come back here."

Bat stared unflinchingly at Russell, "Unfortunately you would have to go through me to do that. Now you don't really believe that you can draw that old pistol out, cock it and get a round off before I draw and fire on you!" Bat said, "You've got a bit of nerve, Russell, but not good judgment. You draw your pistol for occasional use, me on the other hand, I draw and fire mine every day."

Russell straightened a little; he was suddenly bewildered and stunned at Masterson's audacity to question his abilities. "What do you mean?" He asked.

"Why, if I'm not mistaken, I'd say your sidearm is an old Army Colt cap and ball pistol. They can be had at any hardware store for twelve dollars. The trouble with them is that they have a tendency to misfire on occasion, if any moisture has gotten to the powder. My pistol, however, is new, the latest out; it's loaded with a sealed cartridge practically a 100 percent guarantee that the cartridge is good. All I have to do is draw and pull the trigger. You've been out and about for a week outside, crossing rivers and creeks. When's the last time you checked your powder loads?"

Bat did not give Russell a chance for a reply; instead quick as a flash he drew a silvery Colt .45 and leveled it at the youth. "You also got to know when to draw!" Bat said.

Russell and his cousins were each sentenced to five years prison time and housed in the correctional facility at Leavenworth.

Evelyn Tiggs was soundly reprimanded by the judge for shooting Avery Welky, but was not given any prison time. At a later date she married a freight hauler and the couple moved to Colorado.

Avery Welky, though wounded by bird shot, mostly in the legs, recovered and was awarded half the reward money for the capture of Russell Tiggs. It is believed he went back to Texas and returned to herding cattle for his living.

For the next two years Dodge City was a quieted town thanks to the disarming efforts and influence of Bat Masterson. He was defeated for sheriff in the election of 1879, but remained in Dodge for a time as a saloon owner and card dealer.

DEAD WOMEN TELL NO TALES

By W. Michael Farmer

Slater's elbow gently pokes in my ribs. He thumb-points over his shoulder toward the back of the courtroom. Tom Tucker, deputy sheriff for Otero County, stands at the door, waving his big paw for me to join him.

Tom meets me at the foot of the stairs; saying nothing, he jerks his head toward the back door. Outside, he heads for the street across the yard between the jail and the courthouse. I trot to keep up with him.

"Tom! What's happened? Where're we going?"

He looks around to be sure no one is close enough to hear us.

"They took Persia. Sadie wants to see us right now."

"Who took Persia? She driving the stage to Lake Valley this morning. She's not due back here until three this afternoon. How —"

"Three of Ed Brown's boys just appeared outta nowheres in the bend of the road and took her off the stage 'bout three miles north of Harlosa Springs. They made her hike up her skirt an' give 'em that little pea-popper Sadie give her, then put her on a horse, give the driver a note, and disappeared. The driver near drove the team into the ground gettin' to the telegraph. Soon as Sadie got the telegram she sent for us. She's down to the Orchard."

I feel sick. This is my fault. Brown's boys wouldn't have bothered Persia if I'd just left town like they wanted. I swear through clenched teeth as I steam down the street for Sadie

41

Orchard's hotel, vowing to get Persia back safe no matter the cost. Tom runs to catch up with me.

Sadie, who owns the stage line and a couple of hotels here in Hillsboro, sits at her desk staring at a telegram in her hand. Three other telegrams lay in a scattered pile nearby. She looks up, her eyes cold, black, filled with rage, and hands me the telegram while she looks at Tom. The telegram reads:

STAGE STOPPED 3 MILES NORTH OF HARLOSA SPRINGS. THREE MEN TOOK PERSIA. DISARMED HER. RODE OFF TO EAST. SAID SEND FOLLOWING NOTE FROM LAKE VALLEY:

WE GOT PERSIA. PEACH GOES TO ENGLE BY MIDNIGHT. STAYS UNTIL TRIAL OVER. IF HE DON'T PERSIA AIN'T COMING BACK.

Handing the note to Tom, I say, "Of course I'll go. What's the quickest way to get to Engle...where is Engle anyway?"

Tom takes a quick look and hands me back the note, shaking his head.

"You must be makin' Ol' Brown and his boys sweat. They're scared, stupid, and mean. That there is a powerful combination, and it can get down right deadly. Engle is over the river, about forty miles north and east of here, on the *Jornada del Muerto*, far side of the Fra Christobal and Caballo Mountains. It's in the middle of big ranch country. Mainly, it's a railroad shipping point for ranchers. Ain't much there, just a few mercantile stores that sell the ranchers their beans, a saloon, a railroad hotel, and a few houses. Ol' Gene Rhodes lived there when he's a kid. Forget about findin' it. You ain't goin'."

"Why not? I can defend myself. I know how to ride. I have to do everything I can to get Persia back. It's my fault they have her."

Tom snorts and shakes his head.

"You got cajones, Quent, but in this here country, guts don't make up for sense. My money says they're setting you up to kill ya. They'll be sure you and Persia disappear before you ever git to Engle. Brown's gonna make sure you two disappear just like he did Fountain and the little boy. Maybe even have you share the same canyon with 'em over in the San Andres or wind up with rocks in yore pockets in the river. You're gonna have to be smarter than they are for you and Persia to survive."

Sadie crosses her arms and nods, speaking in her cockney accent that had made her and her girls a lot of money. "Tom's right. Best thing yuh can do is let this old warhorse help yuh take care of those no good snakes. How many horses do yuh need, Tom?"

"Four good saddle horses and a pack horse. You'll have to lend Quent a saddle and trail gear, and he oughter have a rifle to go with that sawed off Pinkerton shooter you give him."

He scratches his chin and looked at the floor for a moment.

"Maybe you can git Tom Ying to throw us some eatin' supplies in a sack? Can you do that for us, Miss Sadie?"

She nods, her chin thrust out in determination.

"Why, hell yes, Ay can. Tom, yuh go on an' get yuhr gear, Ay'll fix Quent up with some of JW's clothes and a rifle. I'll 'ave Quent, the horses, and yuhr supplies ready in an hour down at the Ocean Grove kitchen door."

Tom pulls down his hat and gives her a little wink.

"Thanks, Miss Sadie. See yuh in a bit."

Sadie points me down the hall.

"Go down three doors and take off yuhr duds. I'll be along directly with some of JW's trail clothes for yuh."

I jump as she bellows, "Sam! Sam! Get yuhr black fanny in here and help me!"

From outside I hear, "Yas'am, Miss Sadie! I'm a comin'!"

Tom, his hat pushed back and pulling on what's left of his shot-off ear, squats by the back door of the Ocean Grove. With a cottonwood twig he sketches a map in the dust.

"The country says how we got to play this game."

He draws a swerving line between two points.

"This here is the stage road between Hillsboro and Lake Valley. Persia was took off the stage about here. There's a line of low mountains just off to the east that runs alongside the road. They'll ride through a pass about here, and then head straight for the river. That's about a three-hour ride. Then they'll turn for Palomas Springs and use the ferry at Elephant Butte. Not far from there is a long winding pass road up between the Fra Christobal and Caballo Mountains that runs over to Engle, about fifteen miles off to the east of Palomas Springs. I'm guessin' they'll nest in that pass and wait to bushwhack ya. They'll figure you'll ride through about dark and be easy pickin'.

"I'm telling you, make no mistake about it, they mean to kill ya. Brown's figurin' you got to go. Just when he thought he was free and clear with Lee bein' tried and all, you, a wet-behind-the ears reporter who ain't got no dog in this fight, could hang him out to dry, even if the law don't. Foller what I'm sayin'?"

I nod, and, with a sinking feeling, I already know the answer to my next question.

"Yeah, I hear you. If they kill me, what do you think will happen to Persia?"

Tom shakes his head.

"Dead women tell no tales. When they're done with you, she's next and I'm bettin' Brown told 'em to take care of business even if she is his niece. When you both disappear, he'll say it's 'cause you run off together. Brown is rid of you both, free and in the clear."

I can't argue with his cold logic.

"I've got to get her back. How do you want to handle it?"

He looks at me from under his brows.

"First thing we're gonna do is to take care of them that took her. It's gonna give me a whole lot of satisfaction to put them boys away. Once they're out of the way, I'll set Mr. Brown straight."

Tom grins as he looks me over.

"Miss Sadie fixed you up right didn't she? You'd pass for J.W. Orchard from a distance. You all saddled and ready to go?"

I hold up the old model 1876 Winchester and point to the saddled pinto Sadie has loaned me. "Let's ride."

As we mount, Sadie steps out the backdoor of the restaurant, her hand shading her eyes. "Don't yuh boys come back without her."

Tom salutes her by touching a couple of fingers to his hat rim. "Don't worry none, Miss Sadie. We'll be back in a day or two."

I tip my hat. "Thanks for the use of the rig Sadie. We won't be long."

She smiles. "Be seeing yuh boys."

Tom alternates the pace of the horses between a fast walk, a trot and a fast gallop that eats up the miles. As we approach the river, the rusty red and brown massifs of the Caballo and Fra

Christobal Mountains loom before us in the golden glare of the mid-afternoon sun. They are huge, breath-taking vertical cliffs, with occasional flashes of black-green near the river and on cliff ledges. I can't imagine how there can be trails and roads across them as they grow more imposing the closer we get.

We water the horses in the greenish-brown Rio Grande. Its flow is fast, deep, and too dangerous to cross at our watering spot. Our horses hang their heads in fatigue and need rest. It's been a hard ride in the heat of the day. Tom tells me to ride the roan and let the pinto rest. He changes off his pony, a tan mustang, to the big black stud, Sadie's favorite. We mount and turn south, following the cool and pleasant trail that twists along through the willows, cottonwoods, and sycamores by the river.

In a couple of miles the river turns toward the west. On the east side, a wide swath of brush under the trees is gone, a sure sign this spot is used as a cattle crossing. Tom doesn't hesitate to ride into the river. I'm right behind him, expecting to get off and swim with the horse, but the water only comes up to the horses' bellies and the bottom is smooth and sandy.

"I thought you said the best fords and a ferry were in Palomas Springs or Caballo."

"They are. The local ranchers know about this place, but don't recommend it. It kinda comes and goes, depending on wet weather upstream. There's another pass through the Caballos close by and a trail that leads over to Engle that'll get us around and ahead of them boys sitting in the main pass waitin' on ya."

The pass trail through the Caballos is long and winding and uses several ledge passages with long drop-offs. Tom tells me to just let my horse pick his way and I'll be fine. The horse makes it easily, but his surefootedness doesn't stop me from breaking into a sweat every time I look off into those long drops into eternity just to the right of his feet.

The sun is fading in diffused orange and purple glory behind the Black Range when we come out on the *Jornada del Muerto*, the high desert country of the great ranches like the Bar Cross. Off to the east, the San Andres Mountains waver in the distance.

Tom stops to rest the horses and have a smoke. The desert is already giving up its heat. The night will be cold. Not used to long horse rides, I'm saddle sore and my legs are cramping. I dismount and try to stretch the kinks out of my muscles.

"Where to now?"

"Be another couple hours until we hit the Palomas Springs-to-Engle road."

"Then what?"

"I figure them boys is waitin' on you close to where the pass road tops out on the *Jornada.* They'll stay there 'til maybe ten o'clock before they decide you ain't comin'. Then they'll saddle up and head for Engle to git some whiskey before they take care of Persia. The road crosses an arroyo about five miles from the pass. We'll wait on 'em there."

"What if they start shooting when you try to arrest 'em? We can't shoot back. Persia will be in the line of fire."

"We'll figure somethin' out. Come on. By the time we git over to that arroyo we'll still have time to make a little coffee and have a couple of Tom Ying's biscuits before we get down to business."

The moon lights up the horizon behind the San Andres and soon rises big, yellow, and brilliant. Its cold glow covers the *Jornada* in white light and inky black shadows falling from the bushy mesquites and tall spiny yuccas. The Engle road ruts look like two pieces of manila rope snaking out toward the weak twinkling lights of Engle far in the distance.

Riding toward Engle, we soon approach a wash. Tom leads us off the road, down the wash and around a bend a few hundred yards away. We dismount, unsaddle the horses, rub them down and give them water and grain.

"Quent, if you'll dig us a fire pit, I'll git some kindlin'."

It's easy to scoop out a hole out of the soft, sandy dirt by the time he returns with an arm full of brush.

"This stuff will burn fast, but it's enough to make a pot of coffee, and that pit'll keep our fire from being seen unless they're right on top of us."

The night is cold and the coffee good. It goes well with cold biscuits, bacon, honey, and corn fritters. Tom checks his watch.

"Our friends ought to be here in an hour or two. Persia'll likely be ridin' between the first two. I want you on the south side of the road. I'll be on the north side. You grab her horse's lead rope as soon as we stop 'em and bring her down here. She's gonna be cold, thirsty, and hungry. We'll stay here tonight and take care of her before we head back for Hillsboro."

I'm cold, but that's not the reason my teeth are chattering.

"What are you going to do if they don't surrender?"

Tom frowns at me like I don't have good sense. "Whatever it takes."

Coffee finished, we kick sand over the fire and gather more brush to make another after we take Persia back.

We take our blankets and walk back up the wash to the road. I find a place on the south side that gives a clear view across the wash and down the road to Palomas Springs. Tom is wrapped in his blanket as I am in mine. He's practically invisible behind a big spreading soap weed. An hour passes. Two. It's nearly midnight when I make out four riders on the road casting short black shadows under the high, silent moon. I feel the hair on the back of my neck prickle. I wonder when Tom plans to step out in the road to say, "Deputy Sheriff Tucker, hands up!" *What'll happen if they put up a fight?* I wish we could just shoot the scum and be done with them.

It isn't long before I'm sure that the second rider is Persia. From the Mexican sombrero, I surmise that the man in the lead is Greco. It's too dark to make out who is riding behind her, but the one bringing up the rear is big, big enough to be Clayton. I pull the hammer on my rifle back a click to safety. I hear Tom's rifle slowly click twice, one to safety, the second to full cock.

The four ride down into the wash. Persia looks haggard and her beautiful black hair a disheveled mess. I grind my teeth, and curse those who stole her.

Across from me a shadow rises in the bright moonlight.

The sombrero jerks toward it. "Wah?"

Flame and thunder come once, twice, three times in less than a handful of seconds. It happens so quickly it's like being struck by lightning. My jaw drops. I'm stunned, frozen in surprise. Greco, on the ground, doesn't move. His terrified horse squeals and races down the road toward Engle. Persia, her hands tied in front of her, tries to hold on to the mane of her rearing mount. The two horses behind her, eyes white with fear, rear and twist in circles trying to avoid stepping on their fallen riders. The rider who was immediately behind Persia rolls on the ground groaning, his hands in the middle of a dark wet spot spreading across his belly. The

47

last rider, a wet spot on the back right side of his coat, is on his hands and knees, trying to crawl up the Palomas Springs side of the wash.

I run for Persia's horse and grab its lead rope. Tom runs to the second man and stares at him a moment before there is the roar of a forth shot. It's still ringing in my ears when there is a fifth burst of thunder. There is no more groaning and the man on his hands and knees isn't moving anymore.

Persia's horse settles as I speak gently to it and reel in the lead rope. I see the moonlight sparkling in the streams of water rolling down Persia's cheeks, and hear her say, "Thank you God! Thank you, dear God!"

Yelling, "Gittin' the other horse," Tom catches a horse, swings into the saddle without using the stirrup, and races past us as I reach up to help Persia down.

Persia sags in my arms. She's trembling, and my shirt grows damp where she buries her face on my shoulder.

"Are you all right? Are you hurt anywhere?" I say as I untie her hands.

She grabs the lapels of my coat in her hands, looks in my face, and whispers, "Now I'm fine, just fine."

I help her to my blanket. "Stay here while I take care of business." She nods as she wraps the blanket around her and I walk back to the bodies.

Greco lies on his back, a perfectly round, black hole dead center in his chest. The gut-shot man has a second shot between his eyes, the back of his skull and brains splattered on the ground in a little halo behind him. I don't recognize him. He wasn't with Greco and Clayton when they beat the hell out of me up just before the trial began. The man who was on his hands and knees lies face down, a bullet hole in the back of his head. I roll him over with the toe of my boot. The top of his head is gone, but I have no doubt it's Clayton.

The flood of nausea is swift, unexpected. I retch and vomit violently, my hands on my knees. I've seen bodies before, but the swift, ferocious slaughter and the iron smell of blood and loose bowels, the smell of death, overwhelm me. I've never imagined murder to be so swift, so unexpected, and so violent.

Persia, concerned, stands up ready to throw off the blanket and come help me. I wave for her to stay where she is as I walk down the wash for the last horse and return to tie it off near the bodies. I motion for her to join me, and we walk together, my blanket over our shoulders, as we lead her horse down the wash to camp. She drinks in long deep swallows from my canteen while I unsaddle her horse, and then make a fire. Soon the coffee pot begins bubbling and she eats Tom Ying's bacon and biscuits like a starving woman, slurping the hot, strong coffee, gaining strength to match her courage.

Back at the road, I've wrapped Greco's body in a blanket and laid it across the horse when Tom returns with Greco's horse.

Saying nothing, he tosses me the blanket roll tied to his saddle. He dismounts, ties his horse to a bush, and takes the blanket roll off Greco's horse.

"Persia all right?"

"Yeah, just wore out and a little shakey. She's eating down by the fire."

"Good. You take the guns off Greco before you wrapped the blanket around him?"

"Yeah."

"Be sure to do the same with the other two – spoils of war. Greco's rig was fancy. You keep it. I'll keep the others."

We wrap the other two bodies in the blankets. Finished, we sit down to rest a minute. Tom rolls a cigarette and lights up.

"Tom, mind if I ask you question?"

"No, sir. You earned answers to all the questions you need to ask this night."

"Why didn't you tell 'em to surrender before you started shooting?"

Tom wags his head. "Bunch of reasons. Mainly, they kidnapped a woman. Any man does that don't deserve no chance to surrender. He's gonna die. Whether by a bullet or a rope, he's gonna die. After them bastards murdered you, they was gonna rape her and slit her throat. They ain't getting any chance out of me, includin' a first one."

"But you're wearing a star. You're sworn to uphold the law."

"Yep. I am and I did. They got all the judge, jury, trial, and execution they deserved. You agree with that, don't you?" His eyes narrow as he gazes at me and blows a puff of smoke toward the stars. "I saw where you puked over there."

49

I look at the ground and nod. "Yeah. Yeah you're right. You won't get any argument out of me."

"Good. Let's throw these bodies over the horses and get down to the fire. It's right chilly, ain't it?"

A few coals glow orange under gray ash. The sky turns to faint pink streaks thrown out from the gauzy bright line following the jagged outline of the San Andres. It's been a long night. Persia sleeps by my side, but the horrors of the past day are heavy on us as the stars follow their great circles around Polaris. I turn from one side to the other, restless, thinking of what might have happened. Trembling, startled by bad dreams, Persia awakens several times. Tom Tucker, wrapped in his blankets on the other side of the fire, doesn't move all night. The snores from under his hat drown out the calls of distant coyotes.

Giving up any hope of sleep, Persia and I build up the fire. Hearing us move around, Tom instantly grabs his revolver, sits up, nods good morning, stretches and yawns, reminding me of an old hound after an afternoon nap. After making coffee and eating bacon and biscuits, we load the horses and set off down the Engle road toward the Rio Grande.

It's still early morning, the sun not far up, when we reach the river. The ferryman, eyeing the blanket-wrapped bundles draped over the horses' saddles, wastes no time getting us across the river. On the west bank, we give the horses a ration of grain and let them drink; Tom refills the canteens and water cask – in this country you never know where the trail will take you. The twinkling glints off the river are bright, sparkling, and the air is starting to warm.

After dipping his bandana in the river, Tom wrings out the excess water and hangs it around his neck.

"Quent, you reckin you folks can find your way back to Hillsboro without me? Just follow the road south an hour or two, and then swing west straight for the Black Range. You'll cross the road to Hillsboro purty quick that way. Ride at a good trot and you'll be back by mid-afternoon."

"I'm sure we can find our way, but where are you going?"

Tom nods toward the horses. "I'm gonna take these here bodies to ol' Ed Brown for plantin'. Before he does any diggin', we're gonna have us a little chat to be sure there's enough holes in

50

the ground for ever'body. He just might need an extry one for his own self. When I'm finished with him I don't expect he'll be sendin' nobody in our direction or botherin' Persia ever again."

Persia, a frown filling her face, shakes her head. "You're not going without me, Tom Tucker! That man tried to have me killed. I kept telling myself yesterday that if by some miracle of God I got away from those killers, my uncle would never do that to me or anybody else again. I'm coming with you!"

Tom, his brows raised in surprise, looks at Persia and then me. "Quent?"

Persia's eyes flash, wide and angry. "What are you asking Quent for? He doesn't have any say over what I do. He can come if he wants, but I'm coming with you. One way or the other – I'm coming."

Feeling a strange mixture of pride that she has such spunk and fear she'll be killed or badly hurt if guns come out, I know I can't stop her unless I tie her up and throw her over her saddle.

"Looks like it's going to be a three-man posse, Tom. I want to have a little eye-to-eye conversation with the SOB myself."

Tom slowly grins and pulls out his cigarette fixings. "You birds can come with me if you're a mind, but I'm wearing the badge and you'd best do exactly what I tell you or old Ed is likely to fill us all full of holes."

Persia and I nod as Tom lights up.

We make good time. An hour before noon we pass through the little town of San Marcial without having seen a soul except the ferryman all day. Tom turns east; the river crossing is wide and shallow and it appears to be used often. After crossing, we stop to rest the horses, eat dinner, and rest for a while in the shade of a big cottonwood. We unload the pack animals. The bodies are stiff and starting to smell. Rummaging in the supply sack for the rest of Tom Ying's victuals, we fill up on the greasy bacon, stale biscuits, and hard fritters. Finishing his dinner, Tom stretches out next to the cottonwood's trunk for a nap.

Persia takes her last bite of biscuit, sees Tom pull his hat over his eyes, and smiles at me.

"I'm in bad need of a bath. Will you guard my privacy while I put some dirt in the river?"

The thought of being alone with her makes me laugh with pure pleasure. "Yes, ma'am. I will if you'll do the same for me."

She giggles. "Wonderful!"

Tom raises his hat off his face and grins. "Don't you folks do anything I wouldn't enjoy."

A quarter mile up river we find a willow grove, the ends of its long green wands dragging on top of the current. They form a green privacy wall around a calm pool. Persia disappears through the green wall while I keep watch for stray eyes and listen to her splash around enjoying the sheer pleasure of being wet without it being her sweat. I'd love to watch her bathing, but I'd never betray the trust she's placed in me. It's not long before she's back, her long, beautiful hair wet, shiny black, a crow's wing in early light.

I take my turn in the river. The water is cold, refreshing, hard to leave. Persia lets her hair dry in the sun while I bathe. When I come out of the willows she has her hair in long blue-black braids that make her look more like an Indian beauty than a rancher's daughter.

Walking back to Tom's shade tree, we're lost in the sweep of the sky's translucent light ranging from turquoise on the horizons to royal blue as it nears the brilliant, glaring sun. In the sweetness of the moment, it's easy to forget about the confrontation we're likely to have in a few hours.

Off to the east we hear cattle bawling. At the cottonwood, Tom is up and has the horses saddled, his horse in a sweat from being ridden.

"Tom? What's going on?"

"Small herd, maybe ten or twelve head, comin' this way."

"Okay. Why is your face filled with thunder and lightning?"

Tom pulls his big Winchester out of its scabbard.

"Two drovers comin'. One of 'em is Ed Brown. We're gonna lay back in the bushes and wait for 'em. I want you and Persia to stay out of sight with the horses. The cattle are gonna be thirsty. They'll stop to drink. Brown and his vaquero will let 'em. I'll come out and have Mr. Brown step down from his horse and send the vaquero on with the cattle. They're likely heading for the shippin' pens in San Marcial. It'd be a good excuse for Ed to 'accidentally' meet up with these here boys in the San Marcial saloon. He'll be wantin' to know about how rubbin' you two out went. Well, he's about to get a first-hand report. When the drover is out of sight, I'll call you, and we'll have our little talk with Mr. Ed Brown."

We pull the horses back into the brush, where we can still see the action, but not be easily seen. Tom steps out of sight behind the cottonwood and waits. Persia and I lever our Winchesters and let the hammers back to safety. The cattle come closer. The air is hot and still, filled with mosquitoes and flies. The smell of death from the bodies is strong and sickening. As we wait, I think, *This isn't a good way to spend a Sunday afternoon with a pretty girl.*

I see two red cows with white faces lope up to the river, splash in up to their bellies, and begin to drink. The rest come trotting up to stand in the water at the river's edge and drink. Behind them are the two drovers. One is an old Mexican, his face lined from years in the sun, slits for eyes, a large, gray-white mustache, skin brown as old gun leather. Hanging against his back is a wide sombrero – dusty and tattered from long wear. An ancient, pitted and scarred cap-and-ball revolver in a well-oiled holster riding on his hip, and canvas pants stuffed in boots scratched from years of wear make him look like what he is – an old-time drover. The other man is middle-aged, his face lined from years in the sun, heavy bushy brows over narrow slits for eyes, a thick black mustache under a straight bulbous nose, his jaw and cheeks, needing a shave for several days, are covered with salt and pepper stubble. He wears bat-wing chaps, a handsome leather vest too small to button around an apple belly that hangs over his belt, and a holster carrying a long-barreled Colt hangs from a gun belt filled with cartridges. He and the Mexican pause at the water's edge to let their horses drink.

Tom steps from behind the tree and levers a round into the chamber.

"Howdy, Brown. Step down. Send yore vaquero on into town. Damn! That's poetic, ain't it?"

Brown's forehead wrinkles in surprise; he starts to reach for his revolver, sees Tom is wearing a badge, and slowly moves his hands to his saddle horn where Tom can see them.

"Well, I declare. Look who's here." A forced smile creeps under his mustache as his close-set eyes sweep the area looking for other guns and his voice wavers trying to sound nonchalant. "What's doin', Tom?"

"I said to git off your horse. Ya lost your hearin'? Send yore man on with the cattle. We're gonna have us a little talk over here under this nice big tree."

Brown speaks to the Mexican and waves him on across the river. I hear instructions to go into San Marcial and wait for him in the saloon. The old man nods and begins driving the cattle on across the river.

Appearing relaxed and affable, Brown swings down and leads his horse over to Tom.

"Unbuckle that shooter and hang it on yore saddle before you sit down here in front of me."

Brown flashes a toothy smile and nods.

"Why shore, Tom, glad to be friendly. You bein' Curry's deputy and all, I'm surprised to see you. I thought you'd be up to the big trial in Hillsboro. Wished I coulda gone, but there's a lot goin' on around the ranch and I ain't got much help."

He hangs his gun belt from the saddle horn and loosens the cinch before tying the horse to a bush. From where Persia and I watch, I can see Brown's eyes, cold and calculating, searching for anyone hidden in the brush. Taking his time, he gives no indication he sees Persia and me. He sits down cross-legged in front of Tom, tips back his hat, and pulls a sack of tobacco and papers out of his vest pocket. He begins to roll a cigarette under Tom's dark scowl.

"What can I do for you, Deputy?"

"We're gonna have us an understandin'."

"Why shore. Always glad to accommodate the law and help out old friends."

Tom doesn't move a muscle as Brown lights up, takes a long draw, blows the smoke skyward, and grins.

It would give me the greatest pleasure to put a bullet hole in his head just to wipe the oily smirk off his face.

"Smell anything, Brown?"

Brown sniffs the air and makes a face.

"Yeah, somethin's dead."

"What you're a smellin' is the three boys you sent to murder your niece and Quentin Peach."

Brown doesn't blink and slowly begins shaking his head. His voice is low and uncertain as he tries to give a glib, too clever-by-half, reply to a man whose voice sounds angry enough to kill him.

"What are you talkin' about? What boys? I used to be my niece's guardian, but now she's on her own. Heard she's workin' in some cantina over to Hillsboro. I ain't seen her for months, maybe a year, and I never heard of Quentin Peach. Who the hell's he?"

Tom points the rifle at Browns chest and pulls the hammer to full cock. A twitch ripples across Brown's face. I see him gulp air and swallow. The cigarette smoke makes him cough.

"You and Miss Persia come on out here, Quent, and bring them horses with you."

Persia and I step out of the brush and tie the horses to bushes near Tom's cottonwood. Despite the cool air, there are streamers of sweat rolling down Brown's face. Persia sits to Tom's right, crossing her legs under her skirt, and all the time keeping an eye on Brown and a hand in her skirt pocket on the little pistol I retrieved for her from Greco last night.

"Surprised to see me, Uncle Ed?"

Brown shows some teeth in his smile. "Shore am, child! You decide to come back home and live with me and Delia?"

As Brown speaks, he gives me the once-over while I study him. Persia surprises me with her steady, cool monotone voice.

"I'm not stupid, you rotten excuse for a man. After I was kidnapped, I heard Clayton tell Greco you didn't care if they had a piece as long as I didn't come back. You knew all about it. You set it up, didn't you?"

Brown's bushy brows go up in surprise and denial as he shakes his head. "I ain't seen Greco or Clayton since, oh, maybe March, and that's God's honest truth."

I can't hold my tongue. "Then, what did you use, telegraph or psychic?"

Browns eyes are wide in denial. "Why no. I tell you I ain't seen or had anything to do with those boys since March. I don't have any idea why they were doing business with you."

Tom squints at him and continues to hold the rifle steady, inches from Brown's heart.

"I ain't listening to no more horse apples coming off your tree, Brown. There ain't no doubt, none at all, that, for whatever reason, you tried to have these children murdered. Them boys wrapped in the blankets an' stinkin' was just doin' what you paid 'em for.

"Besides me, there's a whole lot of folks that's mighty angry about you tryin' to frame Lee for the Fountain murders. These children are ready to hang ya right here, but I ain't gonna let 'em 'cause you ain't worth it. Me? I'd just soon kill you as look at you. Aw don't look so surprised. If Lee hadn't asked me to stay cool, you'd never have made it to the river.

"You're gonna put them boys under the dirt while I think on what I'm gonna do with you. There's a miner's shovel tied on the back of Arch Clayton's rig. Wonder what he planned to use it for? Git it! There's a nice little clearing right over yonder in the brush. Dig three graves first, and then I'll decide if I'm gonna need you to dig a fourth. Now move!"

Tom pokes the rifle barrel right in the center of Brown's chest so hard he almost tilts over backwards, but catches himself by throwing his hands back. Brown puffs hard like he'd been running, and his face is covered with sweat. He jumps up, twisting to his feet and away from that rifle quicker than a cat dropped upside down. He holds up his hands up, palms out, as he stammers, "I'm...I'm gettin' it. I'm gettin' it."

He scrambles straight to Clayton's rig and takes the shovel. Tom walks him over to where he wants the graves dug. "Git busy, Brown! Faster you dig, more likely I'll be in good spirits when you finish. Dig, damn you!"

The earth where Brown digs is soft. He flails away with his shovel like a kangaroo rat digging a tunnel. Even in the relatively cool air, his shirt is soaked and sweat falls off his face like a gentle rain. He works for a couple of hours while we sit and watch.

Persia's hard eyes follow his every move, waiting, hoping he'll make a life-ending move. Tom squats resting the rifle on his knee stoically following Brown's frantic labor. As I watch Brown, it's hard for me to believe that this seemingly innocuous, middle-aged man is the source of so much grief for so many people. He looks perfectly harmless compared to the best-known gunman in the country, Oliver Lee. But, I know better.

When Brown finishes the three graves, he stands up straight, stretches his back and implores, "Can't I have some water, for God's sake?"

Tom pitches him a canteen. Brown drinks most of it and pours the rest over his head, then continues to stand in the last grave, looking hopeless as Tom stares and thinks before he thumbs back toward the bodies.

"Get them men! Bury 'em! Now!"

"You gonna help me with 'em?"

"Hell no! But I'm lettin' Mr. Peach go with you to watch you work 'cause he's right eager to settle up accounts for all the grief you caused him. Now git!"

In another hour, Brown has the bodies buried. He's soaked in sweat all the way down into his chaps, and looks like he's about to collapse from heat exhaustion. Tom asks Persia and me to tighten saddle cinches and mount while he waits in the shade of the cottonwood with Brown.

The horses saddled and the gear on the pack horses, I call out, "Ready!"

Tom nods. He stares, eyes cold and lifeless, at Brown.

"Ed, this here ain't a threat. It's the way it's gonna be. I ever get word anything violent happens to those two, you be ready 'cause I'm comin'. Anybody ever comes after me with your money in his pocket, you be ready 'cause I'm comin'. Any more tales comes out about Lee and his boys, or any kind of smear job at all, you be ready 'cause we're comin'. Anybody follows us outta San Marcial, I'll come back and you'll never see the light of another day. You been mighty, mighty lucky today. Do we understand each other?"

Ed, his face and hands covered in thin brown mud, sits by the graves staring at the dirt and nods. Tom mounts and we ease into the crossing. I look back when we're on the other side. He hasn't moved. Persia watched him all afternoon and said nothing. I wonder what she's been thinking, certain her anger will last a long time.

Tom lays a beeline for Hillsboro. Lost in the wilderness of our thoughts, none of us says much of anything the entire ride back.

DON'T JUDGE A BOOK

By Dave P. Fisher

The town of Flint Mesa lay quiet under the Texas panhandle sun. The hot July winds blew sand across the flat country, interrupted only by the buildings of the growing town. The wood sided structures were ground and pitted. Their owners had given up the fight to keep them painted. Remnants of white, yellow, and red still clinging stubbornly to the wood were evidence to the only compromise the people had made with the country. The newest buildings made of red brick defied the winds and stood as a defiant symbol that Flint Mesa had come to stay.

In the thirteen years since Charles Goodnight had brought the first herd into Palo Duro Canyon the country had grown to cattle. The sparse grass that had once supported thousands of buffalo now fed the equally tough longhorns. The towns of Amarillo, Panhandle, and Canadian grew up around the cattle trade and were prospering. The Panhandle and Atchison Topeka railroads had criss-crossed the panhandle, opening trade and providing a source for shipping cattle to all parts of the country.

Flint Mesa began life on the rail line northeast of Amarillo. It didn't exist before the iron rails, like their neighbor Mobeetie had, but unlike the dying Mobeetie, Flint Mesa was not only growing, but prospering. They were competing with Amarillo for the corner on the cattle trade and giving the larger town a run for its money.

Michael Black, owner of the First Bank of Flint Mesa, was a wise businessman who organized the town leaders in a drive to bring the cattle trade to Flint Mesa. Black's bank was the first brick structure in town, demonstrating his determination to stay. Several businesses had followed his example having had tons of red brick brought in by rail. Cattlemen saw this as a positive sign that they would always have a ready market and buyers in town. Many ranchers began shifting from Amarillo to Flint Mesa much to the celebration of the town's businesses.

Black's bank sat centermost on Flint Mesa's main street; beside it was a print shop that produced a small four-page newspaper, as well as printed hand bills and advertisements for the business community. The remainder of the street was made up of dry goods, clothes, liquor, and tobacco stores. The best hotel in town, the Flint, was a three-story brick structure promising the finest in modern accommodations. A courthouse for all county and city business was under construction; it would be a brick structure as well.

On the furthest east end was the livery that doubled as a blacksmith shop. Wolf Murphy was the owner and blacksmith. His father had come into the country with the Army to fight the Comanche and Kiowa. He stayed on as a buffalo hunter, being one of those who settled in Hidetown, that later became Mobeetie. He named his son Wolf figuring it would make him strong.

Wolf had made his way around the Indian Territory and on across Texas. He had been a cattle drover moving a herd to Abilene, a buffalo hunter, and along the way fought some Comanche. He learned the blacksmith trade from a man in El Paso. He also killed his first man there at twenty years of age. There had been a few more since then. He was a man who had lived the rugged life of the wild lands and it showed.

He eventually became a lawman and put in several years at that before moving to the growing Flint Mesa and settling down with his own business. Wolf was one to stay to himself; no one in town knew him intimately. He was friendly but reserved, which made some suspicious of him. Little was known of his past which led the town's story spreaders to come to the conclusion that he was an outlaw living under an alias.

Like all western towns, Flint Mesa had saloons. The Cattleman Saloon was directly across from the bank. It was well furnished and catered to the better citizens, cattlemen, and wealthier customers. The Cattleman didn't have fights or shootouts; in fact there had never been a shootout in the town since its conception. Ranchers made their cowboys behave in town, not wanting to spoil their good standing with the town leaders.

A quarter mile out of town, past Wolf Murphy's Livery, was the Comanche Saloon, a rougher establishment where cowboys could blow off some steam without upsetting the citizenry. As long as the Comanche kept its business out of town they were tolerated. The community leaders believed that the Comanche was actually good as it kept the rough stuff out of town; if the Comanche wasn't there the crowd would drift in and cause trouble. Anyone wanting to open another saloon was discouraged from doing so.

The biggest news of the day was the successful business venture that Michael Black had pulled off. He had convinced a prominent cattle purchasing company to move their office to Flint Mesa. They were sending in two buyers to staff the office. The men were due to arrive in town in a week and preparations were being made to set them up with an office appropriate for their positions. They would come in together on the train.

A welcoming celebration was planned for their arrival and the town was alive with excitement. The item that was being kept as secret as possible in a town with loose talkers was the fact that the buyers were also bringing two hundred and fifty-thousand dollars in cash to deposit in the bank for cattle purchases.

Evan Willis had come to town a month back following up on an advertisement that Flint Mesa was hiring a town marshal. He met with Black and several of the other town leaders and laid out his history to them. He had been a lawman in several Texas towns, as well as a Texas Ranger. Once his commitment with the Rangers was up he headed north and upon seeing the advertisement he knew a nice town like Flint Mesa was just where he wanted to settle. The town hired him on the spot.

Marshal Willis made himself popular throughout the town. He made friends with all the business owners, spoke kindly to the ladies, and kept the peace, which was a simple matter. If a patron of the Cattleman became too drunk he would kindly escort them to a room at the hotel where they could sleep it off. Everyone in town loved their new marshal.

The only man in town who didn't like Willis was Wolf Murphy. Willis kept his horse at the livery and had let Wolf know all about his background, emphasizing his Ranger work. Wolf would only look at him and give no reply.

Willis had been told not to bother with the Comanche Saloon, to let them do whatever they wanted as long as they stayed out of town. On most late nights Wolf watched Willis ride out of the livery and to the Comanche. He would be gone for hours and return walking unsteadily, leading his horse and smelling of liquor. He fell asleep in one of the stalls one night and explained to Wolf that he was keeping an eye on certain members of the Comanche crowd and had spent the night in the livery so he could watch them closer. Wolf's only reply was a dead stare.

Willis decided he didn't like Murphy and had learned that most of the town thought he was odd and possibly an outlaw. Willis promised to keep an eye on him and make sure he didn't cause any trouble. The people of the town praised him for his diligence.

Three days before the train carrying the cattle buyers and their money was due in, three men rode down the main street of Flint Mesa. They were sun browned men with eyes like chips of stone, hard and trail toughened. Their clothes and unshaven faces were covered in dust, as were the horses they rode. It was noticed that they were armed with pistols and rifles and those guns were well worn and wiped clean of dust.

Buddy Frank, the town's lead story monger, ran into the Cattleman and directly up to the bar. He slapped the bar for his usual beer. The barkeep put the beer down, but Buddy grabbed his hand before he could pull it away. "Henry, did you see them three mean looking hombres that just rode into town?"

Henry shook his head with a tone of annoyance. "No Buddy, I can't see much from behind this bar."

"Well, they come riding in armed to the teeth. Mean looking bunch they are. I'd lay my summer wages they're outlaws and they're here to rob the bank when those buyers come in with all that money."

"Quiet, you old fool, that is not information for the whole world to know about."

"The whole world already knows. Why do you think those men are here? You watch, mark my words, you watch, they'll join up with that odd Murphy fellow. Trouble's a comin' I can feel it."

Henry had to wonder about that. Surely something like the money on that train couldn't be kept a secret for long. He would keep his eyes and ears open.

The three riders drew attention as they rode along the street. The town's people were accustomed to seeing dust-covered cowboys riding up and down, but these men weren't cowboys. They looked dangerous and to a peaceful town like Flint Mesa that had none of the wildness of other towns, they stood out.

The three men dismounted in front of the Flint and walked inside. The clerk behind the desk looked up and froze in place. The man in the middle asked for three rooms.

The clerk shook his head, "I'm sorry, we're full up."

The man looked at the wall behind the clerk and saw several keys hanging out of the pigeon-hole sorter. "All those rooms taken?"

"Yes sir."

"Let me talk to your boss."

The clerk disappeared into a back room and came out with a gray haired man dressed in a suit. "Yes, may I help you?"

"It seems strange that a town this small and a hotel this big has no rooms available."

Sweat began to pop out on the man's forehead. "Most of our rooms are actually offices, only a few are sleeping rooms and those are occupied."

The man glared at him, "Where else can we stay?"

"There is another hotel on the west end of town, try that one."

The three men glared at the two behind the counter and walked out. They stepped into the street, pulled their horses loose, and mounted. The youngest man looked at the others: "That went well."

They rode west to the second hotel. It was a windblown, unpainted two-story building. A barn was behind it for horses and a pump in the front yard. The men walked in the door to find a sixtyish man sitting back on a chair reading the newspaper. He looked up, dropped his paper, and walked up to them. His head was mostly bald and his face weathered, he had the look of a man who had been across the prairie and lived to talk about it.

"Do you boys for a room?"

"Three if you got them."

"Got 'em." He grinned, "Bet you boys got turned down at that fancy place."

The man nodded, "That a regular thing around here?"

"Oh yeah, pretty uppity bunch there in town. Me, I've seen the elephant, fought Comanche and Kiowa on this very spot before them white-livered city dudes came in on the train. I take in them they don't want."

The man grinned, "Probably like it here better anyway."

He handed out three keys. "Watch out for that new marshal, he'll be asking you questions because you don't fit in."

"You don't care for him?"

"Nah, he's a four flusher. Pretends to be the saintly type, but I've seen him getting liquored up at the Comanche. Claims he's a former Texas Ranger, bah."

"Bah? You don't believe him?"

"I've seen enough Rangers in my time to know the difference and he ain't never been one."

"Then that's good for us."

The three men signed the register and the man spun it around and read the names. "Morgan, Pete, and Jack. Nice to meet you boys, I'm Jeff Taylor."

The men left the hotel and mounted back up. Pete glanced at Morgan, "You figure he knows?"

Morgan shrugged, "Pretty sharp old coon, he can likely read the sign."

Jack tossed Pete an irritated glance, "You ask more questions than a kid."

Pete grinned back at him, "I am the kid remember?"

Morgan moved his horse on, "Let's check out this town."

Heads turned and talk quickened as the three men rode back down the street. Pulling up in front of the Cattleman they dismounted and went inside. All heads in the room turned to stare at them as they walked toward the bar.

Buddy leaned into Henry, "That's them."

The three men stepped up to the bar and ordered drinks. Henry gave them what they asked for. "We don't see too many new faces around here, you passing through?"

Morgan shrugged, "We might stay on a few days until our business is completed."

"What might that business be?"

Jack was leaning his elbows on the bar; he looked at the barkeep and growled, "A man's business is his own, nosy girl."

Henry frowned, "Just trying to be friendly."

"Just trying to learn why strangers would be in your town, you mean."

Henry moved to the end of the bar to wait on other customers. Jack growled under his breath, "Nosy dude."

As they stood at the bar Marshal Willis came in. He looked around and walked toward the men. He pulled in alongside Pete. "Marshal Willis. Are you gentlemen on business here?"

Jack stood up straight, "Our business seems to be of almighty importance to you folks."

"It is important to me. I run a quiet town and want to keep it that way. I want to know when men like you come in and why."

"So, what is 'men like you' supposed to mean?"

Willis glared at Jack. "It means what I said. Finish your drinks and head out of town."

"We like it here and figure to stay a few days. Our money's as good as anyone else's."

"As long as you don't cause trouble."

The three men finished their drinks and walked across the saloon and out the door. Pete grinned at Jack, "You have a real way with people."

"It gives the right impression."

They mounted up and rode east stopping at the livery.

Buddy Frank ran out to the street and watched them go. He dashed back into the saloon, "Told you. They stopped at Murphy's I'll bet they're all in cahoots together to rob the bank."

The train pulled into Flint Mesa at two the next day. The marshal was on the platform when it pulled in. As the train screeched to a stop it blasted a cloud of steam out of the drivers and blew the whistle. Two men in black suits stepped off the train. Willis walked up to them and they all shook hands. They walked with Willis to the bank.

Walking into the bank, they were ushered into Michael Black's office where several men waited. Willis gave the men the names of each businessman in the room. "Gentlemen, this is Agent Miller and Agent Smith, the railroad detectives we were expecting." The men shook hands all around.

Agent Miller took the lead. "We are here in advance to make sure the money arrives safely and gets into the bank vault. The railroad wants to keep good relations with Flint Mesa and the cattle company; they have sent us to insure a successful transfer."

Black smiled, "And we are happy to have you here. Between you and the marshal we are sure to be safe. I have heard that there are three rough characters in town who may well be scouting the bank and intend a robbery."

The agents both looked at Willis. Willis looked unconcerned, "Drifters. I had a talk with them yesterday. Unfriendly lot, but so far they've done nothing I can arrest them on or even run them out of town. We will just have to keep a close eye on them. I have asked the town's citizens to report any and all of their behavior to me. So far we know they have met with that strange Wolf Murphy down at the livery. They could be planning something, you can never be too careful."

Black nodded, "Yes, that Murphy is an odd character. If anyone was an outlaw it would be him. I trust the three of you will be on top of any attempts to pull a robbery."

Miller smiled, "That's why we're here, don't worry about a thing. You just trust us and all will be fine."

"Mister Black, if it's alright with you I'd like to show Agents Miller and Smith the layout of the bank. The vault, offices, back door, all possible entrances robbers could use."

"Excellent idea marshal, please carry on."

Black returned to his office as Willis gave the agents a tour of the building.

The next morning Morgan, Pete, and Jack came out of Jeff's hotel and rode into town. They went into a café and took a table. As they had expected, heads turned and all conversation stopped. A young woman in a checkered apron made her way slowly toward them. Her boss had told her to take their order so they didn't make trouble, but to get them out as soon as possible.

She took their breakfast order. As she wrote on a pad, her trembling hands were not missed by the men. They exchanged no talk with her other than to speak their order. Jack made it a point to look over everyone in the room. As his eyes met theirs, the person quickly diverted their eyes to other directions.

Finishing the breakfast, it was clear that there would be no second cup of coffee. They took that as evidence that their company was not wanted in the café. Jack was about to demand a second cup when Morgan stopped him. "We don't need to give that marshal reason to lock us up, just drop it."

Together they got up and left the room. The conversation quickly picked back up with excited chatter. They could hear the words 'bank,' 'money,' 'train.' They looked at each other and shook their heads.

Morgan assigned jobs to the men. "Jack, you spend some time down at the train station and get the lay of it and how the trains are running. Pete, watch the bank. I want to know how the customer flow goes. Casually step inside and give it a quick look if you can. I want to know how many doors there are and if there's a back door." The men turned their horses and headed out without a word.

Morgan headed for the Cattleman. He tied off his horse in front of the saloon and went inside. A few men were at the tables drinking coffee and discussing business matters. A couple of early drinkers were at the bar and Henry the barkeep was in his usual place.

Stopping at the bar he asked for a cup of coffee. Henry dropped a cup on the bar harder than was necessary and splashed coffee over the rim as he hurriedly poured. Morgan gave the barkeep a look that made him blanch and hurry away. He turned and faced the room to see Willis and two men in black suits coming toward him. He recognized who they were, but they didn't know him.

The three men stood in front of Morgan. Willis pointed to the men with him, "Just thought I would introduce my friends to you. This is Agent Miller and Agent Smith, railroad detectives. They are here to see to it that nothing happens."

Morgan sipped at his coffee, unimpressed by the introductions. "Just what is supposed to happen that you need railroad detectives in town?"

"Don't play funny with me, mister. We are all aware of your intentions in this town and you can be sure that you will not succeed."

Morgan continued to drink from his cup; it was obvious Willis was playing to the audience. "I have no idea what you're talking about marshal." He put the cup down, "You boys have a nice day." With that he headed for the door.

Willis called out to him, "Hey, I never did catch your name."

Without stopping Morgan answered, "That's right, you didn't." He walked out the door.

Henry leaned over the bar, "Good job marshal, you sure put the fear into him. They'll be thinking twice before trying anything now. I'd be proud to give you gentleman a drink on the house."

Willis held his hand up, "I never drink."

Miller and Smith waved him off, "Thank you, but never on duty and we are on twenty-four hour duty until that money gets in the vault."

"Glad you're here for our town, gentlemen."

The agents both smiled, "We are too." Together the three men walked out.

Buddy came up to the bar, "Now there's three real square gents. I can tell 'em, you know."

Pete was sitting across from the bank in a chair propped back against the Cattleman wall when Willis and the agents walked out and saw him. Willis turned to him, "Kind of an odd place to be hanging out, isn't it?"

Pete shrugged, "Good a place as any. I'm thinking I like this town. I might just stay on."

"Ask your friend what I told him about these two men with me. You try anything here and you will be staying permanently alright...in our cemetery."

Pete grinned up at him, "But, then again, if everyone is as friendly as you maybe I'll move along."

"Good choice." The three men walked across the street and entered the bank.

The people who had been walking by nodded in approval of the marshal's handling of the outlaw. Pete smiled up at them and in return he received frowns and glares. He laughed, got up, and spoke low to himself, "Wonder what the bank looks like from the back." He mounted and headed down the street.

Jack walked up and down on the wooden station platform looking the area over. He read the chalk-written schedule on the wall and saw that a train was due in that morning. The train with the cattlemen on it was due in tomorrow at one. The station master watched him with unpleasant interest.

Leaning out of his window as Jack looked over the chalk board he spoke in an unfriendly tone. "Planning on taking the train out of here?"

Jack scowled at him, "You people sure take a lot of interest in my business."

"We know why you're here; you're not fooling anyone. If you were smart you'd get on that train and clear of here. Our marshal and those detectives aren't to be trifled with. If you know what's good for you..."

Jack cut him off, "Well, I don't know what's good for me, so get your head back in there and shut your mouth."

The man swallowed hard and pulled his head back in the window.

At the end of the day, the three men came together at Wolf Murphy's livery. Loosening the cinches they pulled the bridles and left the horses in stalls with hay and grain. Wolf was watching them.

Morgan turned to him, "Seems that marshal has an intense interest in our business. He's pushing and suggesting, but I don't think he's completely sure we aren't just riding through. I don't think he's on to us yet."

"He'll know for sure tomorrow, won't he?"

Morgan laughed. "Anyone at the Comanche we might know?"

"Head on over and have a look, you'll see a few familiar faces. The saintly marshal should be in there tonight getting liquored up as usual. He keeps it together pretty well in front of the town, but you should see him at night. It's something to keep in mind."

Buddy ran into the Cattleman and shouted across the room, "They're back at Murphy's again. I tell you, that's the whole gang. We should march right over there, drag them out and hang the lot of 'em."

Henry gave the man a disgusted look. "Do you ever shut up Buddy? First off, if we want this town to prosper, we can't defy the law and hang people vigilante style just because we suspect something. This is eighteen-eighty-nine for crying out loud. Second, I'm a saloon keeper and you're a story-monger-saloon swamper. Neither of us, nor anyone else in this town, is a gunfighter. Someone would be killed for sure."

The day of the anticipated train had the town in a flurry of excitement. Banners were hung out on the store fronts; a platform was set up for speech making and a couple of musicians had been practicing for the grand entrance. Willis and the detectives were moving around the town smiling and encouraging the celebration. Willis was carrying a shotgun.

Michael Black was sitting in his office, his stomach a knot of nerves. He wanted everything to be perfect for the cattlemen and above all, he wanted the money to make the three hundred yards from the train to his vault. Once the money was in the vault he would relax and not until. He had also seen one of those outlaws moving around town taking in everything.

Willis and the detectives came into Black's office. "Mister Black, the train will be here in a few minutes. Here's what we want to do. The three of us and you will meet the train. You carry the money bags from the mail car. I will have the shotgun and walk in the lead; you follow me while Agents Miller and Smith walk to both sides of you. They will be armed as well. If those outlaws try anything, we will shoot them to pieces."

Agent Miller added, "We don't believe they will try anything outside as there are too many people about. If they try it will be in the bank and before we reach the vault. I want everyone out of the bank, no employees, no lookers. Should shooting start we don't want any innocent people getting hurt. If only the four of us are in the bank no one will get hurt should things go bad."

Black nodded his head nervously. "Yes, I can see the wisdom in that. I would not want any of my people injured. I saw one of those outlaws looking around this morning; I haven't seen the other two yet."

"Don't you worry about them, let us deal with that. Now, if there is shooting I want you to drop the money bags and get down under a desk for safety. If we know there are no employees inside and you are not in the way we can be sure that our shooting will be directed at the outlaws."

"Yes, yes, I will do as you say. Do you think they will try?"

Willis answered him, "Between you and me, I believe they will. That's why they've been in town. You just follow all the instructions we have given and you and the money will be safe."

The far off sound of the train whistle could be heard drifting across the prairie. Willis checked his watch, "Right on time." He gestured toward the door, "Let's head down to the station and meet the train."

Black was visibly shaking as he stood on the platform with the three lawmen. He trusted them, but was fearful all the same. They watched the train come in with the brakes grinding it to a stop at the platform. The locomotive blew out steam and laid on the whistle.

A crowd had gathered around to watch. The two cattlemen stepped out of the car and were met with a cheering throng. The lawmen eased aside the crowd to let Black shake the hands of the cattlemen and welcome them to Flint Mesa. The men were then escorted by the crowd to the platform in front of the Flint.

Black and the lawmen stood alone on the train station platform. "Are you ready, Mister Black?"

Black nodded to the marshal, "Let's get this done."

The marshal told the mail guard to open the door and give Mister Black the money bags. He handed two canvas bank bags to Black. He slipped his hands into the bag handles, taking one in each hand.

"Follow at my pace Mister Black, I want to do this fast." He set off at a quick pace, his shotgun at the port arms position. Black had to rapidly shuffle his feet to keep up. The agents were close to his sides. His nervous eyes scanned all around them. He felt sick to his stomach.

All the people were moving toward the platform in front of the Flint as they walked along the street. Black was beginning to feel better as they came to within a few steps of his bank. A few more steps and the money would be safe in the vault. He had not seen the outlaws and that reassured him.

They were inside and half-way across the empty bank when the sound of racing horses came from outside. Two men with kerchiefs over their faces slammed open the door and burst in. They pointed guns at the men and began shooting. Terrified, Black dropped the bags and dove under a desk as he had been instructed. Agent Smith shoved him down to make sure he was well under the desk.

The masked men grabbed up two bank bags and ran back out the door. A third mounted man was holding the reins to their horses. Mounting, the men fired several shots around them to discourage anyone from poking their heads out.

As they spun their horses around, Morgan stepped out from the side of the print shop with a Winchester and blew one of the robbers out of the saddle. The remaining two were shocked into temporary paralysis, which allowed Morgan to clear a second saddle. The third man kicked his horse into a gallop and tore down the street. He blew by the screaming and shouting crowd who had heard the shooting. The two bank bags lay in the street beside the bodies.

Morgan watched him go and cussed his luck that the man had gotten away. About the time he figured the fleeing robber was passing Jeff's hotel he heard a single shot. Grinning to himself he spoke low, "You old Indian fighter, you got him."

Pete and Jack stepped out from their hiding places, rifles to their shoulders, at the rear of the bank as the back door swung open. Willis and the two detectives burst out the door, each agent carrying a bank money bag. Jack shouted at them to stop. Looking wildly around, Miller saw the men and fired a shot at them. Jack shot him in the chest while Pete shot Smith.

Willis fired the shotgun at them. As Jack and Pete ducked for cover, Willis grabbed up one of the bags from the ground and took off running. Pete began to run after him, but Jack called him back. "He's headed for his horse at the livery, Wolf will handle him."

The street was suddenly filled with shouts and the sound of running feet. Morgan walked in the front door carrying the two bank bags the robbers had carried out. At the same time Jack and Pete came in from the rear pushing the wounded Smith ahead of them. Pete carried a third bank bag. A crowd had gathered around the dead men in the street chattering excitedly.

Black climbed out from under his desk. His face was pale and eyes wild with confusion. He looked at Smith holding his bloody side. "What is the meaning of this?" Black demanded. "You shot a railroad agent. You'll hang for this!"

Jack snapped at him, "Be quiet you darned fool. I swear you're denser than an Osage orange fence post." He dug into his pocket and produced a badge. "Texas Rangers."

Black stood in shock, his mouth opening and closing with no words coming out.

Morgan opened the bank bags he had picked up from the street. He pulled a couple of books out of them and dropped them on the floor. "They were false bags." He pointed at the bank bag in Pete's hand, "There's the real bag." He looked at his two partners, "Where's the other one?"

Jack jammed a thumb toward the east, "Chic headed for the livery with it. Murph should have him by now."

Willis burst through the open livery door. He came to a sliding stop on the scattered hay grabbing for his horse with one hand while clinging tightly to the bank bag with the other. As he turned the horse, he heard the sound of a snapping gun hammer. He looked slowly around to see Wolf Murphy pointing a Colt at him.

"Howdy Chic, long time no see. Don't remember me, do you?" The man shook his head.

"Texas Ranger. A while back I killed your cousin. I would suggest you drop that bag and the gun or I'll drop you right here on the spot."

With a resolute sigh, Willis lifted his gun from the holster and dropped it. He then dropped the bank bag.

"Turn around and put your hands behind your back." He complied and Murphy tied his hands together with a length of rope. He picked up the bag and stuck the gun in the man's back. "We're going to take a little walk down to the bank. Get funny and I'll kill you, hands tied or not." They walked out of the barn headed toward the center of town.

Michael Black was sitting in his chair with his head down. Comprehension was beginning to take hold. The marshal, the detectives, the men he had trusted and opened the bank to were actually outlaws setting him up. The men they had maligned and suspected were the actual lawmen. He lifted his head as Wolf Murphy shoved his prisoner through the door and handed the second bank bag to Morgan.

Jack grinned at Pete, "Told you."

Morgan pointed at the man Black knew as Marshal Willis. "Mister Black, meet Chic Bowrie, leader of the Bowrie gang." He pointed at the wounded man with Pete, "That's his brother, Ned Bowrie."

Jack broke in, "And out back with a bullet in his chest is Rafe Bowrie; he won't be coming in though."

Morgan continued, "Out in the street we have Buck Stills and Zack Johnson. The last member of the gang you'll find drawing flies down by Jeff's place is Jake Knolls." He looked at Jack, "One shot as he rode past Jeff."

Jack grinned, "That old Indian fighter wouldn't miss either."

Michael Black looked from one Ranger to the others. "I...I don't understand."

"Sergeant Morgan Wright, Texas Rangers. You were duped, Mister Black. Chic came in early to set the whole robbery up. His brothers came in disguised as railroad agents and they won the hearts of the whole town. They gained your trust because

73

they looked the part and said all the things you people wanted to hear.

"The other three came into town last night and hung out at the Comanche. That's where they got together and set their plans. We went in there last night and saw them all together. They had it set up that the men coming in shooting were the diversion. They were to take the false bags Chic had prepared and hid and then make a getaway, drawing everyone's attention to them while the Bowries went out the back with the real bags of money."

Jack grinned, "Only thing is they didn't expect us to be a hitch in their plans."

Black's face was drawn and red with embarrassment. "How did you know?"

Morgan gestured toward Wolf, "Wolf used to be a Ranger in our Company. He recognized Chic as soon as he took over as marshal. He knew the money was coming in and suspected what was happening. He wired us and we came in."

Black looked angrily at Wolf, "Why didn't you tell us we were in danger?"

Wolf's hard eyes looked in the nervous banker's. "Because no one in this two-bit town would have believed me and I didn't want to tip the hand by letting a bunch of loud mouths spread the word."

Black cast his eyes down, "We haven't been very friendly to you, have we?"

Wolf ignored the statement.

Morgan went on. "We came in looking like drifters as we had no idea who in town belonged to the gang. Our lives and the job here would have been jeopardized if the wrong people got wind of who we were. The pretense worked, evidenced by how bad everyone in this town treated us."

Black opened the bank bags and saw that all the money was in them. He then looked at the bags with the books. "They really fooled us all, especially me." He looked at the Rangers, "I for one am ashamed of my stupidity and the way we treated all of you. We fell all over the criminals while the *real* lawmen were treated shamefully."

Jeff pushed his way into the bank. He smiled at Morgan, "Shot me a coyote, figured you like to add his hide to your collection."

Jeff looked at the people around him, "I'm glad I could see this. You're a lot of uppity snobs, thinkin' you're too good for

74

common folks. You got took in and took in good. I'm glad you did, it'll teach you all a lesson about how smart you all think you are. You obviously never heard the old saying about 'don't judge a book by its cover.' I knew they was Rangers right off."

Black looked at him, "How could you and we couldn't?"

"Because, you don't know how to look. You see a fancy suit and right off you think you know. There's one tell tale sign that anyone who's been around could see. They was covered in trail dust and needin' shaves, but their guns was as shiny as if they just come out of the store. A Ranger never lets his gun stay dirty."

The two cattle buyers had come on the run at the first shots and had pushed their way into the bank. They each put their hands out to Morgan. "We appreciate what you men did. That's a lot of money to lose."

Morgan shook their hands. "It's what we do."

Jack and Pete pushed Chic and Ned Bowrie out the door. "We'll be locking them up in your jail. We have a prison wagon on the way to pick them up. Wolf has agreed to watch them until it does."

Black approached Wolf, "We could use a real marshal in this town. We've got some ground to make up to you and we'd sure like to make amends. Are you interested?"

Wolf looked at the hopeful faces around him. "I'll think on it."

The owner of the Flint stepped forward. "I have our three best rooms available for you gentlemen."

Morgan looked at him and then at Jeff. "We've got rooms."

The Rangers moved out with their prisoners as the crowd parted and watched in silence as they walked away.

The next morning the town's people stood in silent embarrassment as the three Rangers, now washed and shaved, rode down the main street. The sun reflected off the badges that were now worn in the open. They looked neither right nor left, but straight ahead, leaving Flint Mesa behind them.

ESCAPE FROM THE HELL HOLE

By John Duncklee

T he blistering hot wind intensified the burning heat of June on the Yuma Sand Dunes whipping billions of tiny sand particles into flight, stinging Ben Hammond's face as he waited in the scant shade behind a dune. Another three hours until nightfall and he could continue his escape without being cooked alive.

In spite of its discomforting punishment, Ben was glad for the wind. The blowing, drifting sand would quickly fill the tracks he had left as he plodded northward. He followed his escape plan. "The search party from the prison will look for me on the way to Mexico instead of on the Yuma Dunes heading north," he said, as if talking to the wind. Nevertheless, he scanned the horizon between the sapphire sky and the rounded buttocks of endless sand, cupping his hands like binoculars to shade his eyes from the afternoon sun and pelting sand, making sure he was not being followed.

It had taken over a year to think out his escape plan with minute care. Since receiving his last letter from Martha he knew he must flee his incarceration and find her. Find her if she still lived. She had told him of her marriage and her move from Tucson to her husband's ranch east of Yuma on the Gila River. Her telling about the way her husband beat her bothered Ben the most. "Why does she write that to me when I cannot do anything about it as long as I am in this stinking prison," he had said to himself when he had finished reading the letter. "Maybe she is asking me to attempt an escape," he mumbled.

77

Hammond also feared that the Quechan Indian trackers might be hired to find him. He knew they were paid fifty dollars to bring in escaped prisoners dead or alive. The Indians had never been known to bring in anyone dead because, as they reasoned, they would have had to carry the body back to the prison to collect their earnings. Besides, a live prisoner might escape again and they could earn another fifty dollars.

Ben had studied the confluence of the Gila with the Colorado River just outside the walls of the prison. He knew that he must follow the Gila eastward, but to avoid detection he would have to walk a long way north before turning east to the Colorado. That would mean a day or two, maybe more, of plodding his way through the heavy sand of the dunes. Once across the big river he needed to travel eastward until he could meet the Gila at the top of a large bend that it made before angling southward toward the town of Yuma. Following the Gila would get him to the ranch where Martha lived with her husband. Following the Gila meant water. By following any other route the possibility of finding water was as remote as being pardoned from his life sentence at the Hell Hole. Kevin Randolph's father continued to influence the territorial governor. Other prisoners sentenced to life had been pardoned after serving a mere four years of their sentences. Not Ben Hammond. He knew that many prisoners received early pardons because the Arizona Territory needed voters. When pardoned instead of paroled, the prisoner regained all his rights including voting and bearing arms.

Now, however, the challenge for him was to survive the heat, the blowing sand, and the inevitable hunger on his way through the dunes and the bleak, sandy desert to the eastern bank of the mighty Colorado River. After fighting the blazing heat all day he began to wonder if he would be successful in his escape or end up a broiled stiffened corpse buried beneath the ever shifting dunes.

The scorching heat had made Hammond drowsy. He fought the strong desire for sleep. Resting in the lee of the dune his thoughts flew back to before his life in the Hell Hole.

He had gone two blocks from Martha's house when Randolph pulled up next to him in his buggy, yelling, "You should stop pestering Martha. She deserves more than a down and out cowboy."

Ben and Kevin were slightly acquainted, but nobody would consider them friends. Randolph had only those friends who enjoyed the rounds of drinks he would buy at the local cantinas. Even then, the recipients tired of his pompous attitude. By his slurred words, it was obvious to Ben that Randolph had been drinking.

"You're the one pesterin' Martha. She would appreciate it if you left her alone," Ben retorted.

Randolph had jumped down from the buggy, and weaved his way toward Ben, who stood his ground at the side of the rutted, dirt street. Randolph stopped two feet in front of Hammond wavering in an unsteady way that made Ben think the banker's son might fall to the street.

"Listen to me carefully, Hammond," Randolph said. "Martha Redmond is probably the most beautiful girl in Tucson. You are a forty-dollar-a-month cowboy with no future. Someday I'll own a bank. You have nothing to offer Martha, so leave her alone."

Angered, Ben replied, "You're drunk, Randolph. You ought to get back in your buggy, and go home to your daddy before I mess up that pretty face of yours."

Randolph reached for a revolver in his right hand coat pocket. He had the weapon halfway out, and had cocked it, when Ben jumped at him, grabbed his arm and twisted it with all his strength. During the scuffle the gun discharged, sending a slug into Randolph's gut. He slumped to the street, groaning and gripping his belly with both hands.

Ben stood over the profusely bleeding playboy, gazing down at him. After one last groan, the banker's son expired.

"Crazy bastard killed himself," Ben muttered.

Just before first morning light he decided to change his direction to northeast and make for the river. He knew that success depended on his stamina and time, because the small amount of water and food he carried might not allow another day. He stood the chance of becoming a pile of gray, bleached bones in the shifting sands.

At daybreak he became discouraged that the chocolate-colored mountains still seemed a long distance away from where he stood and turned to travel north again. By midmorning the wind began again, lifting the sand, and throwing it against his face. He resisted the temptation to take any more water from the nearly empty canteen. The baking heat, the fear of capture, and the exertion from almost wallowing through the heavy sand caused dizziness at times and he slowed his pace to avoid heat exhaustion.

By midday the water was gone. "Hell's fire, I've got another day at least until I reach the river," he mumbled.

The sandy dunes began to change their personality. Small wind-varnished stones began appearing on the surface and gradually the sand beneath the stones became firmer under his steps. He felt relieved that the heavy sand would no longer impede his progress toward the river.

He felt his stamina starting to weaken and decided to sleep in the relative coolness of night. Finding a small arroyo, he made a bed of sand and fell into a deep sleep.

A family of coyotes singing to each other at daybreak awakened him and he started his journey eastward to the river again, shading his eyes with one hand from the morning sun.

By midday his tongue began to swell, and he wondered if he had been walking in circles. Spells of dizziness slowed his progress. Finally he lost his balance completely, stumbled, and fell sprawling on the ground.

The wind had changed and the sound of water broke the deadly silence. Ben lifted his head and listened.

"The river," he muttered.

He began crawling toward the sound, resting periodically to regain his strength. His entire world spun continuously when he reached the six-foot-high bank of the river. His nearly limp body rolled down the steep embankment until he landed face down on a small sand bar with his head in the water.

The cooling water brought him back to consciousness.

"My God," he mumbled. "I made it."

He began to drink, but the water caused his stomach to cramp and he doubled up with pain. He began to writhe and then retched, vomiting into the river. When the spell ended he took a little water into his mouth and swallowed it slowly. He rested for a while, regaining his strength before easing himself into the cooling river. After a while he felt a little of his strength return and made up his mind to cross the river before some paddle-wheeler came by and found him.

The current was slow at that point because the riverbed was wide. Nevertheless, Ben found himself drifting downstream. Swimming enough to keep his head above water he slowly made headway toward the eastern shore. The current took him almost a mile downstream before he arrived at the eastern bank. He reached for a tree branch that extended low out over the water, grabbed it, and pulled himself onto a sand bar where an arroyo made confluence with the river. He lay still with his exhaustion, and slowly drank more water. A nearby grove of willow and arrow weed provided him with shade. He crawled into it and slept.

Ben thought he might be dreaming when he opened his eyes and saw a mule looking at him from just a few feet away. The mule, curious, head down with ears forward, peered at Ben. The animal dragged braided rawhide reins attached to the hackamore on its head, and the long ears flipped back and forth as Ben pushed himself to a sitting position. The mule backed away from him as he stood up. "Mule, what are you doin' a way out here?" Ben asked as he eased toward the animal and picked up the reins. "Where's your rider, Mule? All saddled up and out here alone? Now come on, Mule your rider must be around here someplace."

The mule looked around at Ben as he talked and it made Ben wonder if the animal understood. Maybe this wasn't a one-sided conversation after all.

The mule was saddled complete with riding harness that included a breast collar and breech strap to keep the saddle from sliding off the animal's rump or over its neck. A pair of bulging saddle bags tied behind the cantle piqued Ben's interest, but opening them could come later if the mule proved to be alone. Ben looked up and down the river and through the brush as far as he could see, but could see nobody. He tied the mule to a willow, and began following the fresh tracks along a small trail that led upstream. He moved cautiously in a half crouch keeping his eyes in the direction the mule had come from.

The sight of the black robed body supine in the middle of a cottonwood grove made him stop short in amazement. A black, broad-brimmed hat laid crown up four feet from the man. Ben wondered what a priest could be doing so far from civilization. He approached the figure slowly, trying to determine if the man was breathing. Nothing. As he looked down at the body, he saw a hole in the black robe over the heart. The fabric showed a large ring of dried blood when he examined it at closer range.

Ben shook his head wondering who would kill a priest. He unbuttoned and pulled back the black robe to examine the wound. The hole in the priest's chest was too large for a bullet, and he saw where the flesh had been ripped away as if an arrow had been extracted after it had accomplished its goal. The material in the robe showed the same. An Indian had killed the priest.

Ben's thoughts came together. He left the dead body and returned to the mule. "Let's go, Mule. It looks like I am your new owner." He led the mule back to the cottonwood grove. Exchanging his striped, prison clothing for the black robes of the dead priest, he washed the bloodstain from the robe before buttoning it on. A silver cross on a silver chain around the priest's neck tempted Ben, but he left it where it hung. When the swap was done he dragged the prison-dressed body of the priest to the riverbank, and shoved it into the river, then watched as the current took it downstream toward Yuma. As he walked back to the mule he heard a faint jingling.

He searched for a pocket. Nothing. He unbuttoned the robe, and on the inside he found a flap. He reached in and found four gold coins and a folded piece of parchment. He unfolded it and his eyes opened wide. Strange looking lettering said *"El Tesoro de Tumacacori"*. The parchment was a map to a Jesuit treasure cache, a familiar legend around Tucson and southern Arizona. Ben remembered the story that the Jesuits, during Spanish colonial times, had supposedly buried gold and silver in the Tumacacori Mountains before they were banished by the King of Spain in 1767. The Mine With The Iron Door in the Catalina Mountains north of Tucson, where Ben had taken care of the Z Bar K cattle, was another legend that kept circulating wherever the fables of buried treasure were told around campfires or in the many saloons of Tucson and southern Arizona Territory.

Refolding the parchment, he returned it to the flapped pocket, buttoned the black robe, and pulled down the broad brimmed hat until it was snug on his head. He walked over to the mule and looked through the saddlebags. "What luck!" Ben said. The saddlebags held coffee, beans and an ample supply of beef jerky in a threadbare flour sack. There was also a set of hobbles for the mule. With two full canteens of water, and his hunger satisfied, he lengthened the stirrups, mounted the mule, and headed east.

"Now, Mule, I don't know if you understand what I'm telling' you, but I reckon that don't matter. Maybe that padre who rode you before I found you talked to you in Latin. I can't talk Latin, but I'll sprinkle in a little Mexican if it'll make you feel more at home."

Shortly, Ben could see over the riparian vegetation and felt happy to see that he and the mule traveled with a small range of hills between them and Yuma.

"Well, Mule, I know you'll live a lifetime to get a chance to kill me once, but let me tell you, Mule, as long as you and me are friends and you don't get any of those fool ideas in your head we'll be fine together. And, by the way, I hope you noticed that I didn't say a thing about owning' you because I know damn well that nobody owns a mule. A mule owns himself pure and simple."

Ben hesitated before riding the mule into the barnyard of the ranch headquarters that Martha had described in her letters. She rushed out of the house and embraced him. She was completely surprised to see Ben and was also happy to tell him that her husband had gone to Yuma with a herd of yearling steers to sell. Ben would have enjoyed spending more time with Martha, but he had no desire to meet her husband or be captured by some lawman. He needed to get to Tumacacori to find the treasure from the map.

Martha gave him her husband's Sharps rifle and some ammunition so that he could hunt for food along the way. She also gave him a pair of Levis and a shirt, cooler than the black robe. They made plans to meet in Tucson once she was able to get free from her abusive husband.

Ben had ridden many days keeping the mule pointed toward the eastern horizon. He knew he must be in Papago country by the look of the brands on the few cattle he rode near.

Seeing some shadowy figures moving across the trail up ahead he reined in the mule. Another traveler? A large male coyote stopped in the middle of the trail and appraised Ben and the mule before loping off into the desert shrub. "Giddup, Mule, we should be at the next *rancheria* by sunup. I hope they have more than *pechita* for breakfast." *Pechita,* ground mesquite beans boiled or fried, was a Papago staple with which Ben was familiar.

First morning light crept into the desert. Suddenly the mule stopped and Ben, almost asleep in the saddle came close to plummeting to the ground. The mule's ears pointed forward and Ben scanned the trail and the surrounding desert to discover what the mule had taken such acute notice of. The faint sound of what seemed like wailing came to Ben's ears. "You heard it first, Mule. What the hell is it?"

He kicked the mule to start him walking again, but turned his head so the sound might be clearer if it focused on one ear. Another quarter mile and the sound became loud enough for Ben to recognize a human crying out. Not for help, but in some sort of grief. He reined in the mule, dismounted and donned the black robe and priest's hat again. "We must be near that *rancheria*, Mule. I wonder what's going on to cause all that noise."

Back in the saddle Ben rode toward the sound, still wondering at the sound that continued unabated. With every step the mule took the morning light grew brighter. Ben saw the *rancheria* buildings, not much different from the last. Dogs came yelping toward him, but nobody came to the door of the adobe house. He reined in the mule and sat in the saddle waiting. The wailing continued and he could tell that there were two people making the sound, one voice deeper than the other.

"*Hola*," he called after waiting for several minutes for someone to come out of the hovel. The wailing from the deepest voice ceased and momentarily an Indian man, hatless, wearing a somewhat tattered white shirt that showed his deep brown chest and faded denim trousers, came bare footed out of the open doorway.

"*Hola*," Ben repeated. He noticed the man's red, tear-filled eyes.

The Indian smiled and motioned Ben to dismount and enter the house. "Padre," he said in Spanish. "How did you know that my wife's mother died yesterday at sunset?"

"I did not know," Ben replied. "I am just passing through on my way to my mission."

Ben followed the man to the small house with no door or windowpanes. A woman, who Ben assumed must have been the man's wife, kneeled by the bed on top of which an old woman with canyons of wrinkles on her face lay face up with her eyes closed. Ben stopped before venturing further than the doorway. The wife turned her face toward Ben and rose from her position next to the bed. She no longer wailed but the tears kept forming in her eyes and running down her cheeks like raindrops on a window.

"Welcome, Padre," she said in Spanish. "You must have known that my mother has passed from this world."

"I did not know until your husband told me just now," Ben said. "I am sorry."

"She was very old. She told me she had lived long enough. I think she had completed ninety years. Please, Padre, say the words for her."

Ben stood in the doorway, almost in a state of panic while attempting to keep his composure and trying to think of something to say. *It has to be in Latin, but I don't know any Latin.*

He went to the bed, made the sign of the cross as officially as he could. "*E. Pluribus Unum,*" he began, and paused trying to think of something else to say that might sound like Latin. "*Longitudum, latitudum...sine, cosine, tangent.*" And then he remembered what his father used to say for "time flies". "*Tempus fugit,*" he said and again made the sign of the cross and placed his hand on the old dead woman's forehead. It felt cold and leathery.

Turning toward the two Indians who watched as he "performed" the last rights, he said, "*Vayanse con Dios.*"

"Thank you, Padre," the woman said. "I will have breakfast ready for you shortly."

Ben went outside to tend to the mule. As he approached the animal he saw, out of the corner of his eye, three children of mixed ages standing under the *ramada* looking at him. "*Buenos días,*" he said after he grabbed the reins.

The children all wished him a good morning in unison. He led the mule to a wooden water trough and noticed that it stood empty. "Please bring my mule some water," he requested of the children.

He thought they would battle each other for the only bucket that had been left to the right of the doorway. The oldest boy won, and hurried to the dug well next to the *ramada*. After attaching the handle of the bucket to the hook on the end of the well rope, he lowered it down and waited for it to fill. Moments later, he raised the bucket to the top of the well, unhooked it from the rope and carried it to the wooden water trough. He repeated the process four times. The mule drank deeply.

The *pechita* with red *chile* took away his hunger. The coffee tasted strong, but it proved to be invigorating. Instead of using their *ramada,* Ben decided that he had best be on his way. He might have availed himself of a comfortable place to sleep during the heat of the day, but having faked the Latin service for the old woman, he felt the need to keep moving in case the family planned to bury her and he might be called upon for more Latin. He remained empty of any further "religious" words.

The man gave Ben directions for the next *rancheria* to the east, and offered to pay him for the services. "*No gracias,*" Ben said. "The breakfast and the water for my mule are plenty of payment. *Vaya con Dios.*" He mounted the mule and headed over the trail east toward the Quinlan Mountains.

Finally rounding the northern end of the Quinlan Mountains, Ben viewed familiar country. He had not ridden this far west of Tucson, but he had viewed the landscape from the Catalina Mountains when he rode for the Z Bar K. He came to a narrow valley between the Quinlans and the Coyote Mountains. Reining in the mule, he looked at the surroundings. It looked like the place the last Papago man had described as the entrance to a small settlement called Pan Tak. Ben dismounted and put on the black robe and hat again. Before riding further into the valley, he rode up a foothill of the Quinlans to see what he might be riding into. Atop the hill he looked down on several adobe huts, similar to those he had visited before.

He let the mule pick its way down from the hill. He came to a fork in the trail and reined south to head for the creek draining the Coyote Mountains. It had not looked like a great amount of stream flow, but Ben hoped that it would be enough for the mule and to fill his canteens.

Heading south, he stayed away from the wagon road to Sasabe until he turned east beyond the Cerro Colorado. He camped along a small stream beneath some lofty ash trees west of the mining town of Arivaca. He was sleeping soundly when the crash of thunder awakened him. He looked up through the trees at the large black cloud, and listened to the strong wind whistling through the leaves. Another storm.

Ben rose, hurried to find the hobbled mule feasting on tall green grass by the stream, and led the animal back to his camp. He quickly built a fire for coffee, hoping the rain would not hit before

86

the brew was done. The Papago woman at the last *rancheria* he had visited had given him a sack of jerky. He took out a handful, and started to eat.

Just as the coffee started to boil, Ben saw a group of four javelinas approaching the stream. He slowly and quietly got to his feet, took the coffee pot off the fire, and stole over to the mule. Without taking his eyes away from the pig-like creatures, he untied the Sharps from the saddle, pulled back the hammer, and sighted the rifle toward one of the smaller one's head as it drank.

Just as he was starting to squeeze the trigger, the javelinas jerked up their heads as if they sensed danger. Ben aimed for the chest, and fired. The animal jumped, fell over on its side, and lay twitching its legs as Ben hurried over to claim his prize. The others had fled the scene.

The Tumacacori mission building looked old and in disrepair as he rode by it. He pondered about the times when the Spaniards arrived with soldiers, priests, cattle and horses. Two miles beyond the mission he saw a Mexican man wearing a straw hat, walking along a field of corn with a shovel on his shoulder. Ben reined the mule off the road, and approached the man, who was irrigating the cornfield from a ditch.

"*¡Hola!*" Ben greeted the man.

"*¡Hola!*, Señor," the man answered.

"Can you tell me where *Cañon de las Tinajas* is?"

The irrigator turned and pointed southward.

"It is maybe a mile. This side of a tall round hill," he said, waving his hand in a circle to further describe the hill.

"*Grácias, Señor*," Ben said.

"*Por nada.*"

Ben waved as he reined the mule around and headed back to the road. As he rode to the entrance of the canyon, Ben saw that it was larger than some he had passed previously. The dry arroyo looked as if it sometimes carried a lot of runoff from the mountains and foothills. He had ridden a couple hundred yards from the mouth of the canyon when a smaller arroyo branched off to the northwest. The major arroyo entered from the south, weaving through the bases of the foothills. Ben followed it around a long, gradually sloping hill to his right. It was not long before he saw a small stream of water disappearing into the sand. The canyon became narrower and the walls almost vertical, especially on the south side where over time the water from the mountains had cut down through the rock.

The stream was a welcomed sight. Ben had followed the arroyo around a sharp bend in the canyon when he saw a cave. Reining in the mule, he sat looking at the large cave in the rock wall of the canyon. "This might be our home for a while, Mule," he said.

Ben studied the situation. A chunky ledge coming down from the cave's entrance would allow him access without making a ladder. The stream of water ran next to the canyon wall on the cave side. A ten-foot high mesquite tree was growing at the sharp bend, a good place to tie the mule or hang a deer carcass. There was plenty of grass on the hills, and he had seen a game trail coming down to the arroyo. He could lead the mule up the trail and hobble it to graze. But, also there was a lot of grass along the sides of the arroyo through which he had just passed.

After riding back to the mesquite, Ben dismounted and tied the mule to the tree. Climbing the ledge proved easy, and when he saw the depth of the cave he was even more pleased with his find. As he stood at the mouth of the cave he said, "Even if someone comes looking for me, I'll be hard to find."

With the saddlebags untied, he climbed back up the ledge and laid them down on the floor of the cave. He looked at the ceiling and saw the blackened rock, evidence that someone, in some other time, had also lived there. Then he made three trips downstream gathering armfuls of driftwood he had noticed on his way up. There was still plenty of daylight for him to ride up the canyon to scout what might be further upstream. He untied the mule, mounted again, and rode slowly up the canyon.

A short way up the canyon he came to the junction of another smaller dry arroyo coming down between two hills. Ben saw a small spike buck deer approaching the stream. All the while keeping his eyes on the buck, he slowly and quietly untied the Sharps from the saddle, pulled back the hammer, and sighted the rifle toward the deer's head as it drank.

Just as he was starting to squeeze the trigger, the buck quickly lifted its head as if it sensed danger. Ben aimed for the buck's chest, and fired. The buck jumped, flipped over on its side, and lay twitching it legs as Ben hurried over to claim his prize.

As he sat by the fire in the cave, Ben thought about Martha in her unhappy marriage at the ranch on the Gila River. How long would she stay there before returning to Tucson? How would her husband react to her wanting to leave him? Once he found the treasure, would she be willing to live with him in Mexico out of the jurisdiction of Arizona Territory? What if he didn't find the treasure? Would he be able to find a cowboy job in Mexico? Maybe it would be better to head for New Mexico or even Texas.

The cooked deer liver tasted better than the javelina. With a full stomach, the urgency Ben had felt diminished, and he was soon asleep on the floor of the cave, using his saddle for a pillow.

Ben had awakened early, made his coffee, and eaten some of the deer heart after grilling it on the fire. With the treasure map spread unfolded on the floor of the cave, he began to examine it in the early morning light. According to the map he would have to travel up *Cañon de las Tinajas* until he reached a point somewhere near the base of the mountains. Then, for the first time, he noticed that the measurements of distances on the map were written in *varas* and *legas*, not miles, yards and feet. "Hell, I don't know how far a *lega* is," he said aloud to himself. "I'll never find this treasure until I find out just how far a *lega* and a *vara* is. I should have done this before I rode in. Maybe, the Mexican at the store knows."

Ben was getting ready leave to bring the deer carcass up into the cave and out of the hot summer sun when he heard his mule bray. He grabbed the Sharps, cocked it, and crept to the mouth of the cave. As he peaked around the corner into the canyon, his eyes caught a man's figure under the mesquite tree where he had hung the deer carcass. Then his eyes picked out movement at the top of the canyon. He looked up as a cougar began its spring from the edge of the cliff. Quickly, he brought the rifle to his shoulder and fired at the plummeting feline. Before the cougar hit the mesquite, Ben saw a red splotch on its side.

The cougar fell on top of the man and knocked him down. Ben cocked the Sharps again, but didn't aim at the man who was rising to his feet.

"Who are you, and what do you want?" Ben yelled.

"Looks like I owe you one," the man said. "I didn't see that cat. It must have been after your venison."

89

The man started walking toward the cave. Ben saw blood on the man's sleeve.

"It looks like the devil sunk its claws in you," Ben said.

"Better its claws than its teeth. Mind if I come up there?"

"You have to climb the ledge. Is your arm all right?"

"I think it's just a scratch. My name is Jake Dunn," he said, and offered his hand to Ben.

"How about some coffee?" Ben asked. "There's some left."

"Coffee will be fine. After that experience I might like some mescal better."

"I can't help you there."

As Ben put the pot back on the coals, Jake stepped over in front of the carbine where it leaned against the wall of the cave. *This man is no killer*, he thought to himself. *Otherwise, that rifle would still be in his hands.*

Ben rinsed the tin cup with water from his canteen, and filled it with coffee.

"I've only got the one cup, but you're welcome to it," he said, handing it to Jake.

"Like I said down there, I owe you one," Jake said.

"That's all right. I'm glad I had the carbine ready. I wouldn't have if my mule hadn't brayed."

"I'm going to level with you, Ben Hammond. I've been following you clear from Yuma."

Ben felt his stomach tighten.

"Are you a lawman?"

"No, just a bounty hunter. Remember, I owe you one."

"So what does that mean now that you've found me?"

"I do not have to take you in, and, as a matter of fact, I do not intend to. But, I'm going to give you some advice."

"I reckon I need all the advice I can get at this point."

"There are efforts being made on your behalf in Tucson. You have friends who are trying to get your life sentence pardoned because they believe you were railroaded. I may be wrong, but my advice is to turn yourself in. You'll have a better chance with the new judge."

"Jake, I was railroaded once. I didn't kill Kevin Randolph. He killed himself. He was drunker than seven hundred dollars."

"I heard the entire story. I can't say as I blame you for being gun shy of territorial justice."

"You sound like an honest sort, Jake. And now, I've got another problem. I found this map on a dead priest near the Colorado River."

The two men continued their conversation. Ben told Jake all about his escape and entire adventure. Mostly Jake listened.

"Now, I'm here where the map says I should be, and can't figure it out because the measurements are in *legas* and *varas*. I don't have any idea how long a *lega* or *vara* is, do you?" Ben asked.

"I reckon that was not part of what little education I have," Jake said.

"If you can find all that out, we could be partners on this treasure hunt."

"That sounds like you are not figuring to turn yourself in, Ben. You got that map off the body of Henry Waters, who never made an honest dollar in his life. I'll bet a year's worth of bounties that he was going to try to sell that map to some unsuspecting easterner as he went around in the robes of a priest."

"Are you telling me that I am looking for a treasure that doesn't exist?"

"That's exactly what I'm telling you, Ben. There's a real beautiful woman waiting for you in Tucson. She wanted me to tell you that she loves you. If I were in your boots, I'd forget about your map. Your real treasure is a woman named Martha."

MARSHAL OF ARIZONA

By Douglas W. Hocking

The sunset blazed red and orange over the Tumacacori Mountains west of Tubac. There was just enough light left in the day to draw a bead on a large target. From the town's lone cantina, two men emerged onto a dusty street. The day had been hot, and men early sought the dark interior of the cool adobe pub. Now tempers flared hot as well.

The larger man, dressed in worn, black, woolen clothing, jacket, and vest, was thought of as a "fast gun" or at least a man fast to use his gun. That he was a belligerent drunk and still alive seemed to indicate that his gun hand was fast. His gun, a .36 caliber percussion cap revolver, short barreled and light for quick handling, was tucked into the belt that held up his trousers. "Poker Jack" had wandered in from California and was reputed to head the list of a committee of vigilance. He undertook no known occupation but always seemed to have money.

His opponent, the stranger, dressed in fringed buckskin wore what was then a rarity, a belt supporting two holsters and a Bowie knife. The holsters, black, military issue, rode high and leaned forward. The flaps had been cut away and replaced with leather thongs tied in loops that slipped over the hammers to keep the guns from sliding free. Both loops had now been slipped off, allowing the pistols to be drawn swiftly. The holsters showed the outline of Colt Dragoon .44s. The only fast way to pull the guns was a cross-draw, right hand to left pistol.

"I don't really want to kill you," said the man in buckskin, "and I don't think I've done anything to insult you, but if I have, I apologize."

In the cantina, the stranger had jovially claimed to be able to snuff a candle flame at 30 paces with a shot from his pistol. It was a foolish thing to say, but, as with the wearing of his pistols, he intended to let people think he was dangerous so that none in this perilous country would think him an easy mark. Two towns, Tubac and Tucson, the Sonoita Creek farming area and Fort Buchanan, were beginning to be called Arizona. The region was 300 miles from the nearest court when it was in session once a year and just as far from the nearest town of Mesilla. Arizona was 600 miles from Santa Fe where the judge made his home. Tucson was a haven for men who had little use for law. Tubac was headquarters for the Sonoran Mining and Exploration Company, owner of the Santa Rita Mines and others.

Belligerent, if not intoxicated, Poker Jack had growled, "Don't mock me, boy!" His pretensions as a gunfighter and marksman were well known.

"I'm not mocking you," replied the stranger civilly enough.

"You callin' me a liar!" blurted Poker Jack. It wasn't a question.

"I've no wish to fight," said the stranger, backing away toward the door.

Out in the street people dodged into doorways, seeking cover from bullets that soon would fly. They guessed the stranger would die, for such was Poker Jack's reputation, but they feared one or the other's shots might go wide.

"But I want to kill you," said the man in black. "It is an affair of honor!" Poker Jack edged around slowly, ensuring that the setting sun was behind him.

When he saw the stranger squint, Poker Jack drew his weapon, or tried to draw it. It hung up on his vest. He'd cocked as he drew, and now his hand pulling upward against the impeded pistol jerked forcefully against the trigger. There was an explosion, a pistol firing, and Poker Jack fell screaming onto the dusty street. There was a hole where the inseams of his pant legs joined.

The stranger stood, both pistols in his hands, his feet braced and ready for action. The word went up and down the street that his draw was lightning, so fast that no one had actually seen him pull his guns.

94

"The stranger shot the wick off Jack's candle," someone yelled, and the stories began as each claimed more knowledge than the next about what had occurred and the stranger's prowess with a gun.

Bastyan Clegg, the stranger, glanced about in the gathering dark. "Get that man to a doctor. Where are his friends?"

"There's no doctor here," someone replied. "And he hasn't any friends here."

"Let's take him to Ehrenberg," suggested another, and with that, several of the people now emerging from doorways and alleys grasped Poker Jack under the arms and began to drag him down the street as he screamed and bled.

Clegg entered the cantina, ordered a drink, and then stood with his back to the wall watching the door. A well-dressed man of medium height and build entered. His energy and self-confidence reflected in the way he scanned the room, unafraid to meet any gaze, willing to look any man in the eye. Locking onto Bastyan, he strode across the room and stood next to him at the plank between two barrels that passed for a bar.

"Buy you a drink?" he asked. "I'm Charles Poston." The new arrival extended his hand.

"Sure," the stranger replied taking the soft, slightly greasy hand. "Bastyan Clegg." Soft, he thought. This is a politician and a schemer. Bastyan would count his fingers later.

"You shoot Poker Jack?" Poston asked.

"Nope," Clegg replied without explanation.

"They say you did!" insisted Poston.

"That's what they say," replied Clegg.

"I need a man with your kind of reputation," Poston said, "a man who's fast with a gun and not afraid to use it, who wears his guns where folks can see how fast he can get them out."

"Why?" asked Clegg. "I'm no mercenary for hire."

"I should explain," said Poston. "I've been appointed *alcalde* here. That's a New Mexico term for something like a justice of the peace, but it's a lot more—mayor and captain of militia. I want to see Arizona made into a territory with some government. Right now, we're part of Doña Ana County, and the county seat is over in Mesilla on the Rio Grande. There's no law or court here, and while I'm a kind of judge, I'm no sheriff."

"What's in it for you?" Bastyan asked rudely.

95

"Fair enough," Poston replied. "I own and am developing several mines in the Santa Rita and Cerro Colorado Mountains. Without government and without law and order, I can't find investors willing to risk their money. Thieves and murderers come up from Mexico and troublemakers down from Tucson, which is no more than a nest of men on the run. And Apaches raid right to the corrals at the edge of town." Seeing alarm in Clegg's face, he quickly added, "But Captain Richard Ewell of the 1st Regiment of Dragoons is attending to that problem."

"I'm thinking," Bastyan Clegg said, "that when Poker Jack is fixed up, he's coming after me and might well go for my back. I think I might not want to be here for that."

A fortyish man in a bloody apron showing the prints of hands recently wiped of gore entered the cantina, and seeing Poston, he approached the pair at the bar.

"Will he live?" Charles Poston asked the newcomer.

"I ist ze mining engineer, Charles, not ze docktor!" the man said.

Poston introduced his chief engineer. "What do you think, Ehrenberg?" asked Poston.

"I think ze news is badt und gut," Ehrenberg replied. "Ze badt news ist dat I think he hast nicked the artery deep in his leg, und I cannot schtop the bleeding zo he vill die. Ze gut news ist dat if ve had a Hebrew zemetery, he could be buried in it." Ehrenberg smiled at his presumed humor.

"So you can shoot the flame off a candle at 30 paces!" exclaimed Poston. Not stopping to hear Clegg's protest, Poston went on. "With a reputation like that, no one will want to tamper with our new marshal. You're perfect for the job!"

"I have to think about it," said Clegg warming to the idea. He needed a job. "What's the pay? And what will my authority be? Where's the jail?"

"Why there is no jail," replied Poston. "You'll have to tie lawbreakers to a tree. But your real job and only authority lies in intimidation. I want you to intimidate rough characters into leaving Tubac alone and going to Tucson to play. We've no justice court and no prison. You just scare them off. It's all image, my good man. Come, we'll talk about it over dinner."

Outside en route to Poston's casa, they encountered Missouri Anne hurrying home in the dark. Light from a doorway showed her to be quite handsome in all respects. Her name, Poston told Bastyan later, was a testament to the pilgrimage of her father, an itinerant preacher. Her siblings bore similar testaments—Mississippi Jim, Texas Tim, and Arkansas Sally. Introduced to Bastyan, Missouri Anne looked up into his eyes in a way that melted his heart and told him he was her hero. Having encountered only Mexican women in the last several years of his travels, Bastyan Clegg was intrigued enough by Miss Missouri Anne to stay in Tubac a spell.

With no badge or official authority, Justice of the Peace Charles Poston made Bastyan Clegg marshal and called a town meeting where the appointment was confirmed by unanimous consent. A salary of $50 per month in U.S. dollars was allowed and would be paid by voluntary subscription from merchants and mining companies. There being no official government apart from that in distant Mesilla, there was no authority to collect taxes. The people of standing in the town felt better knowing they finally had law and order.

"Marshal Clegg, come here, we need your help!" cried the owner of the cantina the next evening.

Entering, Bastyan came face to face with a Goliath of the desert. He towered at least a head over Clegg and was a yard wide across his broad, powerful shoulders. The big man stank of raw alcohol laced with tobacco for color and other secret ingredients, rattlesnake whiskey, as well as of sweat and animal butchering. The man looked at Clegg and couldn't quite focus his eyes. Bastyan ignored him and headed for the bar.

"I'm gonna tear this place apart if that barkeep don't fetch me a drink right now!" yelled the big man. He raised a chair over his head and smashed it through a table. Both objects were local rarities in Tubac, being there was no sawmill for hundreds of miles. "Then I'm gonna tear this town apart. Where's your new law dog? I'll start with him."

Then, for no particular reason, he turned and punched the man closest to him, knocking the man to the ground as he stood laughing. This gave Bastyan his opening. Approaching swiftly from the man's left flank, he hooked a foot behind the man's ankle and hit him a hard upper cut left to the jaw. The big man tumbled to the ground as Bastyan drew his left pistol with his right hand and stepped over the giant. There was no need. The blow to his jaw and the fall to the floor had caused the drunk to lose focus and close his eyes. As so often happens with a drunk already unstable on his feet, he fell and passed out.

"Get me some rope and a horse," said Clegg.

"You're not going to hang him are you?" queried a tremulous voice.

Securely tying the man, Bastyan used the horse to drag him to a cottonwood tree that grew along the wash on the south side of town and secured the big man to it.

"Jail tree," Bastyan said turning to the barkeep who had come with him. "We'll leave him there overnight and in the morning he won't know who or what hit him."

And so life went for several weeks. Subduing and disarming drunks proved easy for a man who tried to approach unseen. Drunks had been a big part of the trouble in town. Men were left with three options for entertainment. Drinking and gambling led to arguments, and the other option to jealousy, though men with their pants down around their knees were almost as easy to subdue as drunks. No one sober wanted to face the man with the fast gun. Those reverse holsters were intimidating, especially when everyone else carried their pistol tucked into their belt or a pocket. There was no way anyone could beat his draw by pulling a pistol out of the folds of their clothing. Besides, the marshal could snuff a candle at 30 paces.

"Apache!" came the cry one evening. "They're stealing Poston's stock."

Bastyan Clegg grabbed up his plains rifle, powder horn, possibles bag—where he kept bullets, patches, and percussion caps. Although he was fleet, by the time he arrived at the corral, the Apaches were already departing with Poston's horses. Clegg raised his rifle and without much hope of hitting anything fired off a shot. It nicked his target's ear. Lucky shot. The Apache turned his horse about and couching his lance charged Clegg.

Caught in the open, Clegg saw nowhere to hide or run. He thought himself a dead man. Calmly, because the dead do not hurry, Clegg reloaded, pouring powder, driving home a ball without patch, and mounting a percussion cap. He raised his weapon. With the Apache's lance tip almost at his muzzle, Clegg fired and jumped to the side. The Apache fell, a black hole oozing between his eyes. Bastyan picked himself up and ran for cover in case any Apache might try for vengeance. None did.

Finding her man, Missouri Anne wound her arms around one of his and looked longingly up into his eyes. They stayed that way in the twilight until the "militia" had been raised. The few intervening moments passed slowly for Bastyan. The girl was warm, and where her body pressed against his arm he could feel her fluttering heartbeat. The girl squeezed tight, setting the hook. Bastyan had drifted through the southwest deserts searching, though he couldn't define that for which he searched—home, purpose, a job, wealth. He hadn't given it much thought, thinking he'd recognize it when he found it. Now, liking this new sensation, he thought Missouri Anne might be the undefined "it."

"If we go after them now," said Poston, "they may turn the stock loose to delay the pursuit."

"You picked us a good marshal," said one of the militiamen. "Can't miss and just as cool as you please under fire."

Some of Poston's stock was recovered that evening without further incident. The Apache had melted into the desert, and Bastyan Clegg's reputation grew along with his fondness for Missouri Anne.

The summer monsoon blew in, bringing humidity and a daily hour of fearsome thundershowers when the heavens flashed with lightning and black rumbling clouds displayed their displeasure with the presumptions of humankind. Gripping his hat against the wind, he tilted the brim to release a torrent of water and then looked around the lantern-lit room. A muscular man was beating a Mexican girl; blood was already oozing from her nose and lips. No one paid the pair any mind.

"You filthy whore!" the man yelled. "You've taken my poke! Give it back!" He slapped her so hard Bastyan was sure the blow must take off her head.

"No! No! Señor. Please," Juanita whimpered. "I took nothing!" Smack! The man struck her again.

Bastyan looked askance at the bartender who said, "You know Joe. He's our blacksmith. Lives at the old ruined mission Tumacacori. He's a pretty good guy. We need him. If he says she took something, she probably did."

"No man should hit a woman like that," admonished Clegg.

"She's new," countered the bartender. "Just down from Tucson. Probably picked up evil ways. Besides, Joe's everybody's friend."

Unnoticed by Joe, Bastyan stepped in behind him and assuming he was drunk, kicked Joe's feet out from under him, following through with a smashing blow to the chin. Joe went down, but with surprising speed and agility was back on his feet, crouched and stable. His first counterpunch—a near miss—bounced off Bastyan's shoulder and impacted the back of his head making his ears ring. The marshal knew he was in trouble with a very tough opponent. He wasn't here for the pleasure of a fight but to enforce order. Avoiding fierce blows that, though crudely aimed, came in rapid succession, Bastyan feinted with his left as he drew his right-side pistol right-handed. Finding his moment, Clegg smashed Joe in the side of the head with his heavy Colt. The man collapsed.

Released by her assailant, Juanita darted out the door never again to be seen in Tubac. Her kind was all too readily replaceable.

"That hardly seemed fair," declared the bartender.

"Wasn't fair," replied Bastyan. "He was beating a woman."

"*Puta ladron*, thieving whore," said a voice. "She weren't no good."

"Somebody fetch a rope," said Bastyan. No one moved.

"Get it yourself!" said one of the men who'd watched the fight.

Bastyan did and after securing Joe, dragged him over to the usual cottonwood jail-tree. The storm abated, and Joe spent the night cold and wet. Releasing the blacksmith in the morning Clegg noticed that one eye drooped and that the muscular man's speech was slurred. He staggered a little as he walked.

The morning was bright and the sky blue. Rain the night before had washed away all trace of dust and haze. For now the sky was clear, but clouds would gather during the day as fresh moisture blew in from the Sea of Cortez and simmered off the desert floor. Bastyan walked the streets without a friendly greeting anywhere. Conversations stopped as he neared, and eyes turned hostile to stare. Even Missouri Anne hurried to the far side of the road.

Reporting to Poston for his week's pay, Bastyan found more disappointment.

"I had a hard time coming up with your pay," admonished Poston. "The cantina owner refused to pay his share. He says you're a menace to good business. Says you didn't give Joe the chance to explain and that you should've been helping Joe get his poke back."

"I saw a strong man beating a woman," responded Bastyan. "I thought he was drunk. I acted to protect her."

"Ehrenberg says the blacksmith may never fully recover," replied Poston. "We need our blacksmith. Right now he can't see straight or steady his tools. He's the only one we've got. Besides he's really a nice guy. Everybody likes him"

"Except Juanita," mumbled Bastyan.

"You were hired to protect the people of Tubac!" insisted Poston. "Joe, the blacksmith, is one of those people. You had a duty to protect him."

Bastyan almost quit right then and there, but thoughts of Missouri Anne kept him lingering. Besides the work was usually easy and the pay reasonable. He might be able to settle down, even get married, if Missouri Anne could just see passed his reputation as a brutal man, one quick as lightning with a gun.

He practiced with his guns daily firing them to ensure that he always had a fresh load. In the summer humidity and storms, moisture could get through the cylinders and wet his powder. So, he kept his powder dry by constant practice, drawing and firing, proving that he could shoot the flame off a candle at 30 paces. Clegg was quite public with his practice thinking this the best way to further his reputation and intimidate would be evildoers.

The blacksmith's speech improved a little and after a week he could hold his tools properly, but he was never quite the same. Bastyan's relations with the people of Tubac followed a similar route—they were never quite the same. He had been a beloved hero. Now he was feared. Men who used to buy him drinks edged away when he entered the cantina. Men were afraid to rile him and even to drink near him for fear he'd give them the "drunk treatment." Hostility ended, but love did not return.

It took weeks, but as the rains became less frequent, Missouri Anne no longer crossed the street to avoid him, and Bastyan was able to invite her to picnic. Taking her down by the slow moving Santa Cruz River, he spread his blanket on a grassy spot under a walnut tree. As she spread victuals on the blanket, he could see that either the girl was a poor cook or her heart wasn't in the food that she'd prepared. Even the cold chicken smelled burnt. The biscuits were misshapen. The adoring looks were also long gone.

"*Pollo quemado*, my favorite," he joked smiling. She either didn't understand or was ignoring his "burned chicken" comment.

"My father said we're headed for California soon," offered the pretty girl.

Stunned by this prospect, Bastyan blurted out, "Are you going with him?"

"Of course," she answered icily. "What's to keep me here?"

"I thought perhaps," he stammered.

"The men hereabouts are entirely too brutal to make good husbands," she said haughtily. "Though Mr. Kirkland seems nice."

"Why is your father pulling up stakes?" Bastyan asked trying to turn the conversation away from rancher Kirkland. "He's the first protestant minister in New Mexico Territory," she stated proudly.

"But this is Arizona," Bastyan responded trying for levity.

She graced him with a frosty stare. "Arizona isn't a territory, isn't anything but a name. It's still New Mexico."

"He's the only kind of a preacher around here in a very long time," said Bastyan. "There hasn't even been a Catholic priest in over 30 years. Folks need him. All us brutal sinners need him."

"More sinners in California," humphed Missouri Anne.

Bastyan also suspected there was more gold for the offering plate. Arizona had some new mines but was still cash-poor. Wisely, he said nothing. The girl might be frosty, but she was talking to him, was alone with him, even if they were only yards from the town. So, he complimented the poor food, her hair, her eyes, playing on a woman's vanity, and as the afternoon progressed she softened a little. The girl got lots of attention being part of an, if not elite, at least, very limited sorority, but the men to which she was accustomed were laborers, farmers, ranchers, miners, and teamsters, all lacking in sophistication and the ability to ply a smooth tongue. He flattered her, and she enjoyed it. On the way back to town, she looped her arm through his and leaned on him just a little.

This isn't my old life, Bastyan thought, but it is getting better. Things are looking up.

"Mornin,' marshal," said a storekeeper the next day.

After a moment's surprised hesitation, Bastyan replied, "Good morning."

The icy stares were gone. If they didn't always greet him, people at least didn't stop talking as he neared. Even the cantina owner began paying his share of Bastyan's salary again, but with the admonition to Poston that Clegg had better watch his step and not be mistreating good customers. As the storms passed, a warm September was born, and life in Tubac seemed good.

With the passing summer, stories came in from outlying districts. Tucson played host to a former Southern Congressman who shot and killed an Irish headwaiter in the Capitol for refusing to serve him breakfast after the stated hour. German mining engineer Brunkow, together with his associates, was murdered at his mine near the San Pedro River. Brunkow, pierced by a star-drill, had been tossed down the mineshaft. The others had been bashed to pieces with picks and sledgehammers by the Mexican members of the crew who then fled for Sonora. Further north, the crew building the Butterfield Overland Mail Station at Dragoon Springs was murdered as they slept by the Mexican members of the crew who then disappeared south. Some of the young men who ranched and farmed along Sonoita Creek took it upon themselves to beat up Mowry's Sonoran workers in reprisal. As far as anyone knew, Mowry's men hadn't been involved in either set of murders. Stock thefts and marauding Apaches along Sonoita Creek were commonplace. In a region haunted by Apaches, Mexican banditos, and California badmen, Tubac was at peace. It was believed marshal Clegg's ferocious reputation kept evil doers at bay.

"Help! Murder!" screamed the man running up the street toward the adobe casa near the cantina that was Bastyan's home and office. The man was covered in blood.

"What happened? Are you hurt?" Bastyan demanded.

"No. Not my blood," replied the man panting hard from exertion and fear. "I found Henry Smith at the edge of town. It's awful. He was hacked to pieces, just all cut up. Machetes, I think." A crowd gathered around them.

Poston came trotting up the street toward Bastyan. "Mexicans, two of them," he cried. "They were seen hacking Henry with machetes. Just now! I gave Henry the payroll to take out to the Santa Rita Mine. They must have known."

"Saddle me a horse, please," said Bastyan turning to the man who kept the stable. Ducking into his adobe, he picked up his rifle and accoutrements and his saddlebags. "Get me some jerked meat and trail bread," he said to the storekeeper when he emerged. "How long ago?" he asked turning to Poston.

"Minutes!" replied Poston.

103

Clegg tied down his equipment and mounted the horse that had been brought. "I'm on their trail."

"Wait!" cried Poston. "You'll need a posse!"

"Good," replied the mounted marshal. "You get them together and send them after me."

"But there's two of them," insisted Poston.

"Armed with machetes," replied Clegg, "and riding hard for Mexico. I've got guns."

"Bring them back for trial!"

Bastyan Clegg looked at him and shook his head in bewilderment as if trying to clear his mind. He wondered what Poston was thinking. A trial was impossibility because of the distance to the annual court in Mesilla. Poston lacked the authority as alcalde to bring in a death sentence, and nothing less would satisfy anyone. He was distancing himself, Bastyan thought, from the inevitable. It was unlikely the Mexicans would allow themselves to be taken alive. Poston didn't want to get his hands dirty. He wanted his payroll back, too, though it couldn't be more than $500. He had only eight men at the mine.

"I'll do my best," replied Bastyan. Some in the crowd smiled at his vow. They knew the fast gun's reputation for brutality.

Bastyan Clegg rode to the south and soon spotted a dust trail in the distance. He followed the dust as it veered eastward toward the river. Soon there was no dust to follow, though it didn't take Bastyan long to locate two sets of tracks in the soft earth under the trees along the river.

They must know they're being followed, Bastyan thought, as the trail veered west into the desert and disappeared again.

He didn't push his horse hard. That would wear it out all too soon, although the horse was well fed. Equally matched in horseflesh, a chase like this could go on forever. Bastyan had to hope he had the better horse. If he were patient, in time he might overtake them. Unfortunately, the border wasn't far away. Pursuing his quarry over the border, he was apt to find himself prey. He needed to end this chase in the next few miles. He needed to hope they had ridden far before stealing the payroll or hope that they would make a mistake. Perhaps they would stop and try to ambush him.

Ahead of him, the dust trail thinned out. One man had stopped, perhaps doubled back. In any event, one man was still giving him an easy trail to follow.

Clegg came upon a horse, saddled and bridled and sweating heavily, its sides heaving, feeding on a patch of grass by a shallow arroyo. The horse stood out in the open. Perhaps the horse was lame and abandoned. He had to go closer to check. One thing was obvious: whoever had left it was certain he would see it. They might lure him in close and then emerge from ambush in the arroyo as he dismounted. As he approached he could see the horse was splattered with blood. Henry's, he thought. He scanned the terrain looking for anything that might conceal his quarry. The small arroyo beyond the mare might conceal a man. A mesquite thicket might offer cover, but surely mesquite thorns would discourage entry. Nothing moved among the boulders to his right. The arroyo seemed the most likely hiding spot. Wary, he drew a pistol, cocked it, and then with his attention on the animal rode forward toward it.

A boulder towered above him. As he rode passed, he was startled by a blood-curdling scream. A Mexican leapt from a stony perch bringing his machete down with violent force. At the sound, Clegg turned and raised his pistol. The move saved his hand, but the machete impacted with heavy metal, knocking the revolver from his grip and briefly paralyzing his arm. The falling body knocked him tumbling from his horse with the Mexican on top. Suddenly shifting his weight and thrusting upward, he dislodged his assailant and found his feet. Crouching, they faced each other. Bastyan tried for his off-hand pistol but found his arm still too numb to grasp it. With his left he drew his Bowie. Facing a machete, he felt that he was unequally matched and could only dance about yielding ground to avoid the other man's blade. He could not hope to parry, but the big knife was heavy and slow in the man's hand. Bastyan could duck and dodge the blows and he could close in as the blade swept to one side or the other.

The heavy blade swung by and Bastyan leapt in, flicking his smaller blade at the Mexican's eyes, taking a knick out of a heavy eyebrow. The man flinched and backed away. Clegg danced out of range. Blood ran into the man's eye. This would now be his weaker side, his vision restricted. But it was also Bastyan's weak side, his right arm still numb but gaining feeling. The Mexican began another broad swing, and Bastyan, judging its pass began to close in again. As he thought, the Mexican wasn't strong enough to redirect the blow once it began, and reaching over the arm, grasping the machete, Bastyan neatly removed the end of the man's nose. The man screamed hideously and bled copiously. The fight continued, but the advantage was now with Bastyan.

To and fro they fought. Bastyan Clegg left his mark on cheek and chin, hand and arm, and a deep cut across the man's belly. Bastyan continued to flick and dodge as feeling returned to his right arm. Cutting the man across his right eye and cheek, he left the Mexican blinded by his own blood. The man backed away, wiped his eyes, and then unexpectedly charged, the machete held high overhead and descending. Able to use his right again, Bastyan drew and fired, catching his assailant between the eyes. A neat round hole appeared at the bridge of his nose as the Mexican fell.

Bastyan grabbed the man's hat and stripped off his jacket. Donning both, Bastyan went after the horses. Catching his own, he was able to catch up with the Mexican's. Leaving the body where it lay, Bastyan mounted the Sonoran's horse and resumed the chase, leading his own mount. Tumacacori lay behind him and the Portrero, Pete Kitchen's fortress ranch, was not far ahead. Clegg suspected that the other Mexican might seek refuge there. Pete was all right, but his family and ranch hands were all Sonorans, and the man he pursued might be a relative, thereby complicating matters. It occurred to him the man he chased might be ahead somewhere waiting for his partner to rejoin him, hence his disguise.

Perhaps a quarter mile ahead, a rider emerged from concealing mesquite wearing a broad sombrero. Bastyan waved and the greeting was returned. Clegg held his rifle aloft showing his 'accomplice' that he'd killed the hated *gavacho* and had captured his arms as well as his horse. The distance closed. At 100 yards, the Sonoran began to suspect a cheat. At 50 he was sure of it and departed at a gallop. Close enough, thought Bastyan, spurring his horse after the man.

This would be the final chase. They were just beyond pistol range, so there was no point wasting ammunition. True, Bastyan's Dragoon Colts had greater range than most pistols, but aiming from a galloping horse he was unlikely to hit anything 50 yards away. He could dismount and use his rifle, but the range would increase, and Bastyan in losing the advantage of close range would only get one shot. So they would ride hard until one man or the other's horse proved the more fleet or gave out, or one of them made a mistake.

The mistake came when the Mexican's horse stepped into an arroyo—one of those odd little things born of the violence of the last storm no more than a foot wide, hidden by overhanging grasses, but several feet in depth. The horse tumbled brutally breaking its leg and rolling over the Sonoran who didn't get away in time. Bastyan thought the man might have died. As he neared, he saw horse still quivered, barely alive, and there trapped under the dying beast, was the moaning Mexican.

"*Señor, por favor,*" he whimpered, "you must save me. The *caballo*, he crushes my chest, I can't breathe. *Un bondad!*"

Bastyan looked down at the man. "Did you show Henry Smith any kindness when you hacked him to pieces?"

"*Señor*, I beg you, please," wheezed the Mexican.

"Tell you what." Bastyan said. "Tell me where you hid the payroll, and I might help you."

"Have you looked in my *amigo's* saddlebag?"

The cash was there, and good to his word Bastyan helped the man out from under the horse, a process that became quite gruesome and left the Mexican covered in blood. The horse could not rise, and its efforts nearly crushing the man under him. Clegg put the beast out of its misery and then dug into earth and horse to open a path. Disarming the man, Clegg assessed his injuries. Ragged breathing suggested a few broken ribs. An arm that wouldn't move seemed to be due to a broken collar bone. He was bruised from head to foot and appeared to have landed on his face, for a great deal of skin had been scraped away. The Sonoran's nose was broken—more blood and blacked eyes.

Tying the Mexican and allowing him to ride his *compadre's* horse, Bastyan mounted his own and led them back to his partner's dead body.

"Time to get off," Bastyan said. "From here you walk, and your friend rides."

"But *señor*, I am stiff from my wounds. I can barely move."

Pulling and leveling a pistol, Bastyan replied, "You'll find a way."

And so they went, the Mexican stumbling and begging the long miles back to Tubac. Each time the Mexican fell, he removed more skin from his elbows, palms, and shins. Late in the evening, they arrived in town the man looking more like a beaten corpse than a human. Bastyan gave him water and tied him to the jail-tree before heading to Poston's casa. There he stopped by the doorway and cut the bindings that held the dead man to his horse, letting the body drop unceremoniously to the ground.

Bastyan knocked, and when the door opened, he handed Poston the payroll. "Here's your money. It's been a long day. I'm going to bed." He turned and walked in the direction of his home.

"You can't leave that body here!" Poston cried.

Not responding, Bastyan continued his walk to home and bed, too tired even for food. Things were bound to look better in the morning.

The October morn dawned unseasonably cold and crisp. At mid-morning Bastyan emerged in search of a large breakfast to find the dead Mexican propped against the side of his house looking ghastly. Passersby whispered and pointed. Damn Poston, thought Bastyan. He overheard the word, "tortured."

At the jail-tree, he found Missouri Anne kneeling beside the Mexican cleaning his cuts as she fed him tortillas, eggs, and *refritos*.

"Oh no, *señorita*," squealed the Mexican taking sight of Bastyan. "Here comes *el diablo*. He will beat me and torture me as before. Surely he will make you go away, leaving me here to starve and bleed!"

Missouri Anne rose and slapped Bastyan, causing his head to snap sharply to the left. "How could you? How could I ever have thought I loved you? The word is out. You tortured them both! You're inhuman! Everyone knows your evil reputation. They only stole a few dollars. How could you be so cruel for just a few dollars?" Apparently she was overlooking the murder.

Saying nothing, Bastyan turned and walked toward town. The hostility will pass, he thought. Continuing on his original mission, Clegg went in search of breakfast. No one greeted him; instead, they crossed the street to get away from him. Conversations stopped at his approach, and the good citizens of Tubac blessed him with icy stares. He caught snatches of conversation—"murder" "torture" "brutal" "bad reputation" "cruel."

Entering a café the host looked up and said, "We're closed!"

"But, there are people here," replied Bastyan.

"Closed."

"Look, I only need a few tortillas, eggs, bacon, whatever you've got," said the marshal.

"Fresh out!" said the host with finality.

Rolling his eyes, Bastyan turned and went back out into the street. From behind him, Bastyan heard words hurled by people he could no longer see—"beast" "monster" "son of a…" *"puto"* *"cabron!"*

The dead Mexican was still propped against his house; he was starting to stink. I guess he's not going anywhere, Bastyan thought and then headed for Poston's. Perhaps the alcalde would offer him breakfast…or lunch. The morning was fast passing.

Poston came to the door but didn't invite Clegg in. Instead, he handed the marshal some money. "Your pay up through today and I've thrown in two weeks' severance. That's more than I should do, I believe, but…"

"What?" asked Bastyan.

"The town decided this morning," said Poston. "You're fired. They refused to put up any money for your pay, so this is out of my pocket."

"Why?"

"Isn't it obvious," Poston replied. "This is a nice town, good people, not Tucson. They won't stand for torture and murder. They can't take your brutality!"

"What are you talking about?" asked Bastyan.

"The Mexican told us everything," replied the alcalde. "How you captured them, tied them, beat them, cut them with knives as a lesson. Then you murdered his compadre. You told him how you had to as we had no authority to hang them and no *juzgado* to lock them up. So, all you could do was torture them as a lesson and kill them. But you wanted people to see the lesson."

"This is nonsense!" insisted Clegg. "Nonsense. I shot the one because he tried to kill me. The other had his horse roll over him."

"The dead man is all cut up," replied Poston. "It's pretty obvious how you tortured him before he died, just like the other Mexican said. And as for him, making him walk was torture! Especially after what you did to him. What a fine lesson in intimidation you've made. It's too much. You're fired."

Bastyan Clegg saw the futility of further argument. Poston's mind was made up. So apparently were the minds of everyone else in town. Missouri Anne would marry rancher Kirkland, he guessed. Oh well, he sighed. He had no deep investment in this town, his home for only a few months. Walking back into town, he gathered his possessions and his horse. Mounting his steed, Bastyan considered his options.

Tucson was out. He'd been the marshal of Arizona. Likely as not, that crowd would kill him, shooting him in the back if they feared his fast draw and prowess with a gun. There was nothing for him along Sonoita Creek. Butterfield had a string of stations stretching from Tucson back to Mesilla and was always looking for help. Each station was manned by two or three men. Tucson to Mesilla was Chiricahua Apache country. Three men alone twenty five miles from the next station and over a hundred from military help were not odds Bastyan cared for.

Santa Fe then, Bastyan thought. There were plenty of possibilities in the Rio Arriba, especially if he didn't brag about his fast gun and ability to shoot out a candle flame at 30 paces. He'd find something, and the Mexican girls up that way were right pretty. Bastyan rode east, the setting sun behind him.

Author's Note: The Gadsden Purchase, Arizona and New Mexico south of the Gila River, became part of the United States in 1856 when four troops of the 1st Dragoons rode into Tucson to raise the flag. This story was inspired by real events. There was no law enforcement until Tubac hired a marshal and assistant. Motivated by a series of gruesome murders, the pair beat up two innocent Mexicans and were promptly fired. In 1861, a year after this story takes place, the Army was withdrawn to the Rio Grande. The Apaches attacked Tubac, the people ran for Tucson, and the next day Sonoran bandits arrived to loot and burn the town.

RIDING LONESOME

By Jason H. Campbell

Some men are born of trouble; such was the case of Flint Hawk. He was tall and rugged in a handsome way. Though, he was born easy to laugh, and quick to fight. There was not very much extra weight on him. His arms bulged with muscles from wrestling steers, and splitting firewood.

There are some things that a man can't step away from. It would keep eating at your mind, and soul until you had it to do. A drifter by nature after his parents had died, when he was a child. He had simply saddled up his horse and moved on, not looking back.

He had worked several jobs as a ranch hand, and had basically raised himself. He had one fault: his temper. When he was riled he would tackle anything, with a fist or gun. It didn't matter to him if he was out numbered even, he wouldn't back down. When he knew he was in the right. Different times in the past he had lost his temper, and his job only to drift again.

What drove him on he didn't know. But he felt there must be some place where he could find a home. A place of his own, to raise a few animals. Where a man could lay down at night, and not worry about anything.

There was not much law at this time in Texas. The Texas Rangers had just started, but they hadn't brought law and order to the good folks of Texas. There were always vultures in any society, people who would steal and kill, taking whatever they

111

wanted. If a man had a problem he handled it with a six gun or a rope, what ever was handy.

Though too, there were always some good men. Who would stand up, and fight for what they believed in. Even die for their beliefs if necessary. His ancestors had fought in the Revolutionary War, demanding freedom from England. "Give me liberty or give me death." He could remember his father telling him the stories. Their brave blood flowed through his veins. It would not be the weak-kneed people who settled this country, but good honest, hard working people. God fearing folks, if you will. Who came all this way across the seas, for their religious freedoms.

Flint was working now for a rancher named Russell; an old man who had took him in when he was broke. There were five other men working with him. It was not a real big ranch, but it was growing. Despite the cattle thieves who kept stealing Russell's cattle every chance they got. If things kept going on as they were though, they might put the old man out of business. He had got the south range today, by bad luck only. In fact their foreman, Ike, had offered to trade with him.

"I drawed her. I might as well do the job," Flint said, saddling up his buckskin gelding, Lonesome.

He had ridden away into the silence, disappearing from view. Sometimes he felt so lonesome he thought he could cry. For that reason alone, his horse had got his name, Lonesome. He never turned aside for any job; no use to start today.

The day was about gone now. He had pushed a few head of cattle back down the ridge, heading them towards home. In a few days they were going to start their branding. Putting a brand on the young calves, that had been born in the spring. If they didn't brand them soon, somebody else would.

Kind of like a good looking woman, you had better grab her fast. They are few and far between, especially a woman of good character. He could still remember the Bible stories when they had attended Sunday school. Funny though, there weren't many things he could remember. His dad had been a church-going man, and had put the fear of God in him. Maybe some day he would find a woman like that, like in the book of Proverbs.

Though, he was getting close to thirty now, and felt like he was running out of time. "Maybe God wants us to be lonesome all of our lives," Flint said, rubbing his horse's neck. His dad had given him his Bible as he lay dying with the fever; it was all he had left of his family. Sometimes, when he was alone he would read it some. It felt good to know that somewhere up above, maybe God was watching out for him. He had no one else. There might be a time eventually where a man could lay down his arms. Live at peace with his fellowman, though now was not the time.

One steer cut through the brush, going over the ridge. Lonesome quickly turned that way and started over, instinct kicking in.

Flint heard the low bray of cattle as he eased down the brush. He normally didn't come down this way, but stuck to the trail overhead. The riding was a lot easier. What he saw surprised him. There in the corral were a lot of their cattle that hadn't been branded. A branding iron lay there beside a fire that had just about gone out.

It was then that he heard more noise. Somebody was driving more cattle down to the corral now. Riding Lonesome on down behind some thick pine trees, he held him in there to see who it was. He hadn't come all this way for nothing. The steer was there and he intended on getting them. The three riders approached at a hurry, driving before them thirty head of unbranded cattle.

A lot of times a man's herd could increase rather quickly, by how well he could brand. No matter whom the cow belonged to. Opening the gate, the men drove them inside, and then rode over to the fire, getting down off their horses. "We have got to get these branded quick, before the boss finds out," a familiar voice said.

Flint was riding forward slowly on Lonesome now. His guns he held ready. He was almost upon them before he saw who it was: Ike their foreman. Ike saw him about the same time. He tried to give a warning to his two friends, as he drew his pistol. But Flint was already shooting, and he was deadly fast. He put a bullet in Ike's shirt pocket, then two more for good measure. Ike got off one shot, shooting into the campfire. The men started to move, but Flint had them covered and he was mad now.

"You boys drop those guns, or I'll shoot you full of holes!" They looked deep in Flint's eyes, and let them fall.

"You wouldn't act so big, if you didn't have the drop on us," the youngest one said.

"Shut up Red, that is Flint Hawk, the gunman."

"Red, if you want a chance, march out in the field there. I will give your gun back. Only I will tell you quick, that I will kill you if you draw on me!" Red's face got red, but he didn't say anything else.

"You boys saddle up. We have got some cattle to deliver, and you are going to help me."

"What about Ike?" The older one asked.

"Load him on your horse behind you. I won't deny a man a funeral. You all move on ahead of me. And if anybody looks back, I am going to shoot him."

"What about our guns?" Red asked, hate in his eyes.

"You boys can come back for them, now let's move out." Flint unhooked the gate turning the cattle loose, and they were on their way driving slowly.

"I have another gun," Red whispered to the old man, when they were close.

"Son, you had best forget about it."

They made the drive to the ranch about midday. Russell came running out to greet them, opening the corral gate. "What have we here?" He asked, pointing at the two men. "Did you bring me some more hired hands?" He stopped with a cry and ran forward, seeing Ike lying over the saddle tied down now, and very much dead. "What happened here, Flint?"

"You boys tell him!" Flint demanded.

The old man spoke. "We were rustling your cattle, and Ike was in on it. When Flint stumbled upon us, Ike drew first and Flint shot him."

"Should we hang them?" Russell asked Flint, grabbing for his rope.

"No, hanging won't do them any good. They need to learn a lesson is all I think," Flint said.

"Well, have at it. You are my new foreman anyway," Russell said laughing. "Do what you will."

"Alright boys get off them horses. As my father used to say a man comes into the world naked, and leaves the same way."

The men quickly obeyed.

""It is a long walk to town Flint. Please don't make us walk all the way," Red said.

"If you get tired walking, you can always run," Flint laughed. "Now boys get them clothes off. I meant what I said. You are leaving here naked, or you are not leaving at all."

"Why, you are crazy!" Red said shocked.

Flint shot once; underneath his feet it was so close. "Get moving boys! And if I see either of you again. I am going to assume you are hunting me, and I will start shooting. When you get to town just keep on riding, clean out of the terriority!"

The men stripped quickly throwing their clothes down on the ground, boots, pants, shirt, hat, and long underwear. They also left very fast, at a run. "We are lucky—we're still alive!" the old man snapped. "Next time leave me out of your quick money schemes!"

Russell was laughing so hard, he almost missed the stage which was unlike him. It came pulling in fast, a team of six matched black horses. The stage stopped as a very pretty young lady, got out escorted by some of the men.

"Dad, what in the world is going on?" She roared. "We just saw two men running from here naked as a jaybird."

"I don't know," Russell said, with a sly smile. "You must ask my new foreman here. He is the one that is responsible for that!"

"Well, of all the low down dirty deeds. I had forgotten that men of the West were such a low breed of character." The girl roared, looking Flint right in the eyes. God, was she mad, but still pretty, very pretty.

"Good day to you, ma'am," Flint said grabbing his hat that had fallen off. He swung up on his horse, and rode away.

"Come inside Dakota. You have been away from home too long, in that finishing school. I hope you have not run away the best man I have ever had working for me. Why the man has just practically saved my ranch from being bankrupted. What ever else that school learnt you, it sure didn't teach you much about men!"

"Oh dad, I am sorry. I didn't mean to jump to conclusions," Dakota said.

"About like a female, think nothing of it," Russell said grinning.

Far off the man named Flint was saddling up Lonesome, and getting ready to ride out. He stocked his saddlebags full of supplies, and ammunition. "Tell Russell I will be up at the line camp, working for a little while. I will go up and relieve Benjamin," he told Frank one of the best workers on the place.

Right now he needed to be alone, needed it badly. Russell and Dakota came out later to talk to Flint, and Frank gave him the news. He had done ridden out; only the shadows remained.

* * * *

115

The day passed slowly. Flint working from sunup to sundown, rounding up what stray cattle that he could. He was miles from nowhere, but that was the way he liked it. If he was hurt here all alone, chances are he wouldn't make it. Many a cowboy had died from snakebite, or when a horse had fallen on him. It was a rugged life; the stillness, so quiet and all alone. It gave a man time to think, to reflect.

It was on the second day that Benjamin's horse wandered into camp. It had fresh blood on the saddle horn. Saddling up Lonesome, Flint rode out back tracking the horse. The horse was shod with metal shoes, which helped track him better. He wasn't the best tracker in the world, but this was easy.

After tracking him over an hour or so, Flint found the boy dead. It looked like he had been shot in the back. He loaded the boy on his horse, then headed back to the line camp. He would have to bury him there. A man could look over an occasional steer wandering off, maybe folks were hungry. But the thieves were now stealing the cows in large numbers. They had murdered an innocent boy; maybe he had ridden too close to them.

"I'll make sure that they pay for this," he told Benjamin.

Flint was hammering a wooden cross in the ground hours later. It was then that he heard a horse and buggy coming, traveling very fast. He was surprised to see a young woman driving it; Russell's daughter Dakota. She had harnessed the mare and buggy up by herself. She had grown up here, and could ride and shoot, though her mother had thought it not proper. She was coming his way now.

"I came out here to apologize, for the way I have been acting. Father explained everything to me."

"You are just in time for the funeral; Benjamin was shot in the back."

"You have killed another man?" She roared. "Why you are an animal!" She slapped him hard across the face, with a leather glove on her hand; what a lady.

"Ma'am, I look over a woman insulting me once, but not twice," Flint said mad now.

He pulled her to him quickly to ward off another blow. Pulling her in so close her eyes widened. Flint smiled and kissed her lips roughly, and he did not let her go. Her body felt surprisingly good in his arms. When he released her, she hit him fast, slapping him again.

"Lady, it looks like you are having trouble learning. Either that or you enjoyed the kiss," Flint grinned. "Two slaps for two kisses?"

"You wouldn't dare!" she said.

"Yes, but the next one, you are going to have to ask for," Flint said.

"That will never happen!"

"Flint, what is the meaning of this?" Russell roared, riding up. He had two strange young men riding with him.

"She slapped me, sir. So I figured, I deserved a kiss for it," Flint explained.

"He was burying a man he had shot in the back!" Dakota said, mad still.

The two men came over, to examine the grave. "I found Benjamin dead. Somebody shot him, and left him laying. If you think I did it I will be drawing my pay," Flint said.

"Calm down Flint. You're too good of a man for me to lose. I hired some extra help. These men met some naked men running into town," Russell said winking.

"My name is Joshua, and this is my cousin Jaron. We would be glad to track the shooter for you. Russell, if you want us to, Jaron, here is an excellent tracker. We both are from Tennessee where you learn to track before you learn to walk."

"Alright you boys get you a fresh horse out of the corral. Then see what you can find out."

"There have been a lot of cattle rustling going on down here. I wonder who is responsible?" Jaron asked curiously.

"I don't really know," Russell said. "But they have gone too far this time."

The boys saddled up, taking a little extra gear with them. "We will see you in a few days," Joshua said as they rode out.

"They seem like pretty good boys," Russell said. "I wonder if they can find out anything."

"Take me home dad, right this instance!" Dakota snapped. "Soon as I tie my horse on the back of the buggy," Russell said, getting down. He waved once as they quickly left, though, the girl wouldn't look his way.

* * * *

The boys were back a few days later. They stopped in to see Flint. He was breaking a wild horse in the corral to ride when they rode up.

When the mare had finally calmed down, and quit bucking, he saw the boys watching him.

"Did you all find out anything?" Flint asked.

The boys exchanged a look between them. "Yes, we tracked the shooter all the way back to the Big Bar Ranch," Joshua said.

"I figured it might be them," Flint said. "Chad Logan runs the biggest spread in the country, and is trying to get more land. But it could be anyone there at the ranch that shot him."

"Well, the killer left behind some evidence. We will know him when we see him. There was no other horse, ridden down this way," Jaron said.

"When the time comes, I will ride with you," Flint said. "So will the rest of the boys."

"That is what we wanted to hear," Joshua said, extending his hand. "You are a good man, Flint."

"I don't know about that. Though when I take a man's money, I ride for the brand," Flint said.

"That is all you can ask of a man, to do his best," Jaron said.

"Well, a man does have to live with himself," Flint said.

"We are going to head on down and talk to Russell. We need to tell him, what has been going on," Joshua said.

"I will be down in a few days. The boys should have all the cattle rounded up by then. I think Logan is going to take some in and sell them at the stock yard," Flint said. "You boys are riding some fine looking horse flesh."

"We only ride the best," Joshua said smiling.

Their horses looked well bred. They both had four while stockings, blazed face, and a white mane and tail. The boys kind of dressed alike. With a white handled Colt on their sides, and a white cowboy hat on. If Flint was a betting man, he would bet that they could shoot as well. Though they didn't flaunt it much, but a real man never does.

"I knew a man once that bred horses like these," Flint commented.

Jaron froze suddenly, "what was his name?"

"Mort Davis, I pulled a bullet out of him once when we worked together. Though, I heard Mort has joined the Texas Rangers now," Flint said.

"Well, I'll say one thing. Mort breeds the best palominos in the country," Joshua said smiling.

"That he does," Flint said.

* * * *

Two days later Flint was done combing the back range. There were no more cattle back this way that he knew of. He took his time just traveling slowly, pushing the thirty head of cattle back towards the ranch house. A man couldn't handle many more cows by himself than he had anyway. He certainly didn't want to spook them.

He was surprised to see a full roundup in progress when he got there. The yard was packed out, with people from other ranches. They had all come to help with the branding, of course. And to make sure that none of their own cattle didn't get the wrong brand put on them by accident.

Dakota was there wearing a new dress, red and checked. The young men were swarming around her, likes bees after honey. She gave him a mean look, tossing her hair back as she walked on. Suddenly twelve riders came riding in fast, Chad Logan and his men. He was a very big man, over six feet tall and very heavy. He swung down, walking forward like he owned the world. By his side were some people that looked like they knew more about guns than horses. His boy, Luther, walked along behind him with a mean look in his eyes.

"We heard there was a roundup, so we decided to help," Chad said loudly.

"I think I would rather dance with her," Luther said loudly, pointing at Dakota. A few cowboys were playing a fiddle and a banjo while some people were dancing.

Dakota's face got red, but she didn't reply, just walked away quickly.

"You behave yourself, son," Chad told Luther.

Jaron and Joshua had been talking to Logan. They waved at Flint to join them, as they walked toward the men. Suddenly Logan pulled his pistol out, and shot it in the air. Everybody got quiet now the dancing was forgotten.

"Everybody gather around now. We have had a man shot in the back while riding for me. And we have had a lot of cattle stolen," Logan said.

119

"So have we," Chad said. "It could be anybody doing the rustling. I can promise you one thing. It wasn't any of my boys."

"Well, you are wrong," Joshua said, stepping up. "We have the proof that we need."

"Who in the world are you, and why should I listen at you?" Chad snapped. "I know the men that ride with me."

Jaron opened his vest then, along with Joshua. There on their chest was a Texas Ranger Star. "We are Rangers, sir. Sent down to figure out what has been going on with the cattle rustling."

"Alright, but how do my men fit into this?" Chad demanded. His men had spread out, looking for a gunfight. Flint came quickly and stood beside the men, along with the rest of their men all packing firearms.

"There is just one man responsible. As far as the shooting that occurred. We don't know who is responsible for the cattle rustling just yet. Though whoever it is, had better quit while they are ahead," Joshua said.

"Who is responsible then? Just point the man out and I will turn him over to you," Chad said.

Jaron pulled a silver riding spur out of his pocket, then handed it to Chad. "The killer dropped this spur. And we have the shells from his gun."

Chad gasped, looking down at Luther. One of his spurs was gone. They were pretty expensive; besides him, nobody else had any.

"Do you know anything about this Luther?" He gasped.

"Oh shut up Dad. I did it for you. Boys shoot them!" Luther yelled, going for his gun. Only his dad hit him on the back of the head with his pistol, and down Luther went, knocked out cold.

The other three gunmen had gone for the guns. Flint only saw a blur, as Dakota walked out in front of Russell to see what was going on. She was right in the line of fire. Flint tackled her hard throwing her to the ground as a gun went off. He felt a slight tug, then he was shooting back. It took three shots to bring one gunman down, as the man emptied his gun at them.

"What in the world are you doing?" Dakota asked. As the two young rangers, were empting their pistols.

"Lay still," Flint said, holding her firmly.

Finally all was silent, as three men lay dead. Luther was in handcuffs now.

120

"What will happen to him?" Chad asked. "I knew he was a little mean. But I honestly didn't know he could do something like this."

"He will have a trial, and it will be fair. You might want to hire a lawyer," Joshua said.

"Anyway I think the cattle rustling is over with around here," Russell said.

Flint helped Dakota to her feet, but she was still mad. "What in the world got into you, knocking me down?"

"Nothing ma'am," Flint said quietly, grabbing his hat. He saddled his horse and rode away.

"Shut up girl, that man just saved your life!" Jaron said, shaking his head madly.

"Looks to me like, he was in love with you," Joshua said smiling.

"Where is he going now?" Dakota asked. Flint was riding out on Lonesome, leaning over the saddle some.

"If I know him, I do not think he will be back," Logan said. "He probably feels like there is nothing here for him now."

"Oh my God, where did all this blood come from?" Dakota gasped, looking down at her shirt.

"That bullet he took was meant for you!" Logan snapped.

Far off the man named Flint was riding on. Lonesome was carrying him on slowly. He was holding on to the saddle for dear life. The pain had come now. Though, he thought the wound wasn't a great one. Every time he felt like he could care, something bad had always happened. He must be cursed, doomed to forever walk alone like the lonesome gods. Nobody would ever care for him, except maybe his horse. He would keep riding forever this time. And he wasn't going to stop for anything.

He fell slowly to the ground then, and the world turned black. When he woke up he was laying in the lap of a beautiful woman, in the back of a wagon. Russell driving now, followed by some young men that looked like lawmen.

"Where is Lonesome at?" He gasped in pain.

"Lay still son. We took a bullet out of your side," Russell warned him.

"Did you think you were getting away from me, without giving me that second kiss?" Dakota asked, smiling.

"No, ma'am," Flint said.

121

"I am getting old, so if you two get married I am going to have to deed this ranch to someone," Russell said laughing.

"And, Flint?" Dakota said.

"Yes, ma'am."

"You don't have to worry about being lonesome anymore. I will see to that," Dakota said, as a tear rolled down her cheek.

"Is that a proposal?" Flint teased, though he couldn't move much.

"Well, you will have to court me properly first. And then we will see," Dakota said.

Lonesome neighed coming along behind them, tied to the wagon. Flint, hearing it, smiled. He had never heard a more beautiful sound in all his life. He couldn't leave now, not just yet. He had looked into Dakota's beautiful eyes, one time too many.

THE DAY DELGADO RODE IN

By Lori Van Pelt

Alate January moon shone on Amelia Beasley as she stroked the soft calico fur of her beloved cat, Miss Lucy, for the last time. With delicate hands, she laid the frail body in the shallow grave she dug in the fenced plot beyond the garden. She replaced the dirt, wiping tears from her cheek with the back of her hand.

"It's no small thing when a cat chooses you to be her friend," she said. Her words caused a fresh torrent of tears as she remembered the day the wary stray walked to her wooden gate and meowed. The tiny cat had soulful golden eyes that seemed, to Amelia, to have been gentle replicas of her mother's kind hazel ones.

Robert, of course, laughed at what he called her foolish notions and left most of the cat's daily care to his wife. "These strays will get the best of you one day, my dear," he scolded. But he treated Miss Lucy with such affectionate tenderness that when he lay dying, the cat cuddled at his side in a loyal display of friendship. In the two months following his death, Amelia often saw her sitting near his grave as if she, too, grieved his loss.

Amelia rose and brushed dirt from her knees. As she did so, an owl swooped from its perch on a low-hanging branch of a cottonwood, chanting a low-pitched *whoo-whoo-whoo* as it skimmed the creek. She wiped soil from her hands and rested her palm on the top of the spindly wooden cross marking Robert's grave.

She intended to go back inside the house, but the false daylight of the moon gave her some comfort. She pulled her shawl closer around her shoulders, clasping her hands together and rolling the fabric around them for warmth, and then headed down the hill to walk beside Gem Creek. The gurgling stream shimmered in the delicate light.

Some erstwhile miner was rumored to have found garnets in the alluvium near the deep-cut creek. Amelia and Robert settled here with fond hopes of unearthing their grand fortune. Instead, she lost everything she held dear.

She knelt and washed her hands in the freezing water, splashing some on her cheeks to dissolve the stinging salt of her tears. A strange sound—half-growl, half-moan—emanated from behind her. She froze at the creek's edge. People had reported seeing bear nearby. But it was winter. Bears should be hibernating.

The odd guttural noise came from her left. She rose. Her heart pounded so hard against her chest, she swayed. Taking a deep breath, willing herself to stay calm, she tracked the sound. Something rustled. The moonlight revealed a bulldog entangled in twisted willows near the bank.

Hand at her throat, cloak pulled close around her, she said, "Oh, there now. I won't hurt you."

She moved closer. The frightened dog gave a ferocious growl, and then uttered the same keening noise she heard earlier.

Amelia made a loose fist. She held the back of her hand toward him. They stayed that way for what seemed like forever, but could have only been a minute or two. She was just about to lower her hand and back away, fearing he might be sick with rabies or distemper, when he licked his chops, thrust his lower teeth out in a sheepish grin, and stretched toward her. She spoke gentle endearments. He stopped and turned, moving away. She urged him to follow her. When he did not, she beckoned again. He came toward her and then moved away again. He could not escape the willows.

"What are you going to get me into?" she asked, inching closer. He allowed her to come near and nosed her hand, snuffling. She slipped two fingers beneath his leather collar, feeling warmth and prickly fur. A rope tied to the collar was wound round the slender branches. "Ah, this is why—"

The long rope led to the saddle of a dark horse picketed beyond the willow clump. The dog made its mournful growl once more, and she saw the man. He lay nearby, murmuring to himself, his incomprehensible banter covered by the soughing of the creek. She approached with caution. What if he were one of the robbers said to haunt these canyons? He could easily overpower her. But the dog whined when she turned away.

The man continued his talk, whispering, "?Quien sabe? ?Quien sabe?"

Drawing near, she saw an ominous dark stain spread across the upper right of his shirt.

With strength she didn't know she had, she boosted the man onto his horse. He was not much larger than she, but his wiry muscles went limp after only a brief struggle. She untied the rope from the saddle horn, and led the horse back toward the dog. The bulldog, mission to protect his master fulfilled, allowed her to approach and sat patiently when she slipped her fingers beneath the rope at his neck and released the knot. He licked her hand. She began leading the horse toward her house. The dog, worn out from his encounter with the willow clump, struggled to keep up with them. She turned, waiting for him to waddle closer. They followed this frustrating stop-and-go pattern all along the creek and up the hill toward home. Amelia was glad when they reached the top, and passed the garden. As they did so, both the dog and the horse raised their heads and sniffed the air, recognizing, in the way of animals, the smell of death in the fenced plot just beyond.

She led the horse to the door of the house. From there, she managed to get the man inside and into bed. When he was situated, the dog curled up on the rug beside him. She hurried to stable the horse in the barn with her own sorrel and bay, and then rushed back inside to tend the stranger.

She cleaned the man's wound as best she could, pouring some of Robert's whisky across it, and cleansing dried blood with a dampened piece ripped from one of her late husband's shirts. The bullet had gone clear through the fleshy part of this man's chest, just beneath his shoulder. Placing a folded square of the material across the hole, she bound it in place with the remnants of the shirt. To lower his fever, she sponged him with tepid water. She tried to get him to drink cooled tea. When that failed, she drizzled a thimble full of whisky across his lips. After awhile, he quieted and slept.

She had done what she could. A man who had been shot should see a doctor, she knew. Yet now that he was resting, she hated to move him again, afraid that doing so might start the wound bleeding again. She could ride the mile or so into Arrow Bend to fetch the doctor, but she decided that leaving the stranger alone in her house at night was not a good idea. What if he awoke and tried to leave? His own movements could cause the blood to flow again, and he might die. She would have to watch over him.

She remained alert well into the early morning hours, but fatigue overcame her. She fell asleep in Robert's favorite horsehair chair.

* * * *

The creaking of wagon wheels startled her awake. Mildred Brewster, her nearest neighbor on the creek, stopped in front of the house with her buckboard. Amelia grabbed her shawl and ran outside to greet her.

"Ham sent me to warn you," Mildred said, reining her horses. "Billy Schulz has been shot. Delgado. They think he got shot, too, this time."

Amelia shuddered. Delgado! Even his name caused goose bumps to rise on her arms, for he was a gunfighter of unparalleled reputation. He'd murdered so many that people no longer spoke of the dead as men, talking instead of the dozens of them. She rolled her hands deeper into the wool of her cloak.

"Ham's out with the posse already." The Brewsters were Amelia's nearest neighbors. They lived half a mile from her. "The sheriff's sent his best deputies." She lifted her chin a little higher when she spoke of her husband and his inclusion in the prestigious group. Ham Brewster was also the town's telegraph operator.

Amelia stepped toward the wagon, ready to confide that the wounded Delgado slept in her bed so that her neighbor could get the doctor, but Mildred spoke first. "Billy's in a bad way. They took him over to Doc Watkins."

The words died in Amelia's throat. She couldn't ask for the physician's help. Someone would send the sheriff for Delgado. Despite what dastardly deeds the gunfighter had done, she dared not allow Sheriff Royal Spinner to come here.

"I've got to get back to tend our horses," Mildred said. Her rapid chatter told Amelia how frightened she was, for the older woman usually enjoyed lingering over gossip. "You should come with me."

126

"Oh, he's probably miles away by now," Amelia said, trying to act like nothing out of the ordinary had happened to her.

"Might be," she said. She stared at Amelia. "I don't like leaving you on your own like this."

"I'm fine. I've my own horses to tend."

This satisfied Mildred, for the time being. She pressed her lips into a line and nodded. "You should move to town. This is no place for a woman alone."

Perhaps she was right. But Amelia recalled Robert's warning that Ham Brewster, who raised Thoroughbreds, coveted the Beasley property with its fine meadow snuggled up next to Gem Creek. Robert so loved their land that he insisted on being buried there instead of in the town cemetery, and Amelia honored his wishes. Ham had made offers to Robert take the property off their hands several times. Now, Ham might take advantage of her circumstances. Especially since she was assisting an outlaw

"I'll be fine, Mildred," she said. "You take care of yourself."

Inside, the man she rescued at the creek slept, faithful bulldog at his feet. Any sane woman would have climbed into the wagon with Mildred Brewster and headed straight to the sheriff's office. The man sleeping in her bed, with his chestnut skin and twin six-guns, must surely be the notorious Delgado.

Despite her fear and her protesting conscience, she could not bring herself to turn him in. To do so meant she must fetch the sheriff. She vowed never to be in the same room with Royal Spinner ever again. She felt so uncomfortable in his presence that she even stopped going to church. The parishioners had taken to hugging each other in greeting there. Most meant no harm by it, intending those embraces for friendliness. But Royal Spinner took undue pleasure in his actions. And she could not bear it.

On her wedding day to Robert Beasley, she had gone to Maggie Simson's house across the street from the church to change into her traveling suit. Unbeknownst to her, the sheriff followed her. Just after she slipped out of her wedding dress, he stepped inside, grabbed her from behind and swung her around toward him before she knew what had happened.

"Time to kiss the bride," he said, pulling her close and kissing her lips long and hard. He rubbed her breast through the thin cotton of her camisole. She stiffened like a board in his arms, but he was oblivious to her disgust.

Ham Brewster unknowingly saved her when he knocked on the door. "Amelia, Maggie's been delayed with that gabby Francis Emory. She'll be a few minutes, but she'll come help you with your dress. She sent me to tell you so you wouldn't worry."

Spinner released her as if he touched hot coals. He stood, smirking, between the pine door and Amelia, clad only in her camisole and petticoat.

"Thanks, Ham," she called back, desperately trying to keep her voice from shaking. At the very least, she should have slapped Spinner, but she dared not. The lascivious look in his bulging eyes told her he would welcome such punishment. And she wanted to protect Robert. If he ever learned of Spinner's despicable behavior, he would do whatever was necessary to defend her honor.

Ham's footsteps receded. Sheriff Spinner cracked open the door, looked both ways and sauntered outside as if nothing untoward had happened. Amelia stood there, shivering and hugging herself. She fumbled with the buttons on her traveling suit, but managed to get dressed. When she finally gathered courage to go outside, she opened the door and saw Maggie Simson descending the church steps.

"Oh, I knew you'd be waiting on me," Maggie called, smiling.

Beyond Maggie, at the church door, stood Mildred Brewster. Eyes narrowed and lips pursed, her expression reminded Amelia of a red-tailed hawk targeting a common field mouse before swooping on its prey. At that moment, Sheriff Spinner appeared from the side door of the church. He smiled and tipped his hat when he nodded toward Amelia. And then, he shook Mildred's offered hand.

The mere memory of the ugly incident disturbed her so that now she curled her hands within the soft folds of her cloak, pulling the wool tighter around her.

She returned to the house and opened the bedroom door. Slender bronze fingers stroked the bulldog's head with gentle affection. The animal gazed up at his master with fierce expression, but grateful eyes. She had not heard the dog bark. Since their first meeting, he had not even growled at her.

Her patient felt well enough by the second day to take more than the hot broth and tea she had been spooning into him. Although he winced when he moved his shoulder and arm, his wound appeared to be healing. She dared not fetch the doctor, who would involve the sheriff. This man, she decided, most needed rest and food to regain his strength. He had shown no hostility toward her. She must not think what might happen if she were wrong.

"I thank you for your kind treatment," he said, speaking in English, as she brought him a tray with toast, bacon, and tea. His voice was gruff, but his words flowed in a lilting way that reminded her of music. "And for Boris." He slipped a morsel of bacon to the pleased bulldog.

"I meant to help your dog," she admitted. "I have taken a great chance by helping you."

"That is true. But kindness of itself is a noble motive."

"And you? Are you a man of noble motive?" she asked.

He chewed the toast. "You must decide that for yourself."

She did not know how to respond and remained silent as she replaced a towel and freshened the water in the pitcher. "They say you shot Billy Schulz."

His eyes glittered. He snapped off another bit of bacon and fed it to Boris. "Perhaps it is true."

"He could die, Mr. Delgado."

"I had no quarrel with him." His answer surprised her, but although he had no reason to explain, he continued, saying, "He got in the way when I was trying to help a friend."

"And your friend?" Amelia was afraid to ask what might happen if she "got in the way."

He patted the dog. "Animals and little children," he said. "They know the true soul of a person."

"Yes," she said, a shiver of fear rising in her as he deftly avoided her question. Would this "friend" soon come looking for Delgado?

"This is why you help me."

She turned away, busying herself with the pitcher and basin. "Perhaps."

"Then you are a woman of noble motive."

She did not feel noble at all. She felt as if she had betrayed her friends in Arrow Bend. "As soon as you are able, you must leave," she said. "I can't keep you—"

He raised a hand to silence her. "You have placed yourself in danger on my behalf. That is enough." He paused. "But I must ask more of you."

"I can't—"

"Boris, he belongs to my daughter. He followed me. This is why I failed my friend. I intended to ride into Arrow Bend for a fight, but I had to watch the dog. Boris nosed through a patch of dead leaves. Schulz heard his wheeze. Billy Schulz ran toward us and fired when my attention was on the dog. I was injured. I dared not allow us to be discovered."

He turned and swung his legs onto the bed in a swift motion. The movement caused him to grimace, distorting his surprisingly fine-featured face.

"Now, I need you to send word to my wife, Consuelo, and my daughter. They will come and retrieve the dog, and I will go. I have only this request. You understand it is better if I do not attend this matter myself. I wish you no harm."

She did not reply.

"If not for me, for Boris."

"He doesn't bark," she said.

"He knows he must be quiet."

A silence fell then. She rubbed her arms to rid them of the gooseflesh that appeared at his words. The man had not done her harm. He made no move to attack her or hurt her in any way.

"If not for the dog," she said, "you would not be alive now."

"We each do what we must." He shifted his position again, reaching into his pocket with his good arm. "You have not turned me in."

"How do you know?"

He shrugged. "The sheriff has not come. He would be here if you sent word to him of my presence." He handed her a piece of paper with a message scribbled on it.

"If I take care of this, will you turn yourself in?"

"I will do what is best." He nodded toward his empty gun belt, slung haphazardly across the chair back. "I must have my pistols."

"Rest is probably best for you now." She averted her eyes.

"I have no quarrel with you. I will not harm you."

"I don't like guns," she said.

"You are a wise woman." He sighed. "You will have to go to town to send the message. I will be alone here, and I will need my guns for protection."

Amelia stood there, silent. After a moment, she said, "Yes, I suppose so." She retrieved the ominous pistols from the bin where she stored flour. She dusted the flour from the linen towel she wrapped the weapons in when she brought Delgado here. She hesitated. If he were here, what would Robert tell her to do?

There was no answer to that question. She must accept that Robert would never again be coming back to help her. He'd been gone for two months now. Amelia bit her lip and took a deep breath. There was nothing to stop Delgado, except his word, from shooting her when she returned his pistols. And yet, she could not bring herself to turn this man in, because she already died a hideous internal death at the hands of Sheriff Royal Spinner on her wedding day. What could be worse than that?

Amelia returned Delgado's pistols. He took one by its grip, aiming it at the foot of the bed. Even though she was standing beside him, she gasped. He blew flour from the barrel, and then placed the gun on the blanket beside its mate.

"I don't like guns," she told him again.

"I know," he said and closed his eyes.

Amelia berated herself all the way to town, feeling anything but wise. There were unexplained gaps in his story. What if his story was a ruse to get her to assist him in further killing? Any woman in her right mind would fetch the sheriff. But Delgado had not harmed her. He could have simply shot the dog and told his daughter some tale of woe to console her. Instead, he had taken good care of Boris. At the outskirts of Arrow Bend, she hesitated for a brief moment, and then turned toward the train depot where the telegraph office was located, on the opposite side of town from the lawman's quarters.

Her hands trembled as she handed the note to Ham Brewster. He glanced at her. "You all right today, Amelia?"

"Oh, yes, Ham. Fine. Just someone walking over my grave, I expect."

"Can't be too careful these days, Ma'am. They say that Delgado fellow's hiding out in these parts, probably in the hills. Runs with the train robbers these days. He's the one shot Billy Schulz."

"I doubt that he'd care to hurt me," she said, more to convince herself than him. "How is Billy?"

"Holding his own, so they tell me. Well, you just watch yourself. You never know what people are thinking. Never hurts to be careful anyways."

He addressed the message to Consuelo Paz, Rock Springs, tapping the words with quick confidence. "Come. Bring Carmen.

Will meet you." He signed Amelia's name. He returned the paper, peering intently at her over his wire spectacles. "I didn't know you had relatives in Rock Springs."

Amelia paid him. "Thanks, Ham," she said, without further elaboration. "I'll keep my eyes open." She hurried outside before he could ask any questions.

* * * *

Early the next morning, before Amelia finished cooking breakfast, Mildred Brewster knocked on the door.

"Ham thought I should check on you," she said, "what with you being alone and all." She entered the cabin without being invited and strode past the bedroom door to the table by the cook stove. Several biscuits were warming and a sizeable helping of bacon sizzled and popped. The bedroom door was slightly ajar.

An extra plate and mug sat on the table. Delgado had felt well enough to start taking his meals there instead of in bed.

"Oh, my," Mildred said. "Do you have company?" She peered around the room as if she might have missed something.

"I—I sometimes set the table for two," Amelia stammered. "Habit, I suppose."

"Oh, you poor dear." Mildred's tone indicated that she considered Amelia to be far inferior to herself. "You are lonely."

Amelia held her tongue.

"Ham said you'd sent a wire…" She paused to give Amelia a chance to comment further. When no explanation was forthcoming, she changed the subject. "The pastry chef at the Bower Hotel mentioned that he could use a helper there. I know you're an excellent cook, Amelia, and—"

"Thank you for your concern, Mildred, but I'm fine here. This is my home." A tinkling crash and strange snuffle came from the direction of the bedroom.

Mildred started. "Whatever was that?"

Amelia, keeping her expression as even as she could, said, "Oh, nothing to worry about. Sometimes—the cat—knocks things over."

"That didn't sound like a cat to me," the older woman said. To Amelia's chagrin, she strode to the bedroom door and pushed it open. The bedclothes were mussed. The wooden chair sat empty beside the bed. A crystal perfume bottle had fallen from the bureau onto the floor.

"As you can see, Mildred," Amelia said, "I haven't even seen to my chores this morning. Ah. Look." She pointed to the broken bottle. "That cat. Dear Miss Lucy," she continued, her tone sharp and scolding. "You must be more careful."

Mildred cocked an eyebrow. "I know you better than you might think, Amelia Beasley. You can't fool me. You're hiding something. It wouldn't surprise me a bit if it were some stray animal. Ham says those strays will be the death of you yet." She turned from the bedroom. Amelia pulled the door closed. "You never know where they've come from or what they've gotten into. They may well be sick."

Amelia shrugged and smiled. "I can't help myself." As was her usual custom, she invited Mildred to join her. "I'll have a time eating all of this myself."

Mildred, though, declined the meal as she was on her way to town. Amelia stood in the yard and waved until Mildred's buckboard disappeared over the hill. Then she rushed inside. She opened the bedroom door and came face to face with Delgado, his pistol poised to shoot.

She gasped. His eyes were cold. He laid the pistol on the bureau.

"You wouldn't have—?"

Boris snuffled again, apparently having breathed in too much of the rose water. Delgado leaned down and patted the animal's shoulder. He said, "You have not turned me in. Why is this?"

"I—your dog," she stammered.

But the gunfighter shook his head. "No. It is more than the dog."

The words tumbled out before she could stop herself. As if she were a child guilty of misbehaving in a school yard, she told him about her horrible experience with Sheriff Spinner. "I know the right thing to do, but I can't bring myself to do it," she admitted. "And you haven't hurt me."

His eyes narrowed and his lips twitched. For a frightening moment, seeing his menacing expression, she worried that he might accost her. She stepped backwards.

"Things are not as they appear," he said. "You took care of me and Boris. I have no reason to harm you. To be grateful, yes. To injure? No." He strode past her. "The bacon burns."

As she bent to retrieve the shards of glass, she remembered his words, "I will do what is best." The sweet scent of roses wafted from the shattered crystal.

* * * *

Consuelo Paz and her little girl, Carmen, arrived later that day. Amelia, leading Boris with the rope so they would recognize her, met them at the crowded train depot. To her dismay, Mildred Brewster waited among those gathered there. After greeting her visitors, she glanced around the group, taking stock of everyone in sight, and her gaze eventually landed on Amelia. Before she could make her way through the throng, Amelia turned away, hurrying toward a clot of well-wishers surrounding a man who wore a military uniform.

Consuelo and Carmen descended the steps from the railroad car to the platform. At the sight of the youngster, Boris's stout body struggled against the rope as he attempted to wag his blunted tail. Carmen ran to them and reached to scratch his ears. The little girl's delicate features mirrored her father's.

Consuelo said, "You have found our beloved pet. We are most grateful." Her unblemished skin was the bronze color of fallen cottonwood leaves still visible in the snow-spotted meadows on the outskirts of town.

Amelia relaxed a little. At least part of the gunfighter's tale was true. When she turned to take them to the wagon, though, she was uncomfortably aware of Mildred Brewster watching them from the opposite end of the platform, and of Ham's piercing observation from the ticket window.

* * * *

Amelia's parlor became the sight of a happy family reunion. Consuelo, a dainty slender woman, rushed into Delgado's arms with such force that he nearly toppled. After enjoying a lingering kiss with his wife, he stroked the round cheek of his daughter with tender admiration and murmured endearments in Spanish.

Watching them, Amelia suggested that Carmen and Boris sleep on the rug near the fireplace in the parlor, and she could sleep in the horsehair chair as she had been doing. The lovers would have the privacy of her bedroom.

134

Consuelo tucked Carmen into the makeshift bed, and Boris circled a couple of times and snuggled next to her. Consuelo hummed a lullaby, waiting a few minutes for Carmen to fall asleep. This task done, the woman brought her hairbrush and seated herself near Amelia.

"Consuelo," Amelia said, "how did you ever marry a gunfighter?"

"He did not always live by the gun," she replied, brushing even, patient strokes through her long, wavy black hair. The firelight gave a blue cast to her shining locks. "After Jorge and I had fallen in love, another man—a lawman—had his way with me," she said, her voice quiet. She glanced toward the bedroom. "When my father found that I was with child, he disowned me, but despite everything, Jorge took good care of me. He married me."

Amelia's eyes fell on Carmen, whose breathing was rhythmic.

"I lost that baby," Consuelo whispered, "it was a blessing, because that man ran away. Besides my father, Jorge was the only one who knew. He promised to kill him whenever he found him, but that day has not come. I told Jorge that no good could come of him killing someone like that, but I've regretted that."

Amelia stared at her. "Why? Do you know where the man is?"

"No," she said. "And that is the reason for my regret. Because of my reluctance, he got away and could hurt someone else." She sighed. "But we soon had Carmen, and she has kept me busy." She sighed. "But as she grows older...I fear I made a mistake in allowing an evil to go unpunished."

"So why did your husband become a gunfighter?"

"We had nothing. Jorge is an excellent shot. The money was good..." Her voice faded away as she pulled the brush slowly through her hair. "He shot some men before we married. This, I try not to think of," she said. "We all do what we must." She pulled the brush once more through her thick hair.

"What will you do now?"

She laid the brush down. "We will do what is best." She stood and went to her husband, leaving Amelia to wonder at those words, an echo of what Delgado said when she spoke with him about his guns.

In the morning, Amelia awoke to the comforting smell of boiling coffee and saw their traveling bag sitting beside the door. Consuelo had prepared breakfast. They ate round her table like

135

a normal family. Jorge Delgado made Carmen laugh, a sound brimming with happiness, uplifting as church bells chiming on Christmas Day. Boris sat at her feet, now and then cocking an eyebrow as if to ask, "Are we done yet?" But always, he faced the doorway, watchful and protective of his young charge.

After they had eaten, Consuelo poured coffee for Jorge. She ran slender fingers across his back as she leaned over his shoulder. He caught her hand and kissed it. Their eyes met and held.

Amelia realized that, despite what he had told her, Jorge Delgado did not intend to leave with his family.

"Come along, Carmen," Consuelo said. "It is time for us to go." She withdrew her hand but her eyes remained on her husband's face. "Kiss Papa goodbye."

Consuelo's eyes filled with tears when she kissed her husband goodbye. She turned to Amelia. "You're a good woman," she said. "We go now." She picked up her bag and strode through the door.

Amelia took them to the Arrow Bend depot. Ham Brewster saw her bidding them farewell as he walked across the platform and raised a hand in greeting. He did not stop to speak to her.

Delgado remained at her home. He did not turn himself in. To Amelia's unspoken question, he said simply, "I prepare. I must ready myself."

"For the fight you came here for?"

His eyes glittered. "Yes. It has been one I've let go for far too long."

They passed the day as they had the others, speaking to one another with practiced wariness and only when necessary. Later, Amelia slept fitfully in the chair. She awoke in the darkness when she heard the front door open and close. She pulled the blanket around her and peered through the curtains. A nearly full moon illuminated the landscape. The gunfighter to whom she had given charity and succor simply walked out in the middle of the night.

At least he left without confiding in her. If anyone asked, she could truthfully respond that he rode away in the same direction from which he had come. He did not steal her horses. She watched him go, the outlines of his wiry form softened by the lustrous moonlight.

* * * *

136

The next morning, Thursday, her usual day for errands, she rode the bay to town. A crowd gathered at the sheriff's office. She dismounted from her horse and tied him to the rail at the bank.

Ham Brewster caught her arm. "They're bringing someone in. Best not look too close. Think he's shot up bad."

Sunshine silhouetted a stout man on horseback, his hat brim rolled up on both sides and broad shoulders straight and even. As he neared and the sun's glare receded, she saw that the rider was Herman Schulz, Billy's older brother. Another horse walked alongside his, a body draped across its saddle. Ham Brewster pushed closer to the horseman, unaware that Amelia followed.

Herman held his bloodied wrist against the saddle horn. He said, "He got the sheriff, Ham." Ham stepped forward to look. "No way I could stop it. He took the sheriff just like that," he said, wincing, as he moved to snap his fingers and then thought better of it. "It was like—it was like he meant to do it. I saw him first, and I tried to take a shot, but Delgado was too quick. He hit me before I could pull the trigger. Knocked my pistol to the ground! I don't know why he didn't kill me, he could have done it right then, but I don't think he wanted to hurt me. The sheriff's bullet hit Delgado's horse, but that didn't stop Delgado. He said, 'For Consuelo and the others!' and fired. I don't know what that meant, but Royal never had a chance."

"But you're still alive," Ham said. "Anyone who has gone against Delgado and can say that, well, it's a victory, of course."

Herman nodded. "But Delgado is still out there." He looked behind him. "He's still out there. He could kill someone else."

Fighting tears, Amelia turned away. She knew what Delgado's words meant. The "lawman" Consuelo had spoken of was Royal Spinner, and the "friend" Delgado came here to help was his wife. He must have always meant to avenge her, and he finally tracked the sheriff here, without Consuelo knowing it. Amelia's story simply added fuel to the fire, and she became one of "the others" that the gunfighter mentioned when he pulled the trigger.

* * * *

According to Mildred, almost all of the residents of the town and many people from the surrounding region attended the funeral

137

of Sheriff Royal Spinner. Amelia pretended she caught cold and stayed home. Mildred provided all the details while drinking tea in Amelia's parlor after the service. A marble monument stood at the head of his grave in the cemetery, engraved with the words, "Loyal Protector," and a local soloist sang, "I Would Be True," as they lowered his coffin.

Delgado had not yet been found. "But when they find him, and kill him, he'll not deserve any such rites," Mildred told her, with a little too much fervency for Amelia's taste. "They'll toss his bones out in the sagebrush with the other rattlesnakes. He won't even deserve that much attention."

Among residents of Arrow Bend, Amelia knew she alone would carry the image of the tenderhearted father and friend she had met.

* * * *

Buds began appearing among the willows on the bank of Gem Creek and the grass was showing tinges of green when Consuelo Paz knocked on Amelia's door.

She carried a small basket. "For you," she said. "A pup from Boris. And from Carmen."

Amelia gathered the wriggling mass of dog in her arms and invited Consuelo inside.

"She does not know what her father was, the great, feared Delgado," Consuelo continued, once she was inside the house. "She knew only his work took him to many places we could not go."

"Was?" Amelia shivered. "Is he–?"

Consuelo smiled. "No, he is not dead. Jorge has given up the life of the gun," she said. "After staying with you, he said that he wanted only to be home with us."

"He is a man of noble motive," Amelia said, stroking the puppy.

Consuelo touched Amelia's arm. "Yes." Her wide brown eyes remained on Amelia's for a long moment. "He said the same of you," and then, abruptly, she nodded at the bulldog. "We raise them. Many want them. They are prized for sport, for dogfights. We do well. But you—you will care for this dog. Jorge chose this pup especially for you. He wished you not to be so lonesome after all you have lost, but he could not bring the dog here himself."

"I understand," Amelia said, and she also understood now she was right. With gentle movements, she scratched the puppy's ear. He barked.

Consuelo nodded with satisfaction. "The animals know," she said.

CONTEMPORARY WEST

GROUND TRUTH

By Rob Kresge

Hard wind drove burning snow against my cheek. I turned my head to let my long brown hair and black hat catch the stinging missiles.

The little old ladies standing by the body didn't fit the stereotype. They were lean, fit, and dressed in Gore-Tex parkas. Wish to hell I had mine.

Emily was the taller of the two. "We're librarians from Pittsburgh. We always came to New Mexico on our vacations. When we retired two years ago, we decided to move to Santa Fe."

"You're a ways from home. What're you doing on the Jicarilla Reservation? And how did you find this body so far from the main road?"

I gestured at the deceased. Female, early 40s. Not Indian. Face down, but turned a little to her left. No visible marks on her powder blue down parka, but I hadn't examined her. The captain would be sending out the crime scene van.

Sarah, the more suspicious one, spoke. "Where's your uniform if you're a reservation cop?"

"It's my day off." She glanced at my obviously unarmored chest. "I didn't have time to put on my vest." Called out on my only free Saturday this month.

"Do you at least have some credentials?"

I pulled the badge case from my jacket and flipped it open in a practiced gesture. The effect was spoiled somewhat when my numbed fingers couldn't hold onto it.

143

Emily picked it up.

"Sergeant Jo Ann Barefoot. Are you an Indian? You don't look Apache."

"Half Cherokee. The Jicarilla are equal opportunity employers." They took me in after the North Carolina State Police let me go last year. I stamped my feet to keep warm. My bolero jacket, flimsy broomstick skirt, and dressy boots weren't meant for three inches of snow.

"Let's start again. How do you come to be here? When did you arrive?"

Emily handed my badge case back.

"The last part first. Sarah and I got here about an hour ago. We came straight to the site. We didn't want to linger, because the snow looked to be getting worse. When we found that poor woman's body, we didn't touch anything. Other than to confirm she was dead."

"I said we should go back to the warm car and phone the police," Sarah added. "We had to drive to the top of that big hill to get a decent signal."

"That's the Rez for you. Navajos have it worse, I hear." The snow was beginning to slack off. Maybe the sun would break through this afternoon. I glanced around. No purse. No footprints, except mine and the little old ladies. Did she die last night before the snow began to fall?

I crouched and lifted her left arm. No rigor now, but some snow under her arm. Maybe she died only a couple hours ago. I heard the crime scene van as it labored over the hill. It'd be a few minutes yet.

"You still haven't said why you're here."

They began to fidget and looked at each other out of the corners of their eyes.

"For heaven's sake," said Emily. "We have to trust her. She's a cop. The Jicarillas are supposed to know all about these places."

Sarah sighed. "We're site monitors. For the State Archeological Conservancy. There are so many ancient sites in New Mexico that professionals can't excavate them all. They record them and hope to explore them some time in the future."

"They don't publicize the locations," Emily added. "In fact, they're actually closely held secrets. They have volunteers like us visit our assigned sites every couple of months to look for evidence of camping, vandalism, or digging. We take photos and write reports."

The van crunched to a halt on the gravel road a hundred yards away.

"So there's some ancient ruin here?"

"You're almost standing on the wall of an old *kiva*," Emily said.

"Apaches never built any of those, but they gave me a crash course on Anasazi dwellings and customs. I'll have our crime scene team print your shoes for reference. Then you can get back to your warm car. Do you have any identification I can keep?"

Sarah handed me a business card. Internet research consultants. I got contact information and let them get their boots printed.

After that, Gus Tuayaysay and Billy Whitewolf brought a crime kit and stretcher. We got to work.

No purse or i.d. under the body, but Billy thought he'd seen her at the museum and trading post in Dulce, the tribal headquarters. He took photos.

Nothing in her hands but a piece of leather fringe, butterscotch in color and shiny finish. We bagged the little leather bit.

No wounds to the body. But under her long reddish hair was sticky bright red. She'd been clubbed from behind. Shovel maybe. Something with an edge. Not a tomahawk, please. The likely cause of death, if she hadn't died of exposure.

Speaking of which, I crossed my arms over my chest. An unlined bra, black turtleneck, and a bolero jacket might lead to my death, from exposure. I caught Gus grinning.

We wrapped things up and got her onto the stretcher. I followed the two men, holding my jacket as closed as I could. I might have to cancel my date with Roy in Chama. As we walked, I noticed something I'd missed on my way in. Brush marks in the lee of a rock. Someone had swept this area before the ladies arrived. It was snowing and the killer didn't want to leave footprints. No footprints and no purse left behind. A very methodical murderer.

* * * *

Sure enough, Captain Klosen had me cancel my date. As I worked on my preliminary report, Billy came in with photos of the deceased.

145

"Gladys at the gift shop recognized her and looked up her credit card receipt. She bought some jewelry and a few baskets yesterday. Mary Baer. An art dealer from Taos. Must have come over Route 64."

"Sixty-four was closed yesterday," I said without looking up from the sole police computer. "Snow was heavier the last two days in the San Juans and closed the pass. She might have come south of Tres Piedras to Abiquiu and up Eighty-four." Or been on this side of the mountains—Chama or here in Dulce before the snow. I'd been doing my geography homework.

"Now that we have a name and a hometown," the captain said, "I'll check with State Police for a car and see if we can find it. You gonna be all right handling this, Barefoot? It's only our third murder in twenty-six years. I handled the first two myself."

"I'll be OK. This'll be my third one in nine years. More killings in Carolina."

"Since it's a three-day weekend, let's hold off on telling State Police and the FBI we have a homicide until Tuesday. Try to clear the case by Monday, would you?"

He grinned and left. "Clear the case." That was big-city cop talk. I knew the captain had spent a few years on the Albuquerque force before returning to the Rez.

"Billy, when he gets the make and model, would you get Patrol to look for her car? Our killer may be driving her wheels."

I glanced out the window as a local ambulance took the body to Farmington, to the hospital and medical examiner there.

* * * *

Roy Sanchez was understanding about my breaking our date. He offered to come over tonight instead of my going to Chama as we'd planned. He was beginning to grow on me. But I had to work the case.

The captain learned Baer's car was a five-year-old red Hyundai Sonata, a car that should stand out. When I asked Gus to alert Patrol, I caught him looking at my chest instead of my face. I regretted taking off my jacket as I typed.

"Gus, you have to stop looking at me like that. I want to know you'll have my back when I need you, not my front."

Apaches don't blush, but he stammered and went out to Dispatch.

* * * *

146

Two hours later, I caught my first break. Patrol caught Calvin Estebanito driving the Sonata and brought him in. They didn't need to print him or read him his rights. Calvin was our most prolific and inept car thief. Quick prints from the car matched him and the victim. Gravel in her tire treads. Maybe her car had been to the crime scene and the killer had switched cars after ditching hers somewhere near here.

My suspect was wearing an old, dirty leather coat. Hard to tell what the original color had been. Lots of fringe missing here and there.

"Calvin, this has to stop. Your mother worries about you."

"You talk like my mother. I don't wanna talk to no woman."

"All right, you don't have to. I'll talk, you listen. Just nod to me. Where did you pick up this car? At the market?"

Head shake.

"The casino?"

Grin.

"The Best Western?" The hotel housed the Wild Horse Casino.

Nod.

"Last night?"

Head shake.

"This morning?"

Nod and grin.

"What time? Was it before eleven o'clock?" That was when I'd gotten the call.

Nod.

That might mean she stayed at the hotel last night. Progress.

"Take him home, boys, and tell his mama."

Sufficient punishment for the moment, I thought. I knew where to find him. Cocky, he hadn't seemed scared enough to be worried about a murder charge.

The patrolmen left with Calvin. I grabbed my purse and jacket and headed for my truck. I wanted to talk to the desk clerk.

The cold wind still blew powder across the parking lot. I detoured to my apartment and made myself more professional— jeans, boots, uniform shirt, pistol belt. And the Kevlar vest I'd brought from North Carolina. It was hard for a woman to find a good-fitting vest and I treasured mine.

Wilma Cordova checked the registry cards. No Mary Baer last night. That was a puzzle. She couldn't have come all the way from Taos to be killed this morning. Too far, too early, too much snow in the passes. But she'd been attractive. Maybe she'd stayed with someone. A man? I was about to leave when I spotted Wilma's copy of last week's Chama paper turned to a page I knew well. A photo of Roy's Chama Valley Art and Framing gallery. I took her copy. There was a parked car in the photo.

Back at the station, I dialed the paper.

"Editor."

"This is Sergeant Barefoot of the Jicarilla Police. Could I speak to your staff photographer?"

"Speaking."

"Aren't you the editor?"

"I wear every hat on this tiny rag, lady. What can I do for you?"

"Did you take the photo for the profile of Roy's art gallery that ran this week?"

"Sure did."

"How recent is the photo?"

"Lemme see. Got the photo file right here on my...here it is. Four weeks ago."

That set me back a little. Just before my first date with Roy.

"The photo in the paper is black and white. What color was that Sonata?"

"I'm looking for it on the computer. Ah, here it is. Marilyn Monroe lipstick red."

I called Roy again.

"I've changed my mind, Roy. Can you come here after all?"

"Soon as I get some fuel."

"Not tonight. What about tomorrow morning?"

"Wanna play mysterious, huh? Can I bring some wine?"

"No, it's sort of a 'come as you are' party. I'll text you directions."
I thought about it for a moment.

"I'm good at my job. I want you to see something here, appreciate what I do as much as I value your art gallery."

After I signed off, I thought about Mary Baer and Roy Sanchez. I went to the State Police website. I got the password from Captain Klosen's desk drawer and entered the compartment reserved for law enforcement officers. I looked up Mary Baer and whistled at the results. Then I considered my suspects—two little old ladies, a car thief, and my new boyfriend. Clear this case by Monday, my ass. Maybe I'd get lucky tomorrow.

* * * *

"You're probably wondering why I've asked you all here this morning."

That old line went over like a lead balloon.

"Who are all these people, Jo? And why drag me out here? I thought we'd—"

"Maybe later." I cut him off before he got too explicit. I'd kept everyone waiting for a few minutes after they must've heard my truck tires on the gravel. Nobody was happy to be here. Emily and Sarah shivered. I'd asked them to stay at the Best Western last night so they could be here this morning. Calvin seemed upset. He'd had to borrow his mother's car. Bummer for a car thief. Roy had driven his big SUV and I'd timed my arrival after they'd all arrived.

Calvin wore the same fringed jacket I'd seen him in yesterday. I'd seen a fringed shirt peeking out from under Emily's parka yesterday. And Roy had a warm fringed leather coat, but he hadn't chosen to wear it today. I'd need a little something more in the way of probable guilt before I could justify asking for a search warrant to see clothes two of my suspects weren't wearing today. I'd planned for that.

I'd explained to Roy that I asked suspects back to this crime scene and wanted him here purely as a witness today.

"Let's get down to it, so the innocent can be on their way."

They all began to speak at once. I scanned them through lowered lids, snug in my insulated raid jacket today. And my Kevlar. I'd made sure not to wear my equipment belt today, in order to appear non-alerting. My small-frame automatic snugged my right calf comfortably in its holster. Skirt again today for ease of access and my non-alerting image.

I gestured toward the box that covered where the victim's torso had been the previous day. I'd come out and positioned it last night. Another few inches of snow covered my tracks and made the scene look much as it had the previous morning.

"Mary Baer was an art dealer from Taos who also sold stolen antiquities. She was struck from behind. No struggle. Probably someone she knew.

149

"Each of you had some connection to her. You two because you're volunteers to safeguard native artifacts." Before Emily or Sarah could interrupt, I charged on.

"I found someone at the Archeological Conservancy. You're not supposed to be here. The Jicarilla monitor this site themselves, even though it's not their culture. You have sites near Galisteo, south of Santa Fe. You were up here to scope out a site you have no reason to visit. Did you find Mary Baer ready to dig?"

I held up my hands to keep them quiet and charged on. Roy was grinning.

"You," I said, pointing at Calvin, who looked up. "You stole the victim's car. But there's something peculiar in that. Unless you rode out here with her, there should have been a second car. The killer left hers at the Best Western, where you stole it, but she wasn't a guest there." Calvin put his eyes back on his boots.

"Then there's you, Roy." I didn't have to point to him. "You knew Mary Baer, and had...dealings with her." No doubt he'd had at least one kind of dealing with the pretty redhead before I'd come along. Had art dealings led to a falling out? Or a falling out over me?

Roy opened his mouth, but closed it without saying anything.

"I asked you all out here because we found another clue when we moved the victim's body yesterday morning. Ms. Baer was wearing an expensive—and very efficient—down parka." They looked puzzled.

"Her jacket insulated her body from the cold ground. It also performed another function. It insulated the ground beneath her from her body heat. When we moved her, we found a footprint." Everyone looked at each other.

"The killer tried to brush away all evidence that might link him or her to the scene. But that one clue remained." I was running a bluff. I'd gambled that everyone would wear the same footgear today as they had yesterday. I squatted and touched the box. I got more than I bargained for.

Sarah fell against Emily and they both sprawled against me. Calvin stepped back. I struggled to my knees. Roy disappeared up the path that led to the cars. I helped the two ladies to their feet.

They looked down at the bare snow where the box had been.

"My, that was a clever ploy, hoping to smoke out the murderer," said Sarah. We all heard a vehicle door slam and an engine come to life. I keyed my radio three times to alert the blocking unit to move in on the gravel road.

"You'd better hurry, dear, if you're going to catch him," said Emily.

I unsnapped the pistol from my calf.

"He won't get far. I let the air out of one of his tires."

"I thought you didn't know which one of us was guilty," said Calvin.

"I didn't. Not for sure. I'm afraid I let the air out of one of everybody's tires."

THE ROAD

By Wesley Tallant

On a hot, sunny July afternoon, a semi truck rumbled down a dusty winding gravel road. It was supposed to be a shortcut that would save the driver, Mark Johns, several hours on the route to his destination. He was already a day late because of mechanical problems, but the load was needed in Yuma, Arizona by eight-o-clock in the morning.

He had driven from Denver to Flagstaff to Phoenix when an axle broke. The mechanics couldn't get to it for two days, so he spent the day under the truck's trailer doing the repairs himself.

His job depended on him getting this load through on time. His boss had told him that if he was late again, he'd be fired and no excuse would be accepted. Only intervention by the hand of God would save his job if he were late one more time.

He had a bad habit of exploring the older small towns he came to. He would get lost in time as he marveled at how things must have been in the days of the Wild West. On more than one occasion, his exploring the old ruins of a town had cost him a paycheck for missing a delivery time.

So he checks his GPS and it shows this dirt road that would cut at least two hours off his drive time. Not fully trusting the modern convenience, he reaches into the glove box and pulls out a well used Arizona map. But the road is not shown on the map. He calls out on his CB radio and asks if other truckers know the road, but nobody knows what road he was talking about. It's a gamble he must take, his job depends on it, so he makes the left turn and crosses his fingers.

It seems to be a well maintained road. The surface is smooth and level without any of the potholes that were found on other dirt roads. It's so smooth that he is able to maintain a rather fast speed. He keeps the diesel motor turning at high RPMs as he sails down the road toward Yuma.

It is well past sundown when he checks his watch and GPS. By all calculations, he should be in Yuma well before the deadline. His eyes are beginning to show the strain of the long day and he can barely keep them open.

He decides to pull over and set his alarm for just a couple of hours of restful sleep. But where to pull over? Each side of the road is strewn with boulders and other debris that would surely do harm to the truck. And where there isn't any rocks, soft sand would surely stop the big rig in its tracks.

He drives a little farther and sees a building come into view. In front of the building is a dirt lot big enough to park for the few hours he needs to nap. He parks on the edge of the lot so as not to block anybody that might come along.

Mark sets the air brakes and lets the engine idle for just a few minutes before he shuts it down. He decides to stretch his legs before setting the alarm and taking his nap.

The moon is shining full and lights up the old building that looks to be maybe a hundred years old. The paint on the sign hanging on the front of the building has flaked off and the porch on the front looks to be about to fall down. It has swinging doors that have fallen off their hinges and the once glass paned double doors behind them are slightly open. The windows that haven't been broken are so covered with dirt and dust that he can't see through them.

He walks around and peers around the corner of the building. The desert has all but reclaimed the area around the building. Weeds and cactus have grown right up to the outside walls. He walks back to the front door. The small flashlight on his key chain lights his way as he enters the old building.

To his right is a bar that runs the length of the inside wall with a large mirror behind it. The mirror had long since been broken when something flew through it. By the back wall is an old broken-down piano and stool. Four wagon wheels hang from the

154

ceiling on rusty chains with six oil lamps perched on each of them. Tables and chairs are strewn about the inside. Only a few of the tables have legs that haven't dry-rotted and broken off. A stairway leads up to the second floor balcony that opens up into a hallway with several doors in it.

It dawns on him that this was a saloon back in its heyday. He could imagine cowboys lining the bar, gamblers sitting and dealing beer-soaked cards at the tables, and ladies of the night escorting cowboys up the stairs for a quick roll in the hay.

'If only this was in the day time so I could explore it more thoroughly,' he thinks to himself. But then his eyes remind him of why he stopped. He yawns and makes his way back out the door and to the sleeper on the back of his truck's cab.

Again he checks the GPS and his watch. Two and a half hours of sleep and the final short distance drive would put him in Yuma well before the deadline. He sets the alarm and settles in the bed.

He barely gets his eyes shut when a noise from outside the truck catches his attention. As he looks out the windows of the cab, he sees that the old saloon is lit up and a crowd has gathered on the inside. Horses are tied to the hitching posts out front and even a few buggies have been parked beside the building where desert foliage was growing just a few minutes earlier. The old broken down piano in the back is making music and laughter is coming from everywhere.

Next to the old saloon is another building that wasn't there earlier. A livery stable full of horses. And on past it are two more buildings, but he can't tell what they are.

He rubs his eyes thinking they are playing games with him but when he looks again, nothing has changed. He sees that he can now read the sign on the front of the building. 'Dusty Dog Saloon' in bright white letters reach his eyes.

"What is going on here?" he says openly. He climbs down from the cab of the truck and turns around to see that he is face to face with what appears to be an old man.

The old man's Stetson is torn and ragged, his clothes are covered with dust, his face covered with at least three weeks of beard stubble, and his eyes appear to be clouded with age.

"Mighty fancy lookin' wagon you got there, mister," the old man says. "I reckon I ain't never seen one as big and fancy as that before."

155

"What are you talking about, old man. That's just a plain old..." Mark turns around and sees not his truck, but a freight wagon. He rubs his eyes again, still no truck comes into view. Just a freight wagon and four strong mules hitched to it.. "Where's my truck?" he asks the old man. "It was just here. I was asleep in it. Where's my truck, old man?"

"Don't rightly know what you're talkin' about, mister. Only truck I ever seen was a little hand cart down at the Yuma train depot. And it wasn't hardly big enough to sleep in."

Mark looks past the wagon towards the road. What was once a smooth road is now a rutted wagon trail. "What's going on here?" he turns and screams at the old man.

"Just people gatherin' for a little spirits and beer and a little female companionship iffin' you got enough in your poke."

"No, no, no. I mean, where's my truck? And that road, just a few minutes ago it was a smooth level road. Now, I wouldn't drive a truck down it if my life depended on it."

"That road's always been the same. It used to be an old Apache tradin' path. Then they opened the territorial prison in Yuma and started transferin' prisoners down it. It ain't much like the roads near them big cities, but it'll do."

"Look, old man. I've got to find my truck. I am supposed to be in Yuma by eight-o-clock in the morning or I'll get fired."

"Then I reckon you're out of a job. Yuma is two days' travel from here. Ain't no way that you can get that wagon there by then."

"But I've been on the road for..." Mark looked at his wrist expecting to see his digital watch. But instead he sees that his wrist is bare and his clothes are dust covered and he is wearing boots. He had never worn boots in his life. When he was younger, he insisted that his mother buy him PF-Flyers and later jogging shoes, but never boots. Plus there is a gun belt with a pistol in it hanging on his hip. 'Where did that come from?' he thinks to himself. 'I don't even own a gun.'

Mark is now visibly shaken. "Am I dreaming? Is this some sort of nightmare?"

"You look like you could use a drink, mister," the old man says. "You just come on in here and I'll get Sandy to set you up with something that'll settle your nerves. By the way, young fella, what's your name?"

"Mark," he answers in a voice just barely above a whisper. "Mark Johns."

"Glad to make your acquaintance, Mark Johns. Folks around here call me Sagebrush Evans. Sage for short."

Mark stopped walking and watched the old man. 'Could it be?' he thought to himself.

Sage turned around and looked at Mark. "What you stop for? Sandy's got some of the best beer and whiskey in these parts."

Mark dug into the memories in his mind's vault. Something rang familiar about the name Sagebrush Evans, but he couldn't quite get a grip on it. It was a name he had heard his grandfather use long ago before he died—when Mark was only a toddler. But what was the story with it? Who was Sagebrush Evans?

Sage stops short of the porch of the saloon and removes his hat and starts slapping the dust from his clothes. "Sandy named the place The Dusty Dog. But the only dust she wants in the place is the dust on her dog. It's one of those rat-sized Mexican dogs."

Mark took the hint and started slapping at his clothes with his hands.

Sage looked at Mark. "That head cover you got there will do a better job."

Mark looked at Sage. Then he felt that he was wearing a hat. He never wore a hat. He reached up and removed the hat and looked at it. It was a gray-felt, broad-brimmed cowboy hat and had seen better days. It was almost as tattered as Sage's hat. But he found that Sage was right, it did do a better job of removing the dust from his clothes than his hands did.

The two men walked into the saloon. What was just a few minutes earlier a dust covered abandoned building, was now a thriving saloon. A clean place with cowboys bellied up to the bar. The bar was clean and shiny and covered with mugs of beer and shot glasses full of whiskey. The broken mirror was now shiny and in one piece. Shelves behind the bar, that had previously been empty, were now filled with bottles of liquor. A bartender served the drinks and wiped at the bar with a towel that he kept hanging over his shoulder.

The broken-down piano looked like it had just arrived on a freight wagon from someplace back east. The man playing it wore a white long sleeve shirt with red garters at the elbows, suspenders over his shoulders, and a derby hat sat on his head.

The tables and chairs were all sitting upright and several card games were in progress. Only a few of the chairs were vacant. Even the oil lamps sitting on the wagon wheels hanging from the ceiling were as shiny as new and every one of them cast a bubble of yellow light.

A lady's laugh filled the room and Mark looked up the stairs as a woman dressed in a frilly dress led a drunken cowhand into one of the rooms on the balcony. Another door on the balcony opened up and a woman stepped out followed by a cowboy that was still buckling his gun belt around his waist.

In the light of the saloon's oil lamps, Mark takes a closer look at Sage. Mark could tell that Sage is younger than he first appeared. The desert sun had prematurely aged and dried out his skin giving him the appearance of a man twenty years older.

Mark followed Sage to the end of the bar and leaned against it. His mind was still trying to figure out what was going on. "This has to be a dream," he said to himself.

"What's a dream?" he heard someone behind him say.

Mark and Sage turned around and saw a woman standing there. She is dressed in a blue frilly dress with lots of lace around the sleeves and neck line. She has long auburn hair and her complexion is ivory white. She is by far the most beautiful woman that Mark has ever seen. And in her arms is a small tan rat-sized dog.

"Hello, Sandy," Sage says and tips his hat.

"Hello, Sagebrush. Who's your friend?"

"Sandy, this here is Mark Johns. He just pulled up in that freight wagon out front."

"Mister Johns, glad to make you acquaintance." She reaches out a dainty little hand and waits for Mark to shake it.

Mark just stared at the beauty before him until he felt something poke at his ribs and heard Sage make a sound like he was clearing his throat.

"Oh...uh...yes, Ma'am. Nice to meet you too." Mark reached out and gently shook her hand. He had never had any trouble with women before, but this one took his breath away. He found himself mesmerized by her beauty.

"What'll you have, Mark?" Sandy had stepped around the end of the bar and placed the little dog in a small bed on top of it.

Mark felt another poke in his ribs and Sage again cleared his throat. "Oh...uh...I'll have a beer."

"Make mine some of that wildcat whiskey you got back there." Sage reached to pet the little dog, but quickly drew his hand back when it growled and snapped at him. "Damned little mutt, never has liked me."

Mark reached over to pet the dog but wasn't as fast as Sage and received a few fang marks from the little dog's sharp teeth on his little finger.

"Chico doesn't like very many people," Sandy said. She sat the drinks in front of the two men and started petting the little dog. "He only likes me and the girls."

"Don't forget Luke and Sam," Sage said as he pointed first at the bartender and then the piano player.

"Oh, he only tolerates them because they work for me," Sandy said as she petted the little dog.

Mark sipped at the cool beer as he marveled at what was going on around him. "This has to be a dream," he said again. But the beer was cool and tasted good. The sights and sounds were clear and not fuzzy like a dream. The smells of sweaty cowboys and roll your own cigarettes filled his nostrils.

Mark looked up at the old regulator clock that hung above the piano. If it was right, his own alarm would be going off in the next ten minutes and wake him up. He sipped at the beer, gazed at Sandy, and watched the minutes tick by on the clock. The time for his alarm lapsed by. Five minutes, ten minutes, fifteen minutes. Still no alarm woke him up.

The three of them had been engaging in idle small talk while he watched the clock. Mark finally gave into the dream and thought, 'Well, I'll wake up when the alarm goes off.' He emptied the beer and asked Sandy for another.

The night wore on. Beer after beer was served and drank. Mark looked up as the clock struck midnight. He heard Sandy ring a bell behind the bar and call out. "Alright folks, it's closing time. Drink up what you got."

Most of the patrons gulped down what was left of their drinks and staggered out the door. Soon everyone was gone but Mark, Sage, Sandy, Luke the bartender, and three men sitting at a table in the back of the saloon below the staircase.

"Come on, fellas. It's closing time," Sandy called out to the three men.

"We'll just have three more beers if it's all the same to you," one of the three men said.

Mark took a closer look at the three men. They looked like outlaws from movies that he used to watch as a boy. Each had a gun strapped to his side and each had a week's worth of beard stubble. They looked like men a normal person didn't want to get mixed up with. An aura of evil seemed to fill the air around them.

"Well it's not the same to me," Sandy said. "You've each got a half a mug of beer sitting in front of you. That's all you're getting. Now, drink that and go."

Mark saw Luke the bartender reach under the bar for the shotgun that lay there. But before he could reach it, one of the three men drew his gun and shot Luke in the chest. Luke fell back and was dead before he hit the floor.

"Now, about them beers, missy," the man said as the smoke from his gun drifted away. "If Joe wants another beer, he gets another beer."

Mark couldn't believe what was going on. He wanted to race out of the saloon doors, jump in his truck, and get the hell out of Dodge, but something was holding him in place, an urgent need to see this through was holding him there.

Sandy had rushed behind the bar and was crying over the dead body of Luke. It was then that Mark's memory vault doors flew wide open and the story that his grandfather had told him came out.

Mark watched as one of the three men stood up, emptied his beer and started for the bar. He then saw Sandy reach for the shotgun. She didn't know the gunman was headed towards the bar. She stood up with the shotgun, but was driven off her feet when Mark dove at her.

Mark felt the heat of a bullet as it passed over his and Sandy's heads and shattered some whiskey bottles behind the bar. The bullet surely would have killed Sandy if not for his fast action. The barrel of the shotgun then hits the mirror and breaks it into shards of falling glass. Fortunately, none of the glass lands on them.

Another shot rang out. Sage had gotten in on the action and had shot the gunman that had shot at Sandy. The gunman spun around, blood leaking from his shoulder, and shot at Sage. But Sage had ducked behind the bar and when he emerged again, the shotgun was in his hands. He let go with both of the sawed-off barrels and the gunman flew backwards towards his companions.

Mark didn't know how or why, but somehow the gun on his own hip suddenly appeared in his hand as he stood and shot the man that had ordered the extra beers. Both his and the man's guns sang out at the same time. Mark felt a burning in his shoulder but saw that his bullet had hit the man square in the chest.

Sage emerged from behind the bar again. This time with his own pistol in hand, but the third man had ducked behind the staircase and was shooting back. Sage went to the end of the bar and began sending bullet after bullet into the wooden planks of the stairs.

Mark crawled to the other end of the bar and peered around the end. He saw the man's foot sticking out from behind the stairs and shot it.

That brought the man from behind the stairs and he shot wildly at the bar as he limped across the saloon floor trying to get to the back door of the saloon. Mark stayed down behind the bar as bullet after bullet hit the walls and bar around him. At the other end of the bar, Sage was busy reloading his own gun. And then Mark heard a click. Then another click. The gunman was out of bullets. Then he heard the boom of the shotgun again.

Sandy had managed to reload the shotgun and the blast from it sent the third man out the back door as he tried to open it.

The gun battle had lasted less than a minute, but to Mark, it seemed like an eternity. He stood and followed Sage to check each of the gunmen. All three were dead. Mark's wound was only a scratch where the bullet had just grazed him.

Sage began going through the pockets of the dead men looking for some form of identity. In the pocket of the man that Mark had shot was a folded up piece of paper. Mark's bullet had gone through the piece of paper and left a clean round hole in it.

Sage unfolded the paper. He was stunned at what he saw. He handed the paper to Mark. It was a wanted poster. The picture of the man that Mark had killed was on it.

It said;

Wanted dead or alive
for murder and robbery
Joe Gladstone
$5,000.00 reward
Collect at Yuma Prison

Mark knew now what was going on. The story that his grandfather used to tell him was how a stranger had driven a freight wagon to his great grandmother's saloon and saved her life from a gang of cold-blooded killers with the help of her future husband, Sagebrush Evans. Nobody knew who the stranger was or where he came from, only that he had to get to Yuma before eight-o-clock. But when the sun came up, both he and his freight wagon were gone. There was no sign that a freight wagon had even been there. No tracks in the road or anything.

Mark then noticed the resemblance that Sandy bore of his own mother. The same colored hair, the same skin tones, and in his mother's younger days, the same bodily build.

"Well, young man," Sage said. "I guess you won't be worried about a job once you collect that reward."

"No, you keep it." Mark handed the poster back to Sage. "I think I'll be okay, now."

Mark began to walk towards the saloon doors. He stopped and looked back at Sage and Sandy. "Your real name is Ethan, but I like Sagebrush just fine. And Ma'am, he's a good man. Don't let him slip away with that reward."

Mark turned and walked out the door. The night was chilly and a slight breeze moved the clouds across a moonlit sky. He stopped and turned around and looked at the saloon. Once again the swinging doors sagged to the sides. The windows were covered with dust and the paint on the sign had all flaked off.

His truck was where he had parked it. "Was that a dream?" he asked himself. Then he felt the pain in his shoulder and saw the dog's teeth marks in his finger. Then the alarm of his digital wrist watch began beeping.

Mark made it to Yuma with time to spare. After his truck was unloaded, he went back to try and find the road but it had vanished.

Mark went back to Denver and quit this job. He bought an off road vehicle and using the GPS, he found the old saloon. The old road was barely visible. The only tracks on it were made by the vehicle he drove now.

Inside the saloon he found the bullet holes in the stairway, the bar, and the walls behind the bar. He continued searching for something that his grandfather had told him would still be there. In a desk drawer in a room in the back of the saloon, he found a folded up piece of paper with a hole in it. He could just barely make out the picture of Joe Gladstone on it. Beside the paper was a small strong box with a note that said, "Property of Mark Johns." He busted open the rusty lock and found that inside the box was $5,000 in twenty-dollar gold pieces.

Digging further through the desk, he found a diary. It belonged to Sandy. The last entry was from June 2, 1913. It said; "Ethan Junior and I are moving on. Business has dried up here since the livery stable burned down and the railroad came through twenty miles south of us. Sagebrush hasn't been seen since he went prospecting in the desert three years ago. I imagine his bones are fairly well bleached by the sun by now. My sister says we can stay with them in Denver until I can find work. It's tempting to take the gold reward money with us, but Sage insisted that Mark Johns would someday return to claim it. So I'll leave it here in case he does. It was a nice little community here while it lasted."

Mark closed the diary and placed it in the box with the coins, and left the old saloon. He sold the gold coins to a coin trader in Flagstaff for over $300,000.

Mark found a receipt for $5,000 in gold coins in the Yuma Prison records, paid to Ethan Evans.

He also found a marriage license issued to Ethan Evans and Sandra Collier dated August 19, 1893. Just five years before his grandfather was born.

When he returned to Denver, the simple marker on his grandfather's grave was removed and a more elegant one was put in its place. He located Sandy's grave in a small over-grown cemetery and placed a marker there. With the rest of the money, he bought a small bar and named it "The Dusty Dog II" and moved his mother into an apartment above it.

He also bought her one of those small rat-sized Mexican dogs.

WILD BILL, A COMEDY IN THREE ACTS

By James Hitt

Once upon a time before I was born, my mother Juliette Florey, joined Warbling Brothers Road Show and Circus. The man who loved her in the wrong way was my father, Rudy Pinelli, a small-time hood in the employment of Bugsy Siegel. And the man who would set things right we knew only as Wild Bill.

My mother first met Rudy on a Tuesday afternoon at Schwab's Drugstore in Hollywood where legend says a producer discovered Lana Turner. Girls were always going there hoping to be discovered, and Jullette Florey was no different from hundreds of other hopefuls, a pretty girl, prettier than Lana Turner, blonde, blue-eyed, a star waiting to be discovered. Everyday after Hollywood High let out—she was a junior in that year of 1945—she took herself down the Strip to Schwab's, slid onto a stool at the counter and ordered a vanilla Coke. She would bring a book from the library, usually a Bronte or an Austin, and would sit for an hour reading and hope to be discovered.

The war with Japan had ended a scant month before, and servicemen were especially prominent. Once in a while, one got up enough nerve to approach, but she discouraged them by refusing to take her nose out of the book. Then in walked Rudy Pinelli, still in his uniform, but already running errands for Bugsy Siegel just as he had before the war. When he sat on the stool next to her, she kept her eyes on *Jane Eyre*, which she was reading for the third time. He said, "Now that's a real good book. Yessir, real good." In reality, Rudy had never read the book—he only read comics and sports in the newspaper—but he had seen the first half hour of the movie until he had fallen asleep.

She lifted her eyes and discovered a sailor who looked surprisingly like Tyrone Power, especially the dark eyebrows and penetrating eyes.

"You've read it?"

"Sure thing," he said.

"I've never known one boy who read *Jane Eyre*." She closed the book but kept her finger to mark the page. "You really liked it? Really?"

"Can't think of one I liked better," he said.

"What part did you like the best?" She sipped her vanilla Coke, her eyes glued to his face.

"The scenes in the orphanage." These were the only scenes from the film he remembered. "Pretty strong stuff."

"But what about Jane and Rochester? I mean, don't you think their love was—oh—just too much to bear?"

"Sure, absolutely. But I grew up in an orphanage, see. So that early stuff hit pretty hard."

On this particular point, Rudy told the truth. From the time he was an infant until he turned seventeen, he was a ward of the Odd Fellows Home for Orphaned Boys in Bakersfield until they kicked him out for extorting money and favors from a dozen younger boys.

"Let me tell you, the people who ran my orphanage make the ones in this"—he tapped the book with his index finger—"look like cream puffs. They worked us like slaves, and all we got for supper was soup and a piece of bread. When we were lucky, we got a bite of meat in our soup."

"How terrible!" my mother said. "How dreadful!"

He glanced at his watch. "Look, it's getting close to five, and I haven't had a bite to eat all day. I've been running errands for this friend of mine."

"Errands for a friend?" my mother said. "I thought you were in the Navy."

"Just waiting on my discharge papers." He smiled and tapped his chest. "Listen, you're talking to a real live hero, see. I was on the *Indianapolis*. Ever hear of it?"

"You dropped the atomic bomb?"

"No, no, I was on the ship that carried the bomb. We sent the bomb on its way, and then on July 30—I'll remember that day like it was my birthday—we were torpedoed, and the ship went down. I was all alone on a raft for six days out in the middle of the ocean, just me and sharks, until a rescue plane spotted me. So I'm a hero, see."

In this Rudy also told the truth, at least to a point. He was indeed a survivor of the *Indianapolis*, he was on a lifeboat for six days, and he was alone when the rescue plane swept down and carried him away. However, an odd fact emerges when one investigates the circumstances. Of the more than three hundred survivors rescued from the *Indianapolis*, only a handful managed to get to lifeboats. In most cases, the boats were so overloaded, men were in the water clinging to the gunwales. Yet Rudy was alone, and when they found him, he appeared, no worse for wear. He still had food and water for another two weeks. Make of that what you will.

When Rudy asked her to have dinner with him, she felt she couldn't refuse a hero who had helped to end the war. She thought of calling home to tell her parents, but her father, a believer in Old Testament retribution and damnation, would have ordered her home. So my mother said yes, she would love to have dinner with him, and Rudy Pinelli told her to wait a moment, he had to see a man about a debt. He took himself off to the back of the drug store where he found the manager, a burly man with a gambling addiction. My mother heard a body crash and bottles and boxes hit the floor. A moment later Rudy reappeared. "A guy back there slipped on the wet floor. Kind of funny, don't you think? I mean, here we are in a drugstore, and a guy almost gets himself killed."

He had a car parked just outside, a big Oldsmobile built before the war, its deep-black finish polished to a mirror sheen. She had no idea where he was taking her until he pulled up in front of Ciro's on the Strip.

Still in her school clothes, she felt woefully underdressed and out of place. Ciro's! My god, she had heard of this place all her life, and she had seen it in movie magazines and newspapers, but she had never really seen it, not like this, up close, in person.

The Maître d' escorted them to a table in the rear. She caught her breath, holding it in disbelief, for there, just two tables away sat Frank Sinatra and his wife Nancy, favorites of the movie magazines. Rudy waved, and Sinatra offered a salute in return.

167

"You know Sinatra?" my mother asked.

"I met him a few times," he said.

Rudy ordered a bottle of champagne and two glasses.

"I don't drink," my mother said.

"Just one glass." Rudy said. "To celebrate us getting to know each other."

So my mother had her first drink, which made her slightly giddy, and she tasted her first lobster. When they finished dinner, Rudy pulled out a roll of bills, peeled off a twenty, and flipped it on the table. He suggested they go back to his place for a little music and dancing, but my mother had the good sense to say she needed to get home. She had Rudy drop her a block from her house. Under a pepper tree thick with foliage, she allowed him to kiss her before she jumped out. Through the open car window, Rudy said, "I'll see you tomorrow at the drugstore, same time. You be there, you hear?"

Her parents had kept the porch light on, and when she walked through the door, she discovered them seated on the couch. Her father stood, his face red with anger. In his hands, he held a folded belt, snapping it twice, each time the crack as loud as a firecracker.

She met Rudy the next day, and he drove them to Hansen Dam, parking under a weeping willow in sight of the spillway. "You've got to get me home before dark," my mother said.

"Why?" Rudy asked.

My mother pulled the blouse from her shoulder, exposing a thick, red welt. "My father—"

"That son-of-a-bitch! Why, I ought to..." Rudy struck his fist into the palm of his other hand.

They stayed there for more than half an hour, kissing and talking, and twice he made moves on her, a hand inching toward a breast, and each time she grabbed his wrist and pulled it away. By the time he drove her home, the sun hung just above the western mountains, casting long shadows that stretched from one side of the street to the other.

Afterward he collected a couple of debts for Bugsy and drove over to a five-and-dime hotel on Santa Monica Boulevard where he delivered fifty-five dollars to Lew, one of Bugsy's bookkeepers. Upstairs was a whorehouse where Rudy spent the night with a girl from Bugsy's stable.

But he couldn't take his mind off my mother. Girls were a dime a dozen for a guy with his looks, and getting them into bed was a done deal the moment he made his move. So maybe this one had held him off for a couple of days, but in the end, she would give in just like all the others. Dropping his head on the pillow, he flipped off the lamp and tried to sleep.

Just a few miles away, my mother sat at the kitchen table and tried to concentrate on her homework. At one point her father—my grandfather—came in to glare at her with undisguised anger and demanded to know why she hadn't come straight home from school. She told him that she had to stay after to work with the drama teacher who was planning to put her in a play. An angry scowl darkened his face. "I've seen the evil the studios bring to this town. I know they can fill a young girl's head with all sorts of sinful thoughts." He laid a beefy hand on her shoulder. "You're a child. You don't know the kind of trouble you're asking for. So no more lollygagging at school. No more daydreaming. No more talk of being an actress."

The next day, Rudy picked her up at school and again drove out to Hansen Dam. A cold wind blew in from the north, and Rudy kept the motor running. They kissed often, and the windows fogged over. His hand again sought her breast, and she allowed him the barest touch before she broke their embrace. In this area at least, she heeded her father's warnings. She would not let Rudy have his way.

Breathing heavily, he said, "Look, I ain't no kid, see. You can't keep doing this to me. What's the problem? You like me, I like you."

"What you want from me—that's for married people."

"Then we better get married," Rudy said, surprising himself.

That evening, my mother packed a small bag with extra clothes and cosmetics, and stealing out after her parents had gone to bed, stashed it under a hedge by the front door. When her alarm clock rang at five-thirty, she leapt out of bed and dressed quickly. Once out the door, she swept up her bag from behind the bushes. Half a block down, Rudy flashed his headlights, and she ran to meet him.

They drove for over six hours until they crossed the border into Roach, Nevada. Rudy parked the Olds before the Forever Wedding Chapel. He still wore his Navy uniform, although the day before he had received his discharge papers. Clutching my mother around the waist, he led her inside.

The minister, his eyes round and bulging, read the wedding vows in a monotone while his rotund wife acted as witness. The ceremony took all of three minutes, after which Rudy paid the requisite ten dollars. My mother left the chapel with a small bouquet plus a gold band Rudy purchased for an additional twenty-five dollars.

Hurrying next door, they entered the Last Chance Saloon and Hotel, renting a room over the gambling hall where all night they heard the slot machines as if they were in the room with them. My mother never divulged the intimate facts concerning that first night, and I have no desire for such information. However, she did divulge one detail. Returning from the bathroom, she passed the dresser where Rudy had emptied his pockets: a bulky wallet, a comb with broken strands of hair curled around the teeth, a handful of coins and a pair of brass knuckles. This last item she lifted with a forefinger and thumb. "What's this for?"

He lay in bed, his hands propped behind his head, and studied her with sleepy, indolent eyes. "They come in handy in my line of work."

It wasn't until their second week together that he hit her for the first time. They had moved into The Crescent Arms, a block off Hollywood and Highland. Each day, even on the weekends, he was off collecting debts and running errands for Bugsy. On a Thursday, he came home early, a bruise under his left eye, and found her reading *Jane Eyre* again. He knocked the book from her hands and raked his knuckles across her face. She cried, and he promised never to do it again.

He kept his word until the day she told him she was pregnant, and cursing, he slammed his fist into her jaw, splitting her lip and knocking her to the floor. He picked her up, laid her on the bed and said he was sorry, that the news was so unexpected. He swore on his mother's life he would never hit her again. She would just need to get a little operation, and then everything would be fine. After a couple of phone calls, he announced that Monday morning they had an appointment in Tijuana. "It's quick, and we'll be back at it in just a couple of days," he told her.

The very next morning as soon as Rudy walked out the door, she packed her one suitcase and went looking for any money that might be lying around the apartment. As she searched through his coats and pockets, she knocked loose a shoebox from the top shelf of the closet, and stacks of bills wrapped in rubber bands cascaded across the floor. By the time she gathered the bills and poured them on the bed, she had over three thousand dollars. She stuffed the money in her suitcase, too, holding back a couple of twenties that she slipped into her purse.

She caught a cab to Union Station where she boarded the Pacific Coast Special to San Francisco. She only began to feel safe when, just past ten, the train rolled out of the station.

And so, in this way, my mother saved my life.

2

At the Oakland train station, my mother purchased another ticket, this one for Denver, making a fuss at the window by pretending that she was about to throw up so the man behind the grate would remember her. Instead, she caught a local bus that ran to Berkeley, transferred to another and another. Well after dark, she stood in the middle of downtown Sausalito.

She found the Bayview Apartments a block from the bus station. A few lights were on downstairs, giving her hope, and she stepped on the porch and knocked once.

The porch light came on, a door opened, and a thin woman in a housecoat peered out from behind a screen. "It's late to come looking for a room."

"The bus just let me off. You do have a room, don't you? Please say you have a room."

My mother's voice was so full of fear and doubt that the landlady, Mrs. Frankel, took pity on her. "I've got a room if you got the money."

Mrs. Frankel led my mother up a flight of stairs, and when she saw the small flat, the one window providing a view of San Francisco and the Bay, my mother paid a month's advance on the spot. As for the room, it wasn't much—a table, a couple of chairs, a sink and a stove. As Mrs. Frankel turned to leave, my mother said, "Where's the bed?"

"Oh dear, you really are a little lamb, aren't you?" Mrs. Frankel pointed to a door that my mother had mistaken for the bathroom. "It's a fold down. Bath and toilet are down the hall. You share it with the other tenant on this floor."

"Other tenant?"

"Wild Bill he calls himself, but don't let that fool you. That's his stage name. He works for a circus, and whenever they're in winter quarters, he lodges with me. But don't worry you're pretty little head. He's older than God and tame as an old church mouse." With that, Mrs. Frankel shuffled out, closing the door.

At that point, her long day's journey caught up with her. She dropped in a rocker beside the window, laid her head against the hard rim of the chair and closed her eyes. She didn't intend to sleep there, but at half past four in the morning, she awoke with her bladder near bursting. Pushing herself out of the chair, she staggered down the hallway to the bathroom. The toilet seat was cracked in three places, and afterward she washed her hands in a sink stained brown. As she dried her hands, she felt a wave of nausea that almost buckled her knees. Swaying, she stepped into the hallway and stumbled into the wall.

The door to the other apartment opened and a man stepped out, most of his wrinkled face hidden behind a white beard. "What's wrong, Miss?" he asked.

She tried to smile, but even that proved difficult. "I'm just—I'm—a little dizzy."

She leaned into him as he guided her back to her room and sat her on the edge of the bed. "When's the last time you ate?" he asked.

More than thirty hours had passed since her last meal. The old man said, "I'll be right back."

He returned a moment later, offering her what appeared to be a piece of leather. "This is jerky. You know what jerky is?" She shook her head, and he said, "It's dried beef. The juice will give you strength."

She took the rough piece of meat. "You're Mr. Wild Bill."

"Don't deserve no 'mister'."

It took all her strength to chew the tough strip of meat, but immediately she began to feel the heaviness leave her arms and legs.

"How long have you been in the family way?" he asked.

"You can tell?"

"I'm old. I ain't blind."

She knew she should be reticent about telling her story—people who knew too much could betray her—yet she needed to talk. "He only hit me twice, and maybe I would've stayed"—her

172

hand caressed her belly—"but he wanted me to do something so terrible—"

"Did you go to the police?"

"Rudy works for some very bad people. There's this man named Siegel—"

"Bugsy Siegel?"

"You know him?"

"Heard of him."

"If I had gone to the police—"

"You're right. It wouldn't have done any good."

"If Rudy finds me—"

"You go back to bed, darlin'. Get some rest. You're safe here. You have my word."

"I'm sorry for disturbing you so early in the morning," my mother said.

"Hell, darlin', I don't need much sleep. Never have."

He closed the door and left her alone. Just before she drifted off, she heard a chair scrape the floor outside her door and a body settle in.

Over the next few months, my mother seldom left the apartment, and when she did, she went down the road to the grocery store or up the road to the drug store. From a second hand shop she bought a dozen books that kept her reading late into the nights. Now you might think she lived a boring existence during this time as she grew bigger with me, but in this you would be wrong. Wild Bill was there, and she later told me that he regaled her with his stories.

As a young man, he had ridden with the great trail herds from Texas to Kansas, and he told her of meeting such luminaries as Wyatt Earp and Bat Masterson, Clay Allison and Doc Holliday. "Earp was a ruthless bastard." He parted his white hair and showed her an old scar. "He buffaloed me with his 45. Split me open like I was a melon. I had a headache for a month."

"Why did he do such a thing?"

"Me and this other waddie got into an argument over a girl. It came to gun play."

"You killed a man?"

"Naw, I put a bullet in his shoulder. Hell, he was a friend of mine. I didn't want to hurt him bad."

"Your friend? But you shot him."

"It was different in them days. We was all a little wild."

In her sixth month, he took her to a doctor for the first time. "Just making sure everything is all right," he said. The doctor asked questions and listened to our hearts, at the end of which he pronounced us both healthy.

As they left the office, my mother said, "I told you I was fine."

"In my day, women lost children by the wagonloads," Wild Bill said. "My own mama had ten kids. Only three lived past five."

"When was the last time you saw a doctor?" my mother asked.

He thought a moment, trying to recall. "I guess it was '88 or '89. A sawbones dug a couple of bullets out of me."

My mother laughed. "Another friendly shooting, I suppose."

His expression hardened. "I robbed a bank in Dalhart, Texas. It cost me two years in Huntsville." In almost a whisper, he added, "And it cost me a lot more than those two years."

Then, in mid-March, Wild Bill announced that the show was about to go back on the road, and he would be leaving within a couple of days. By that time my mother was heavy with me. "An elephant on two tendrils," she described herself.

Several days later while Wild Bill was off buying supplies for his act, Mrs. Frankel came to my mother and told her a private detective was in town asking about Juliette Florey. "It won't be long before he knows you're here. Maybe he already knows." Mrs. Frankel must have seen the fear register in my mother's face, and she reached out and patted her hand. "Wild Bill will be back directly. He'll know what to do."

My mother spent the next hour fearing the worse. Once she peeked through the thin lace curtains. Across the street, a round little man leaned against a telephone pole, his eyes glued to the house. She jumped back, fearing he had seen her. She ran to the closet, pulled out her suitcase, and in a matter of minutes, had packed everything.

The man across the street, an operative for the Continental Detective Agency, had discovered my mother's whereabouts late the evening before, at which time he phoned Rudy, who, at that very moment was on a ferry crossing the Bay from San Francisco. Under a leaden sky, he kept his eye on the house and waited for his client. The only unusual activity during that time was the arrival of a pickup truck driven by a grizzled old man whose jeans were covered in dirt and sawdust, his Stetson so battered it looked older than the man. The old man stayed in the house all of five minutes before he returned alone and drove away.

Ten minutes later, Rudy Pinelli came hurrying up the street from the ferry depot, his dark coat showing a slight bulge under his left arm where he carried his piece. Without a word, the two men crossed to the apartment building. Mrs. Frankel met them on the porch, her arms folded across her chest. "If you men are looking for a room, I've none available."

Rudy glanced at the pudgy detective. "Where is she?"

"She's got a room on the second floor."

"No one's home up there." Mrs. Frankel stepped in front of the screen door, blocking the stairs.

"Well?" Rudy asked.

The detective shrugged. "I haven't seen her. Maybe she's there, maybe not."

"Get out of the way." Rudy grabbed the landlady's arm and jerked her aside. He stomped up the stairs, his anger growing with each step. No one walked out on Rudy Pinelli—no one—and he'd make sure she'd never do it again. He'd teach her a lesson she'd never forget. As for that bitch of a landlady—

Mrs. Frankel said to the detective, "She's not up there."

"Yes ma'am," he said, "I certainly hope you're right."

My mother heard the footsteps on the stairs, and her whole body turned rigid with fear, not for herself, but for me. In one last act of defiance, she snatched up a heavy glass ashtray, ready to bash in the skull of anyone who came to take her back. The door opened, and Wild Bill stepped into the room. "Grab your things, Darlin', and go down the back stairs. Follow the alley up behind the grocery store. I'll pick you up there."

She maneuvered the back stairs as best she could. I was due in only a few weeks, and her belly stuck out so far it threatened her balance. Once she reached the bottom, she waddled down the unpaved alley trying to avoid the muddy ruts made by the garbage trucks.

Wild Bill stood beside the open passenger's door, the motor of his pickup idling. He tossed her suitcase in the back, and taking her arm, steadied her while she climbed into the cab. By then, her breathing was ragged, her back radiated shape bolts of pain, and her heart beat with such ferocity it felt as if it were trying to break free of her body. She began to fear the flight had brought on an early labor, but as Wild Bill guided the truck down back streets and out of town, her breathing returned to normal, the pain in her back subsided, and her heart settled into a steady beat. "Where are you taking me?" she asked.

"You're joining me with Warbling Brothers Road Show and Circus. I told them my granddaughter was moving in with me. I told them your husband run out on you, and you needed my help."

"Sooner or later, Rudy will find me."

"I suspect so. We'll have the welcome mat ready when he does."

Back at the Bayview apartments, Rudy came stomping down the stairs, his anger boiling over, and when he saw Mrs. Frankel glaring at him, he threw back the flap of his coat and showed her the butt of his .38. "Tell me where she went or so help me—" He reached for his piece, ready to pistol whip the landlady into submission.

The little detective stepped between them, his hand on his own piece. "We're leaving now."

Rudy turned his black eyes on the rotund little man. "Get out of my way."

"You sure you want to pursue this disagreement? You're carrying a .38. I'm carrying a .45. Mine's bigger than yours."

Rudy started to laugh until he realized the man wasn't joking—or bluffing. When the boss of the Continental Detective Agency said this was his best operative, Rudy thought the man nothing more than a trained bloodhound, but now he faced a guy ready to pull down on him, one whose eyes were the coldest and most calculating he had even seen. "You're—you're fired. And I'm not paying you one red cent. Not one."

Rudy stepped back trying to put distance between them, but the little man moved with him. "You're paying me right now. A hundred dollars a day for three days plus forty-three dollars for expenses." Rudy's stopped abruptly, his backside pressed against the porch railing. "Shell out," the detective said, "or I'll shove my .45 so far down your throat it'll come out your ass." Without talking his eyes off Rudy, he said, "Sorry, ma'am."

"That's quite all right," said Mrs. Frankel.

His hands shaking, Rudy brought out his wallet and counted out the money. The detective snatched the bills from his hand. "Now get off this lady's property."

Rudy hurried out of the yard and up the street without looking back, his heels clicking against the pavement. The detective peeled off a twenty-dollar bill and handed it to the landlady. "This is for your trouble, ma'am. Sorry to have been such a bother."

Mrs. Frankel slipped the bill in her apron pocket. "You're a nice young man. You shouldn't associate with such riff raff."

"In my occupation you don't often meet nice people. Hazard of the job." He cast a glance at the overcast sky, the sun just beginning to break through. "Looks like it's going to be a nice day after all," he said.

3

By five that afternoon, Wild Bill had my mother safely stashed in his trailer, already loaded on a flatcar. Warbling Brothers had broken winter quarters and was on a train bound the next morning for Oxnard. As before, my mother worried that any minute Rudy would find her, but after nightfall when he still hadn't shown, she relaxed enough to fall asleep in Wild Bill's bed. While she slept, Wild Bill sat by the front window, a Colt Single Action Army .45 cradled in his lap. She awoke the next morning as the train pulled out of the yard, and Wild Bill was still sitting there.

A week later in Oxnard my mother began her contractions, and Wild Bill rushed her to the hospital where I was born on April 1st, a day for fools. If I turn out to be such, I cannot blame my mother or Wild Bill. They did the best they could for me.

Two months after I came into the world, Wild Bill began to train my mother to be part of his act. He was already eighty, if not older, and at a time when his skills should have been in fast decline, he performed the greatest sharp-shooting, knife-tossing, ax-welding act anyone had ever seen. How do I know? When I was ten, Mister Warbling, the owner of Warbling Brothers Road Show and Circus told me. "I've seen all the great Western acts including Sundown Slim and Texas Jack Murdock," he said, "and Wild Bill performed tricks those bums would never even attempted."

To the sound of the William Tell Overture, Wild Bill would rush on stage dressed in a Western outfit full of fringe and topped with a wide-brim Stetson, but the most impressive part of his dress was strapped to his waist, twin pearl-handled .45s, the polished metal reflecting light like mirrors. "The real McCoy,"

Mister Warbling told me in reference to the weapons. "Owned by John Wesley Hardin, the most feared killer in the Old West. From what I've read, each of these .45s was responsible for the deaths of at least ten men."

Wild Bill's act, once my mother joined, started slowly. She threw a tin can in the air, and he picked it off with ease. Then she threw two, and he blew holes in those, too. Then she tossed up three, and once more he took all three out of the air. He holstered his pistol, my mother grabbed another half dozen cans, and with one mighty heave, send them skyward. His left hand a blur, the pistol barked onetwothreefourfivesix—aster than you could say the words. He never missed, not once.

Every other fast draw act used buckshot in their loads, but not Wild Bill. At one point in his act, my mother lighted a cigarette and stood sideways, her profile to Wild Bill. Using his right hand, he drew his pistol and fired from behind his back, cutting the cigarette in half. That never failed to draw gasps from the audiences, but then he shifted his position and did the same with the other hand. If he used buckshot, he would have blown away half her face.

"I could never use buckshot," he told my mother. "That would be cheating."

"Some people are going to think you're a fake no matter what you do," my mother said.

"The day I have to resort to tricks to fool people, that's the day I quit."

His act, as all good acts do, ended with the greatest feat of all. He strapped my mother on a wheel and sent her spinning. True, the wheel was set at a fixed speed that never varied, but that didn't make his feat any less exciting or any less real. On a table, lay five knives and five hand axes. With lightning speed, he swept up one knife after another and hurled them at the spinning wheel, then followed with the axes. When the wheel stopped, the weapons outlined my mother. "I must have seen Will Bill do that trick a hundred times," Mister Warbling said, "and I swear he hit the same exact marks every time."

It wasn't until the spring of '49 that Rudy Pinelli found us. The show was in Hemet, California, a desert community twenty-five miles southeast of Riverside. By that time, Bugsy Siegel was dead and Mickey Cohen had taken over the rackets in L.A. Rudy had not only survived the transition but moved up in the ranks from debt collector to enforcer. The cops attributed at least half a dozen gangland executions—perhaps even Bugsy himself—to Rudy, but they had no proof, only suppositions.

By then, I was barely three, the only child attached to the show. Others had children, but they were gone from the nest or had been left behind with spouses or relatives, and I became a favorite of many, coddled and protected, seldom lacking for a companion or playmate, albeit a grownup one. During the shows, I stayed in my mother's dressing room, chaperoned by one of the acts that went on before or after Wild Bill. At the end of every show, the entire ensemble of clowns, high wire acts, jugglers, and animal acts paraded around the tent to blaring music and applause. I was there, too, carried on the shoulders of one person or another.

It was at the beginning of April at a Saturday night performance that Rudy watched from the bleachers, his gaze fixed on my mother. She was more beautiful than he remembered. She was no longer the sixteen-year-old girl whom he married but a fully developed woman, slender and athletic, confident and desirable. Since she had run out on him almost four years before, he had slept with a hundred women, and he believed he no longer wanted my mother. All he wanted was revenge, but seeing her now, he desired her more than ever.

At the end of the show, the troupe paraded out the rear of the tent, applause dying behind them. Wild Bill lifted me off his shoulders and passed me to my mother, and we headed off to our trailer. She had no idea that Rudy lurked just off in the shadows, taking stock of her every move.

He waited until the crowd drifted away, then followed us. When my mother reached back to close the trailer door, Rudy caught it and stepped inside. She retreated and sat me on the floor, shielding me with her body.

Rudy wore a silk suit, and a diamond ring sparkled on his left pinkie. The three years had wrought other changes as well. His face had grown puffy, especially around the eyes and mouth, and his once hard belly showed a small paunch. When he smiled, he exposed teeth stained faintly yellow.

She was still in her costume, her tanned legs exposed as well as the tops of her breasts, and his eyes devoured her. "You didn't think you could hide from me forever, did you?" he said.

179

"I'm surprised it took you this long."

With a casual nod in my direction, he said, "That my kid?"

"There's nothing here that belongs to you," my mother said. "And you'll be doing yourself a favor if you leave right now and never come back."

"You're my wife, he's my kid. You both belong to me."

"Just remember—I warned you." My mother spoke calmly and without fear.

He seized her arm, his fingers digging in the soft flesh above her elbow. "You're coming back to L.A. with me—you and the kid."

"Like hell." Her nails raked his cheek, drawing blood, and he slapped her, so hard it sent her reeling to the floor half on top of me. I began to cry, and my mother took me in her arms, pressing my face into her shoulder.

Rudy stepped forward, straddling us, his face flushed a crimson red. "You won't run away again, and you won't complain, and you'll do whatever I want. You know why? Because if you don't, something bad will happen to the kid, see."

He reached again for my mother, and she spit in his face. He flinched, his anger exploding, and he drew back his fist, ready to smash her face.

He stiffened, and his eyes widened in shock as a barrel of a pistol was jammed into his back. A voice said, "You move, and I'll put a hole in you I could ride a horse through." With his free hand, the man reached around and removed the piece from under Rudy's jacket.

Still clutching me, my mother climbed to her feet. With the back of her hand she wiped blood from the corner of her mouth. "You poor, dumb bastard. I tried to warn you. We knew you'd come. We've been waiting for you."

Grabbing Rudy by his coat collar, a hand hauled him to the door, and a kick to his backside sent him flying out the door. Stunned, he lay unmoving until his head cleared. He pushed himself to knees. Only then did he discover himself surrounded by more than a dozen men, performers still in their costumes and roustabouts in their working clothes. Determined to show he wasn't afraid, he stood, and his lips twisted into a snarl. "You guys don't know who you're messing with." He turned to the man who had so unceremoniously removed him from my mother's trailer and found himself looking into eyes as ancient as the desert itself.

It was the man who shot the tin cups out of the air. He was still dressed in his Western getup, the Stetson, the fringed shirt, the chaps, looking more like Gabby Hayes than Gabby Hayes. Rudy would have laughed had the old man not held the Colt cocked and pointed at his belly.

"This ain't over, old man." Rudy wiped his mouth encrusted with dust.

"Mister, that was the wrong thing to say." The old man stepped down from the trailer and swung the pistol. The barrel cracked against Rudy's skull.

Rudy awoke with bright lights shinning in his eyes. When he tried to sit up, pain exploded in his head. He groaned.

Hands reached under his arms and hauled Rudy to his feet. The man moved back in front of the lights of the pickup. It was the old man from the circus, and that gave Rudy hope. How dangerous could he be?

Rudy forced himself to stand straight. Dust covered his jacket, and he slapped at the expensive silk, creating small clouds. Rudy said, "You know how many men I've killed, Gramps? You ain't got enough fingers on both hands to count that high. So if you know what's good for you—"

"Yeah, you're a real tough hombre, especially when it comes to slapping around women and little boys. Maybe you're a big shot back in L.A., but to me, you ain't nothing but a pissant."

"If I had my gun—" Rudy began.

"It's under your arm." Wild Bill tapped his hip. "I got mine, so when you're ready, make your move."

Rudy looked down, and sure enough, there was the .38 in his shoulder holster.

"We're fifty miles from the nearest town," the old man said, "so nobody's going to come along to disturb us."

"You're crazy. This ain't the Old West."

"It is tonight."

Rudy swallowed, his throat full of dust, and his voice croaked like a frog's. "All those people back there—they saw me with you."

"They're carny. They're family. No one's going to say anything. Anyway, you're free to go. All you got to do is get by me. That should make it easy for a tough guy like you."

Rudy tapped his chest with a forefinger. "Do you know who I am?"

"A dead man," said Wild Bill.

Rudy reached for his pistol.

At three o'clock in the morning, my mother heard a soft rapping on her trailer door. When she opened it, Wild Bill, hat in hand, said, "He won't bother you again, darlin'."

"Where is he?"

"Right now I suspect the coyotes and buzzards are having a feast. Does that bother you?"

"I hope he doesn't make them sick," my mother said.

AUTHOR BIOS

Johnny D. Boggs

Former Western Writers of America President Johnny D. Boggs is a six-time Spur Award-winner and six-time finalist who has also won the Western Heritage Wrangler Award for his fiction. Currently he serves as editor for WWA's *Roundup* magazine. A frequent contributor to *True West*, *Wild West* and *American History* magazines, Boggs lives in Santa Fe, New Mexico, with his wife and son.

Jason H. Campbell

Jason H. Campbell lives in Jackson, Ky., with his wife Cheryl Campbell, along with their two children, Jaron Campbell, and Joshua Campbell. Jason was born one of eight children to Hobert and Sharon Campbell. Jason writes weekly for a local newspaper, and works for the school system. Writing is a dream he has wanted to pursue since childhood. His first Western novel, *Tex's Bloody Ground,* was recently released.

John Duncklee

John Duncklee has been a cowboy, rancher, quarter horse breeder, university professor and award-winning author of twenty-five books and myriad articles, poetry and short stories. He is a Western Writers of America Spur Award winner and was awarded a $5,000 unrestricted fellowship for writing excellence by the Arizona Commission on the Arts. He lives in Las Cruces, N.M. with his wife, Penny, an accomplished watercolorist.

W. Michael Farmer

W. Michael Farmer lives and writes in Smithfield, Isle of Wight County, Va. He learned much of the rich story life of the southwest through living in Las Cruces, New Mexico, for nearly 15 years. A physicist by training, as an author he has published short stories in two anthologies, won awards for essays at the Christopher Newport University Writers' Conference, and published essays in magazines. His first novel in the Vanishing Trilogy, *Hombrecito's War*, won a Western Writers of America Silver Spur Award for Best First Novel in 2006 and a New Mexico Book Award Finalist for Historical Fiction in 2007. The sequel, *Hombrecito's Search*, was released in July 2007. *Tiger Tiger Burning Bright: The Betrayals of Pancho Villa*, released in December 2011 completed the trilogy. His third novel, *Conspiracy: The Trial of Oliver Lee and James Gililland*, was published in 2009.

Jerry Guin

Jerry Guin is the author of *Matsutake Mushroom*, a nature guidebook, and the Western novel *Drover's Vendetta*. He has also written a number of magazine articles and several anthologized short stories about the Old West. He and wife Ginny live in the extreme northern California community of Salyer.

184

Dave P. Fisher

Dave P. Fisher is a writer of western novels, western short stories, and outdoor non-fiction articles with more than 400 works published. Dave's accomplishments and credits include: Winning the Will Rogers Medallion Award for Western Fiction for his collection of short stories *Bronc Buster – Short Stories of the American West.* He has won eight People's Choice Awards for Western short stories and has been included in 12 international anthologies. He is the author of the *Poudre Canyon Saga* along with several other western novels and books. His outdoor and western writing is steeped in historical accuracy drawing on extensive research and his personal background as a life time westerner, working cowboy, horse packer, and guide. Learn more about Dave's background and his writing at his website: www.davepfisher.com

James Hitt

James Hitt is a graduate of North Texas State University and holds a BA in English and history and a MA in history. In addition to his many articles related to the West and film, he is the author of *The American West, From Fiction Into Film* (McFarland, 1991), which has been called the definitive monograph on the subject, and *Words And Shadows* (Citadel, 1993), an examination of mainstream American literature and its connection to film. He also is represented in *The Louis L'amour Companion* (Andrews and McMeel, 1992). In 2001, Adventure Books published his novel *The Last Warrior.* In 2010 Aberdeen Bay released *Carny: A Novel In Stories*, which won the Grand Prize for Fiction at the 2011 Next Generation Indie Book Awards. He has been a guest speaker at the Gene Autry Museum.

185

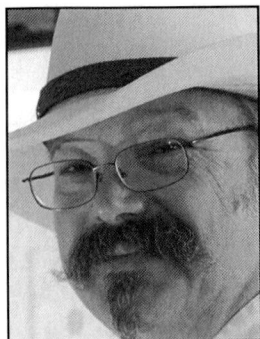

Douglas Hocking

Douglas W. "Doug" Hocking is an independent scholar who has completed advanced studies in American history, ethnology and historical archaeology. He is a retired U.S. Army officer who has lived among the Jicarilla Apache and writes both fiction and history of the pre-Civil War West.

D.B. Jackson

D.B. Jackson is a cattle rancher and a full-time writer. He and his wife, Mary, reside near Oakdale, Calif. on their ranch in the foothills of the Sierra Nevada Mountains. His debut novel, *They Rode Good Horses*, was followed up by his much anticipated second novel, *Unbroke Horses*. Miles Swarthout, screenwriter of *The Shootist*, stated; "D. B. Jackson's excellent second Western brands him as a coming talent in this classic old genre. Unbroke Horses shines with award-winning potential." Jackson is currently at work on his third novel, *County Road 37*.

Robert Kresge

Robert Kresge has lived with his wife in Albuquerque, N.M. since 2002. He's the author of the Warbonnet historical mystery series set in 1870s Wyoming, including *Murder for Greenhorns* and *Painted Women*. Currently he is working on his third book in the Warbonnet series, *Blood and Ice*, to be published in October 2012. The story takes place aboard Grand Duke Alexis' goodwill visit train in January 1872. Prior to moving West, Rob grew up and spent his career in the Washington, D.C. area, working for the Central Intelligence Agency, where he was a senior analyst and founding member of the Counterterrorist Center.

Wesley Tallant

Wesley Tallant was born and raised in Texas. He spent three years in the Navy in the early 1970s. He married his high school sweetheart in 1973 and has three grown sons. In 1976, he went to work for the San Marcos Fire Department and four years later went to work for the Paris Texas Fire Department. He retired from there in 2004 and started writing books. He's a member of the Western Writers of America. Today he enjoys the simple life of retirement.

Lori Van Pelt

Lori Van Pelt won the Western Writers of America Spur Award for Best Short Fiction in 2006 for the title story in her first collection, *Pecker's Revenge and Other Stories from the Frontier's Edge* (University of New Mexico Press). Her short stories have been published in numerous anthologies as well as in online literary magazines, and her short nonfiction pieces have appeared in a variety of publications including *The Writer*, *True West* and *Private Pilot*. Her biography *Amelia Earhart: The Sky's No Limit* (American Heroes series, Forge) was named to the New York Public Library's "Best Books for the Teen Age" list. She received a 2010 Wyoming Arts Council Creative Writing Fellowship in Poetry, and she is also the author of two historical nonfiction books about Wyoming's colorful characters, published by High Plains Press. Lori is currently the assistant editor of *WyoHistory.org*, a project of the Wyoming State Historical Society.

COVER ARTIST

Larry Edgar
Western Historical Artist

Wyoming born and raised, Larry Edgar became interested in history, archaeology and art at an early age. He knew that creating Western historical art was to be his destined goal. He worked under the tutelage of Adolph Spohr and attended Northwest Wyoming College, majoring in Fine Arts. Inspired by Western history and influenced by his friend, the famous artist and illustrator, Nick Eggenhoffer, Larry has been known for his accuracy in clothing, tack, accouterments and firearms in his artwork. This attention to minute detail and careful research of his topics has contributed to his winning of many awards, including the Wyoming State Historical Fine Arts Award in 1984, 1985, 1986, 1988, 1989 and 1990. For more information about Larry and his paintings, prints and bronzes, visit his Website at www.westernheritagestudio.com .

WESTERN WRITERS OF AMERICA, INC.
Qualifications for Membership

WESTERN WRITERS OF AMERICA welcomes all published writers who derive their livelihood, in whole or in part, from writing about the land and the peoples of the American West, past and present. Our membership includes novelists, historians, essayists, journalists, poets, screenwriters, publishers and others. Applications for membership are judged on an individual basis and the requirements for the different levels of membership are somewhat flexible.

BENEFITS:
- All members receive a $30 subscription to the *Roundup Magazine*
- Network with professional Western writers, editors, publishers and agents
- Annual national convention, awards and opportunities for leadership
- WWA regional, state and local seminars and signings
- Professional membership fee is tax deductible

MEMBERSHIP LEVELS AND REQUIREMENTS

ACTIVE: Active Membership in the Western Writers of America, Inc., may be granted to authors who derive their livelihood, in whole or in part, from the writing of books, stories, articles, screenplays, or teleplays pertaining to the traditions, legends, development, customs, manners, or history of the American West, or early frontier, if published or produced without financial assistance of the author. An applicant must have written at least three (3) published books or at least twenty (20) short stories, articles, or poems or three (3) screenplays or nine (9) teleplays. At least one-third of such published/produced work must pertain to the American West, or early frontier. Annual dues are $75.

(continued next page)

ASSOCIATE: Publication of one (1) book about the West or at least five (5) short stories, articles, or poems or one (1) screenplay or three (3) teleplays will qualify you for Associate membership. Such works may be produced with or without the financial assistance of the author. You may also be eligible for an Associate membership if you currently are participating in one of the following occupations, and if your work substantially concerns the West: publisher, editor, bookseller, literary agent, literary reviewer, librarian, film or television producer or director, artist or illustrator. Associate members have all the rights of Active members, save that only Actives can vote for WWA officers or on proposals to amend the constitution and bylaws. At least one-third of such published/produced work must pertain to the American West, or early frontier. Annual dues are $75.

SUSTAINING: Any Active or Associate member who wishes to contribute further support to the WWA may become a Sustaining member by paying annual dues of $150. Sustaining members retain all rights and privileges of their Active or Associate status.

PATRON: Companies, corporations, organizations and individuals with a vested interest in the literature and heritage of the American West may become Patron members by paying annual dues of $250. Eligible organizations include but are not limited to publishing houses, presses, libraries, museums, and wholesale and retail booksellers. Active and Associate members of the WWA who choose to become Patron members retain all rights and privileges associated with their professional membership status.

For more information, visit the WWA Web site at
www.westernwriters.org

Ordering Information

For information on how to purchase copies of *Outlaws and Lawmen,* or for our bulk-purchase discount schedule, call (307) 778-4752 or send an email to: company@lafronterapublishing.com

About La Frontera Publishing

La frontera is Spanish for "the frontier." Here at La Frontera Publishing, our mission is to be a frontier for new stories and new ideas about the American West.

La Frontera Publishing believes:
- There are more histories to discover
- There are more tales to tell
- There are more stories to write

Visit our Web site for news about upcoming historic fiction or nonfiction books about the American West. We hope you'll join us here — on *la frontera.*

La Frontera Publishing
Bringing You The West In Books ®
2710 Thomes Ave, Suite 181
Cheyenne, WY 82001
(307) 778-4752
www.lafronterapublishing.com

OldWestNewWest.Com
Travel & History Magazine

It's the monthly Internet magazine for people who want to explore the heritage of the Old West in today's New West.

With each issue, **OldWestNewWest.Com Travel & History Magazine** brings you new adventures and historical places:

- Western Festivals
- Rodeos
- American Indian Celebrations
- Western Museums
- National and State Parks
- Dude Ranches
- Cowboy Poetry Gatherings
- Western Personalities
- News and Updates About the West

Visit **OldWestNewWest.Com Travel & History Magazine** to find the fun places to go, and the Wild West things to see. Uncover the West that's waiting for you!

www.oldwestnewwest.com

La Frontera Publishing's eZine about
the Old West and the New West